MAGGIE'S GHOST

BY

DONALD MORRISON

Dark Forest Publishing

BISAC: Fiction

ISBN-13: 978-0578773018

Designed by Donald Morrison

Printed in the United States of America

Dedicated to five very real friends, who for a handful of summers, shared in adventures that will never be forgotten.

Chapter 1

"Dude! You're such a pussy!"

Sixteen-year-old Mike Tanner stared at the small stream that crossed a short distance away, carefully plotting speed and trajectory. His bike was heavy, even for aluminum frame standards, and he needed to make sure he could get going fast enough to launch himself, and the BMX he was standing over clear of the six-foot ravine.

"Quit pretending dude. We all know you don't have the balls to jump it. You've wussied out the last ten times."

Mike took a deep breath and glanced over his shoulder towards the friend who jeered him on. Yeah. He'd stopped short or found an excuse not to; his tires were too low; he hadn't oiled his chain. But not today. Today was the day.

"Come on man," another teen called out from behind the boy wearing ripped up jeans and a Pantera t-shirt. "Just do it or he's never gonna shut up."

Mike bit his lip, his gaze settling on the large dirt mound that would serve as his makeshift launch pad. They had built it together, the group, piling dirt for a week during the last summer break. Mike was the only one, Denise excluded because she was a girl, to make the jump. And the others joked that even she was probably gonna make it before him. That was something he couldn't let happen. That, he would never hear the end of.

Behind him another friend of theirs, Todd, a strange kid with the habit of holding his throat as if he was single-handedly choking himself, lifted his hand into place, holding it as he crooked one arm over the other and wrapped it

1

around his chest. "Just do it already, *jeez*. Jeff's gonna lose his virginity by the time you jump."

"Hey," Jeff snapped. "Screw you man."

Jeff was the oddball in the group, fascinated with the macabre, things that generally revolved around forensic science; *Unsolved Mysteries* and watching *Faces of Death* videos. Most likely to become a serial killer was how their 8th grade class had ranked him, much to the displeasure of his mother when she had read it. It hadn't gone into the yearbook officially, but one of his friends had added it and the tally grew during the signing day.

"Good one dude," the kid in the Pantera shirt replied with a laugh. "Totally true."

"Whatever man," Jeff replied. "At least when I do it'll be with a girl, unlike you."

"*At least it'll be a girl*," the other mocked back sarcastically.

"Hey, lay off it, John," Todd said, pausing for a moment before turning his attention back to Mike who still sat staring nervously at the three-foot-deep chasm that awaited the opportunity to swallow him if he failed. "Would you just jump the damn stream already, or not? This is starting to get a little boring."

Mike snapped him one last dirty look before turning his gaze forward and steeling himself for the flight. "This is stupid," he whispered as he brought his foot off the ground and pressed hard against the pedal, starting his momentum forward.

It was twenty feet to the jump that stood at the edge of a field behind the trailer park Todd lived in. The group had adopted the vacant field as their hang out spot. They'd all been friends since elementary, all except John; he'd moved to the United States in the fourth grade from France. His accent, dirty sense of humor and penchant for a rather extensive vulgar vocabulary had earned his rightful place among them.

Mike quickly closed the gap between himself, and the water filled ravine, and in those moments, found himself beginning to regret taking the bet that he wouldn't be able to clear the creek. But before he could finish the thought the thin dirt path leading to the ramp ended and he was ascending the large four by ten sheet of plywood they had laid down atop. He was full speed and moving fast. At the last second, he tensed, lifting the handlebars up as the front tire cleared the lip.

And like that, he was airborne.

The others watched from behind, Jeff and Todd still surprised that he was stupid enough to take the bet. Mike was the worst rider of all of them, but his addiction to video games had proven his weak point, and the promise of the newest action game to come out had pushed all regard to personal safety and reason to the rear. Now all he had to do was land it and each of them would be out fifteen bucks, which meant a week's housework. With that last thought buzzing anxiously in their minds, the three stood wide-eyed, their breath held in their throats as they watched their friend leave the ramp.

Over the ravine Mike felt the wind rushing past and the tears beginning to build in the corner of his eyes. His gaze darted ahead to the flat dirt area opposite the chasm that quickly rushed up to meet him.

His back tire landed first, his front tire bouncing upwards as it connected with the ground. The rebound

3

jerked his hands and instantly all equilibrium was tossed to the wind. He wobbled violently and then his handlebars gave in to the wobbles and twisted to the side. Then his front tire dropped into a small prairie dog hole that had been hidden by toppled weeds, and in that moment, his bike stopped, and he continued forward, flying straight over the handlebars and landing heavy into the dirt, rolling twice before coming to a stop.

"Oh shit!!" he heard as the cloud of dust settled into the air around him. *"Did you see that!?"*

John's voice blasted out above the pain he felt in his shoulder and hip where he had landed.

Across the ravine John continued. "Dude! You just ate shit!!"

Slowly Mike brought himself to his feet, glancing at where his bike had stopped and noticing the hole in the ground. His elbow throbbed, his hip was screaming at him and there was dirt from the collar of his shirt to the bottom of his shoes. Small thorns and foxtails pricked into him as he stood, the tiny jabs only adding to his humiliation.

Mike turned, brushing himself off and walked towards his bike, cursing himself for not checking the area he was going to be landing in. *Rookie mistake... Rookie mistake.*

He could still hear John laughing loudly, a bellowing guffaw that drowned out everything else.

As he tossed his bike up the other side of the ravine and readied himself for the embarrassment that he was about to endure he saw a hand drop down to help him up.

"You alright dude?"

He looked up to see Jeff kneeling down, ready to pull him up.

Mike took his hand. "Yeah." He shrugged, a tiny smirk pulling one side of his face up towards his ear. "I did it..."

"Yeah," Jeff replied, taking his hand. "You definitely did that." Jeff pulled him up as he caught footing and climbed.

"Ow," he grunted as he topped the edge.

As he turned to ready himself for what was guaranteed to be the story retold the rest of summer break, he saw another of their friends riding towards them; a girl with short blond hair that bounced as she pedaled, and a denim button up shirt ruffled loosely around her.

She came to a stop, stepping off her bike and letting it drop to its side on the ground.

"What'd I miss?" she asked as she walked up, her brow raising as she quickly inspected Mike and the thick layer of dust clinging to his side.

"Dude! You *just* missed it. Mike totally just ate shit!" John barked, laughing aloud again.

The girl glanced between the others with an amused smirk. "You finally convinced him to make the jump...?"

"And I landed it," Mike replied, stepping towards her. "Hey Denise."

"The only thing you landed was your face on the ground," John replied with a big shit-eating grin.

"No, dude," Mike argued, the thought of losing the video game dashing forward. "I went like ten feet before I fell. So that counts as landing it."

"Whatever dude," John countered. "You ate it."

"Yeah," chimed in Todd, not for lack of wanting to lose the fifteen dollars, but on the pure representation of technicalities. "Landing implies you stay on the bike until it comes to a stop. That's kind of the rules."

Mike slouched, his shoulders moving inwards in defeat.

"I'm gonna have to side with Todd and John on this one," Jeff said, jumping in. "But it looked freaking awesome!"

Denise shook her head, glancing between them. "You guys are idiots. And one of these days, one of you is gonna end up in the hospital."

"It's cool," John replied, stepping forward. "Todd's mom's a nurse."

"And a pretty *hot* one at that," Jeff added for good measure.

"Dude," Todd replied, his hand pulling away from his neck. "Really...?"

"Just saying man. Your mom's pretty hot."

"Yeah dude," Mike added to his displeasure. "She's kind of a milf..."

"Anyways...," Denise interjected, already fed up with the boy's antics just moments after arriving. "I just stopped by to tell you that Joe Briggs is having another party tonight at his place if you wanna go. His dad's out of town again on some trip and he's planning on going all night."

"Hmph," Mike pondered, his elbow still throbbing as a thin line of blood began to work its way down. "That could be cool." He paused, concern shifting to his face. "I'd have to sneak out though. Who else is gonna be there?"

"I'm pretty sure Russ, David and that one chick that I can never remember her name. You know the one, skinny, kind of a stoner."

"Caroline?" John asked.

"Yeah, that's the one."

"I'm in," John grinned. "What time?"

Denise shook her head. She could almost taste the testosterone laced hormones flooding out from him. "Of course you are... Joe said to tell everyone eleven."

"Yeah, I can't," Jeff said, pursing his lips for a moment. "It was way too close last time, and if my mom caught me sneaking out, I'd never see the light of day again."

"Pussy," John coughed, adding a couple extra fake coughs for good measure.

"Whatever dude," Jeff said, shooting him a dirty look. "Like your parents are gonna let you go out at eleven..."

"I wouldn't be dumb enough to get caught."

"I'll go," Todd said, snapping everyone's attention to him. "I'll meet you there. Want me to bring anything?"

"Whatever you want," Denise said, smiling. "Joe says there's wine coolers and beer."

"Oh, awesome...," John scoffed. "Zima and Bud Light..."

"OK," Todd replied, ignoring John's smartass comment.

"Well," Jeff commented. "Don't get busted." He knew how Todd was going to get the booze...

"I never do," Todd replied with a sly grin.

"Well," Jeff said, reaching down to pick up his bike, "I gotta get going. My mom's gonna be pissed if I'm late for my scout meeting again. The scout master tells her *everything*..."

John chuckled. "Weren't you too old for that like three years ago?"

"Yeah," Jeff grumbled. "Tell that to my mom..." He shook his head with a sigh. "I'll catch you later."

Jeff climbed over his bike and pedaled off, leaving the others to discuss the rest of their afternoon.

Todd stood there, watching Jeff ride down the trail that led to the street opposite them in the field. "Man," he scoffed again. "He's such a mama's boy you'd almost swear they were dating."

"Who says they're not," John replied with a sneaky chuckle.

"Uh… That's gross…" Denise replied, a look of disgust moving across her face.

Mike turned to Denise. "Well, it's kind of true."

Denise shook her head, still struggling to figure out how it was that she became part of their group and quietly scolding herself for allowing it to happen. They were immature, they were crude, and they had no respect for girls, rules or authority. *But* they were all really good guys, and in the end, probably much more fun to hang out with than the jocks or the science geeks she had study class with. "Look," she said, turning back to the others. "I just stopped by to tell you about the party. I've gotta take off too. Try not to kill yourselves yeah."

John smiled at Mike.

"I guess, see you guys tomorrow?" Mike said, the obvious coming in the reflection of a question.

John conjured his best *Beavis* impersonation, sticking his hands in the air in front of him. "Are you threatening me?"

Mike smiled, shaking his head as he picked up his bike and hopped on, turning to pedal away.

Chapter 2

The next day the group met up in town. They had a local spot they called home when they weren't hanging out at *the* spot. Funny enough, the name of the business was Top Spot. It was the local teen hangout; cheap, greasy food, shakes and malts, cherry vanilla coke and a handful of arcade games in the back seating area, the section they always gravitated towards.

Jeff had been the first to arrive, as always. Not only was he generally the first awake among them, his desire to get his chores out of the way as quickly as possible so he could spend the rest of the day relaxing and enjoying the lazy afternoons of irresponsibility, ensuring he was up and out of bed by seven. Even on summer break...

Because of this, the unspoken responsibility had silently fallen to him to be the one to get there early and hold their table. Generally, it would be John or Denise who would arrive next. They both only lived a short distance away. Mike was the one who had to ride his bike nearly forty minutes into town if he couldn't catch a ride from his dad. His dad left for work at six, so unless it was super important, he'd show up around an hour later.

Today, however, it was Todd that showed up first. Jeff had gotten held up by his mom, tasked with helping her pull down boxes from the closet so that she could go through and purge things in order to make a donation to the church. He himself showed up a half an hour later, and by the time he walked in the door it was nearing ten-thirty.

"Hey dude," Todd said as he made his way towards the table.

"Hey dude." He glanced at the second arcade in, waiting a moment until the small video sequence ended and the high score popped up. Then he glanced at Todd and smiled.

Todd nodded. "He's gonna be *pissed*..."

Jeff sucked in air, hissing through the back of his teeth. John had a running battle with some other player. They'd been battling for months for the top spot. And each time John would take it, convinced that he was gonna sit on the throne permanently, he'd come in and his initials would be sitting in second place. There was one time that the owners had unplugged the machines to clean behind them. None of them spoke about that...

Jeff slid into the seat, reaching out and snagging the coffee cup in front of Todd. "Yoink!"

Todd shook his head and smirked.

Jeff took a sip, burning his tongue. "Ow, Jesus!"

Todd smiled, laughing soundlessly. "Well. That's what you get..."

Jeff cleared his throat, taking the lid off and blowing steam off the top before taking another sip and handing the cup back. "Dude... Where the hell is everybody? We were supposed to leave twenty minutes ago..."

Todd raised his eyebrows. "I know, right?"

"Hey man, my mom was up early. Something about having to donate clothes or something to the thrift store... I don't know. I got here as quick as I could."

He glanced out the window to see Denise riding up.

"Well. Now we just have to wait for John and go pick up Mike."

"Just Mike," Todd replied, nodding back out the window.

Jeff looked through the glass to see John crossing the main street a block behind Denise.

A few moments later they were all sitting inside, waiting for Mike.

The group had planned the week before to ride out to this place they referred to as the *pit*. It was about an hour and a half ride outside of town, an hour past Mike's place out old highway Fifty-Six. The pit was an abandoned copper mine from decades before. It was about the size of a football field at the top, with a single road that circled downwards to the bottom. At the base it was filled with water, and not just any water, but the bluest, crystal-clear water you'd ever seen. The story went that fifty years prior, a miner had struck an underwater river and that the mine had filled almost instantly, trapping the miner inside the large piece of equipment five hundred feet down. None of them knew this for a fact of course, the story had been told and retold in likely manner as a game of telephone for generations. But that was the story they held true to. So at least once a summer the group would make the ride out, complete with a packed lunch in their backpacks and bathing suits, and they would spend the afternoon jumping off the fifty-foot cliff into the water and sunbathing on the opposite edge where the road ended. Today was that day. And now that the last of them had arrived, they prepared to saddle up and make their way to Mike's house to pick him up, and then to the pit.

They each passed the coffee between them, each of them burning their tongues, each of them drinking more until it was gone. Then they climbed atop their bikes and started the trek through town, riding down Main Street to Center, and then out to the Fifty-Six.

A half hour later they were pulling up in front of Mike's house.

Jeff was making his way towards the front door when it opened and Mike stepped out, his bag already loaded and in place.

"Yeah Mom," of course," he called back as he stepped onto the porch. "Love you too."

He closed the door and made his way over, slapping hands with the others.

"Awww," John teased, turning his head towards the house. "I love you too Mike's mom."

"Dude, shut up..."

"Awww," he continued, adding insult to injury with a stream of kissing sounds.

Mike pushed him backwards, not aggressively, but enough to punctuate the *shut up*. Then he walked to where his bike was a few feet away and picked it up, swinging his leg over. "Let's do it."

"Yeah," John smiled. "Just keep an eye out. We should probably try to avoid any *jumps* along the way."

"Dude," Mike replied flatly. "Fuck off."

John laughed, Jeff and Todd releasing a chuckle alongside. Even Denise cracked a smile.

Mike pushed off and pedaled past. "Try and keep up!" he shouted back, racing towards the highway.

Behind him the others kicked off, pedaling to catch up.

Chapter 3

A half hour later the group left the smooth pavement, turning onto a long dirt road that led into the middle of nowhere. Plumes of dust rose from their tires and each of them rode spaced out and staggered. John and Todd launched themselves off small embankments, twisting their handlebars and doing little tabletops in the air. Jeff, Denise and Mike just rode normally, enjoying the hot air wafting past and the smell of dirt and sage that surrounded them. Each of them carried their lunch, a couple types of beverages, generally sodas or water. John always made it a point to get some weird ass drinks like Brain Wash of Jolt Cola. The rest of them stuck with Coke, or root beer and cream soda. They also each carried an extra tube with them and a patch kit. It had only taken Jeff getting a flat tire two years prior and having to walk back, an hour ride that quickly turned into a four hour walk for them to all quickly add that to their inventory.

They continued down the long, straight road until they reached a large hill. It was a mass of giant boulders and dirt, pushed into place who knows how many years prior by a bulldozer or backhoe to keep people from driving their cars any further. There were a few rusted out shells of vehicles that people had either driven off the edge or pushed for amusement or insurance purposes. At least that's what Mike's dad had said.

They all climbed off their bikes and carried them over the mound, pushing them to a large BLM gate that stood locked across the entrance of the road downwards. Then they huddled them together and ran two locks around them, securing them in place. The first time they had gone there they rode their bikes down, and then realized what a pain it was to push them all the way back up after a long day of swimming and lounging about. Now they just left them at the top and locked them up to ensure they'd be there when they returned. Though in the last four years of them going to the pit, they'd never seen another person there, and for that matter, had never even heard anyone talk about it. Todd had found out about it one day when he'd been looking at land maps and noticed what he thought was a small lake. Then next summer he'd convinced Mike to ride out with him to check it out, and they'd been coming once a year, sometimes two or three times ever since. They always joked that once one of them got a car, they'd pretty much live at the pit. That had yet to happen though. Mike had his learner's permit, but his parents had told him he needed to wait until he was eighteen. Something about not understanding the responsibility or some crap like that.

"I FUCKING LOVE THIS PLACE!!!" John screamed, his voice echoing back up at them a dozen times.

"WHOO-HOOOOO!!!" Jeff howled.

Even Todd let out a shout, chasing after John and Jeff who'd already started running down the rings towards the bottom.

It was a good mile or so hike to the base, so by the time they reached it they were all back together, walking as a group. They had formed sort of a ritual. They'd reach the bottom, all change into their swimming gear; Denise of course already wore hers underneath, and then John, followed usually by Jeff or Todd, and then Mike, would all take their turn diving off the edge. It wasn't something to scoff at either. It was a fifty-foot drop, over jagged rocks and roots sticking out, straight down into a bottomless abyss.

14

Then you had to swim nearly two hundred feet to the other side. By the time you reached the edge your adrenaline had been spent, your arms were tired and all you wanted to do was lay there for a half hour soaking up the sun and recuperating. Then of course they would do that at least three or four more times.

Denise would make her way around to the bottom and lay out the towels. She liked to swim, but she didn't enjoy the jumping off the cliff part. She was already fairly well-endowed for a teen, and an awkward conversation about *those* hitting the water going that fast, had quickly brought that teasing to an end. *"Imagine jumping in naked, and your balls slapping against the water as you landed..."* They had never brought it up again.

A large splash signaled that their afternoon had officially commenced. A moment later there was another. Then Todd and Mike took what they called a double-barrel and jumped at the same time. That was a risky move, because one time, John and Todd had done it, and when they hit the water, they curved towards each other, slamming into each other really hard and knocking the air out of them. Not something you wanted to have happen twenty feet underwater...

"Whoo-hoo!" Mike shouted as he broke through the surface again.

They all swam back to where Denise had finished laying out the towels.

"Dude!" Mike called out, panting already from the swim. "That was awesome!"

John rolled over and assumed a lazy backstroke, taking water in and spitting it upwards in the manner of a whale.

They sat there for the next two hours, chatting and eating their snacks. They shared stories and John stuck out his bright blue tongue, and effect left from one of his sodas. They laughed and reminisced about their prior year, sharing their lament at returning at the end of summer. They talked about life and basked in their youth. At that moment there was nothing else in the world, only the crystal-clear water, the sound of laughter and friendship.

Chapter 4

The sun drifted overhead, passing slowly as it cast the rim's shadow down across the walls. John and Todd had jumped a few more times, Mike even taking another plunge. John had even surprised them all, being the first to dive in headfirst. That had earned him a standing applause and a full round of high-fives and hand slaps upon returning to the shore. Now they all sat, lounging on their towels, the last of their snacks shared between them.

"No dude," Jeff replied, "Lee Taylor's a fucking asshole. Fuck that guy."

"Wow," Denise replied. "Such hatred…"

"The guy's a fucking prick."

"Yeah," Mike added. "Fuck that guy…"

John looked between them, lifting his hands and pointing at himself. "And *I'm* the one that swears too much…"

"No dude," Jeff continued. "Like Mike said, fuck that guy. Last winter, you know what he did?" He waited. He hadn't told the story; it was just for a dramatic pause. None of them knew. "There was two feet of snow on the ground, and *asshole* smashed a block of ice over my head and shoved me into one of those big plastic garbage cans. Then his *hick* buddies stacked a bunch of bricks on top of it so I couldn't get out."

"What?" Mike replied, shocked.

"Why didn't you say anything?" Denise asked.

"What's the point?" Jeff asked, still hurt at the memory. "So, we can all go find him and beat him up? He'd just have his fucking shit-kicker friends kick my ass when no one was around." He paused. "I stayed in that thing until the snow inside was melted..."

"Dude," Mike replied softly. "How did you get out?"

"The person whose garbage can it was came out to go to work. They took the bricks off and flipped it over." The anger faded slightly, a tiny smile hinting at the corners of his lips. "Scared the shit out of that guy when he flipped it over and came popping up ready to swing."

John chuckled. "Oh God, I can only imagine. The guy's minding his own business and then flips his garbage can over and a frozen Jeffsicle pops up ready to fight." He made the impersonation of someone whose arms were frozen at their side struggling to punch, grunting as he did.

"Dude," Mike said, finding John's impersonation funny, but how messed up it was not allowing for it. "That's messed up dude. Sorry man..."

"It's cool," Jeff replied calmly. "I slashed all four of his tires and cut his brake lines..."

"Jesus, dude!" John barked.

"Damn," Todd said, lifting his eyebrows. "Remind me not to piss you off."

Jeff smirked with a sigh. "I didn't really, but I sure thought about it..."

"Man," John smiled. "That would have been funny. He replaces all four tires and then gets in and crashes his truck at the end of the block because his brakes didn't work." He chuckled. "I like how you think my friend..."

"Dude," Denise replied, still not able to move past it. "I really wanna kick that guy's ass." She looked between them. "Next time I see him you better hold me back."

"Hold you back?" John scoffed. "Shit. I'll be taking bets."

"Yeah," Todd said, joining in. "My money's on her..."

18

"Yep," Mike agreed.

"What an asshole," she exclaimed finishing up the topic.

"No," Mike added. "Seriously. Remember almost a year ago when somebody sugared my dad's gas tank? Every time I saw that douchebag he'd have this shit eating grin on his face. I knew it was him. I still do..."

"Dude," John replied. "You live way the fuck out in butt-fuck nowhere... Why would he go all the way out there, just to put sugar in your dad's gas tank?"

"Dude," Mike replied. "It didn't happen at our house. It happened while my dad was in town at K-Mart. He went in, came out and drove home. The next day the truck wouldn't start. He took it in, and they found sugar in the gas line. It had already killed the engine. The mechanic is the one that told him it had to have happened at least a day before, and he drove it into town with no problems." He paused, the renewed anger flaring. "Then three days later, Lee Taylor passes me in the hall and says, *'Hey sugar'*...? No. he said it because he was the asshole that did it."

"Oh," John replied. "You never said that..."

"What was the point...? Wouldn't change anything."

The group went silent for a moment, each reliving their own interactions with the same person.

"So, guess what," Todd said, changing the topic while bouncing his knees where he sat crisscross applesauce.

They all waited.

"I heard my parents talking. I think they're considering getting me my first car..."

"What!?" Jeff exclaimed.

"Oh shit…," John replied, shaking his head. "Here we go… So much for class. It's gonna be meet at Top Spot and off to Vegas every day.

"Your parents are gonna trust *you* with a car?" Denise asked, doing nothing to mask her surprise. She turned her head to the sky and began glancing in every direction at once.

The others all took cue and looked up as well.

"What?" Todd said eventually.

"Nothing," Denise replied, lowering her gaze back to him. "I'm just looking for the flying pigs."

"Oh, ha-ha…," Todd replied flatly.

Mike chuckled loudly. "That was a good one." He reached over giving her a high-five.

"No," he added. "Seriously. I heard them talking about car prices and if they could afford it. That was like two nights ago."

"If they can afford it?" John asked. "Doesn't your dad work at some airplane company or something?"

"Yeah," Todd replied. "In the factory. My parents don't make *that* much money dude, why do you think we live in a trailer…?"

"Oh… I thought nurses made good money."

"Some do. Like the ones that have been there for years. But my mom's only an assistant."

"Dude," Jeff remarked. "She's been a nurse for like years…"

Todd sighed heavily. "No. She worked at the hospital when I was growing up, but in clerical. She didn't decide to become a nurse until a couple years ago. She's still in school for it."

"Damn dude…," John commented. "That must *suck*, having to go back to school at like fifty…"

20

"My mom's forty-one, dick," Todd replied sharply.

"Still dude... That's getting up there."

Todd sighed heavily, shaking his head.

"I mean I'd still hit it, don't get me wrong," John remarked adding the cherry.

Todd scanned the ground around him feverishly, before settling on an empty soda can, which he picked up and hurled at John.

"AHH!" John yelped rolling backwards.

Todd leapt to his feet, John doing the same, and then chased him into the water.

"You better stay your ass out there," Todd yelled from the edge.

John smiled, treading water a dozen feet out. "All day baby, all day..."

Todd shook his head and exhaled sharply, turning to make his way back towards the others.

"Dude," Jeff said a moment later. "Junior year..."

None of them responded. They sat, their thoughts swirling with the enormity of those two words, and everything they carried with them.

"I'm gonna miss this," Mike said after a moment, glancing out to where John was doing somersaults in the water. "Even his dumbass..."

"Dude," Jeff replied. "It's not like you're going anywhere. You still have to stay here and go to college. You know your parents aren't gonna let you leave."

"Look who's talking..."

"Point made... But what I'm saying is that this doesn't have to end. Just because we graduate high school doesn't mean we have to stop hanging out or coming out here. I mean, sure. We'll be busy with work and stuff like that, but we've been busy this entire time. School, scouts, you and your church. We still find time to hang out. And besides dude, there's still two more years..."

"Yeah, but it's not gonna be the same." He paused, glancing down at the dirt between his toes. "I mean. We're gonna be juniors next year, and then seniors after that. We only have one more summer vacation. And then we're never gonna have this again."

"But we'll still have each other," Denise replied, smiling softly.

"Yeah dude," Todd added. "None of us are going anywhere. It's not like we're gonna stop hanging out."

Mike nodded. "Yeah. I guess."

"You guess," Jeff scoffed, watching as John swam to the shore. "We're friends for life."

"Friends for life," Todd repeated.

Mike looked at Denise who was nodding. "For life."

John walked up, shaking the water from his hair like a wet dog. "What are you losers talking about over here?"

Mike smiled. "Nothing dude. Nothing..."

The rest of the afternoon faded by, the sun dropping the shadow down to the water.

They all packed up, put their regular clothes back on and started the trek back up to the top.

As they circled the rings upwards a small part of them stayed below, waiting for the next time they returned. Each of them had thought the same things Mike had said. It was a doubt that lingered in the shadows, hiding just behind the terrifying thought that in two more years, their lives were gonna change forever. What they didn't know was that *that* was going to happen much sooner than they thought.

Chapter 5

The air was crisp, the summer night's breath beginning to work through the trees lining the highway as Mike rode his bike on the way home. Even in summer there were still nights that reminded you that you were in southern Utah and that it was only a matter of time before the leaves would change color and the snow would return. Winter was never far off, and nestled at the base of the mountains, Cedar City caught the brunt of it all.

Overhead the sky had turned purple, orange and yellow pressing upwards from the west as the sun continued towards its nightly slumber.

Mike pedaled along, still embracing the feeling carried from their day at the pit, and the slight prickle of sunburn that he now wore across his chest, shoulders and back. He had ridden all the way back to town with them even though it meant riding right past his house, forty minutes into town and then the other forty minutes back. But it was pit day, and that was just what they did. They spent the day together and didn't call it done until the sun went down.

They had ridden back to the Top Spot for milkshakes and a round of cheeseburgers which had been lavished like a sentenced man's last meal after the long, sun-beaten ride. They had all shared a smile at John's meltdown when he realized that once again, his score had been overtaken and his initials dropped down to second. Then when eight o'clock crept up and they each had to call it a day, they parted ways, each starting back to their houses. Mike's just happened to be the farthest. So now the sun had fully set, and the starlit sky twinkled overhead.

Mike thought about the day, and what it would be like to miss his friends. He found himself thinking about it more and more as the months flew past. He knew that none of them planned on leaving, and that they all promised to stay best friends no matter what, but he also knew that life had a way of pulling people apart. He had shared his concerns with his mom and dad the year prior and they had told him that unfortunately that was just the way things were. They still had friends that they kept in loose contact with from their childhoods, but those people were all back in California. They sent Christmas cards or the occasional letter, but that was pretty much it. That thought alone scared Mike the most. He couldn't imagine his life without his friends. He had known them since elementary and he felt just as close with them as he was with his parents. *"Blood isn't the only thing that makes family,"* his dad had told him with a smile once. And he was right. They weren't just his friends, they were more. Much more. But this was their second-to-last summer vacation together. After that...

Mike pushed the thoughts away and settled his attention back on the road. It was only a moment before he found himself thinking about the day before, and the failed attempt at jumping the ravine. He was still slightly bitter that he had allowed John and Todd to convince him to make that stupid jump. He knew from the beginning that he was never going to land it, but on the off chance he had, it would have been worth it to see the look on their faces as they had to hand him a week's worth of their allowances. He regretted not being able to see that more than he did making the actual jump.

He smirked, shaking the thoughts and looked up. What he saw in the road ahead brought his feet to a stop.

He continued coasting forward, trying to make sense of what he was seeing.

Standing at the side of the road fifty feet away was a young girl wearing a faded pink dress. She stood staring at him as his bike rolled closer, her gaze wide-eyed and locked to him like a deer in headlights. Her shoulders were huddled inwards, her hands clasped tightly at her waist.

As he closed the space between them, he could see that her dress was beyond dirty, and that beneath the dirt and grime were tatters where slits had been shredded through. Her face was layered in dirt, and he could see where two pink lines cut deep through the grime, dry beds left by faded tears.

Slowly he rolled his bike to a stop, his eyes darting past her into the trees and then back. He turned, looking up and down the road in both directions. Other than the moon overhead and blanket of stars they were alone.

"Are you OK?" he asked, glancing around once more as he struggled to wrap his head around what he was supposed to do.

The girl didn't respond. Not verbally anyways. She looked up, her glassy eyes locking to his. There was flood of emotions held just beyond the glaze, a million silent screams that begged him for help, that pounded and wailed behind two clouded portals.

"Um…" He didn't know what to do and he could feel the icy grip of panic scraping at him. "Uh. Are you… Are you lost?"

Still no response, only the silent, pain-filled gaze. He watched as her eyes slowly lowered to the ground, and for a moment it almost looked as if she was pondering his question.

"Uh. Do you live near here?" He'd never seen her before and he knew, for the most part, a good portion of the people that lived this far out of town. There weren't a lot. "Um. Are your parent's nearby?"

Her gaze held locked to the ground at her feet. Then, when it rose it latched back to his, the same silent pleas pouring out.

"I... I can't help you if I don't know what happened." He paused, looking back up and down the highway. "Crap..."

He eyed her closer. He could see in the moonlight that the darkness on her arms was deep, splotches of purple and brown beneath the grime on her forearms, just beneath where the dress sleeve ended at her elbow. He felt a cold chill work through him. He had seen bruising like that one time, when John had gotten into a fight and the older boy had held his wrists down while trying to keep him from punching him in the face. "Did someone hurt you?" he asked, his words soft as his gaze lifted to meet hers again.

Her hands balled tighter before her, her arms pressing even closer to her sides. But still she said nothing, only the blank, frightened gaze that told him that something was very wrong.

Mike swallowed hard, his mind racing. He looked back towards the trees for a moment and then back to her. "Um. Look. I uh. I live about ten minutes from here," he said. "Fifteen walking. If you come to my house my parents will know what to do. We have a phone. They can call the police. They'll find your parents." He paused, wishing she would give him any kind of response, anything at all. "You can trust me," he continued, lowering his voice and making it as soft and friendly as possible. "I'm not gonna hurt you. I promise."

She held his gaze, the fear held captive in her eyes allowing a single tear to release.

He watched as it rolled down her cheek.

"I promise," he repeated.

Mike glanced behind him one last time and then turned to the girl. "Just, follow me, okay? I'll go slow."

He swung his leg over the bike and pushed it towards her. Instantly she flinched back.

"It's OK," he repeated. "I'm gonna help you."

She didn't retreat any further as he started forward again, simply watching as he pushed his bike past. Then when he was only a few feet away she took her first step and followed after.

"Oh man," he whispered, glancing back at her for a moment before settling his gaze on the road ahead. "This is crazy..."

Mike still struggled to wrap his head around what was happening. There were no cars. He hadn't passed anyone stalled out or out of gas on the way. It was dark and he knew there wasn't much traffic on the highway at this hour, even less after. There were no farms or houses nearby and the woods beyond ran straight to the mountains behind. Beyond that it leveled out and miles of southwestern desert stretched to the horizon. It was almost as if someone had just dumped her there. But it didn't make sense. She was covered in dirt, her dress was torn to shreds like she had just run through miles of woods. And why couldn't she speak? He'd heard stories of kidnappings and crazy abductions where the person managed to get away, but it didn't make sense. This was Cedar City. Nothing like that ever happened there... But something in her eyes, in the way that she looked at him, told him that something really bad had happened to her.

Chapter 6

A short while had passed, and Mike had resolved to make the entire trip in silence after trying a few more times with no avail to get the girl to engage in conversation. Now he walked quietly, wondering what his parents were going to have to say when he arrived home with a lost girl in tow, and the story he'd have for the guys the next day. He was only about a half a mile away now and he could only imagine their reaction...

On the road behind him the sound of a car approaching lifted his attention. He stepped closer to the shoulder and glanced back. A moment later an old, out of commission police car with painted over markings slowed down, coming to a roll at the speed Mike was walking. The man behind the wheel leaned to get a better look, the cowboy hat on his head almost hiding his face.

Then Mike locked eyes with the man and recognized him as one of his parent's really good friends. Recognition flashed through the man's eyes, and he smiled, lifting his hand to tip his hat before accelerating.

"Mr. Brimhall!" Mike shouted. But the man was already out of earshot. "Damn it," he growled. It could have saved him another ten minutes walking, and Joe kept the old police scanner in his car when he bought it. He might have heard something.

Mike turned back to where the little girl stood, ready to tell her that he was gonna try and get them a ride and that they weren't much further now. But as he did, she was gone.

Mike glanced back and forth, coming to a stop, his eyes growing wide as he realized that in the blink of an eye she had disappeared.

"Hey!" he called out. "Little girl?" He paused, his words moving to a whisper. "Where'd you go?"

Mike looked back in the direction they had been coming from and then off to the side of the road, wondering if she had bolted into the trees when Mr. Brimhall had slowed.

"Where the heck...?" he whispered to himself.

Then he shook his head and turned back around.

Standing three feet away was the girl, still staring blankly at him through fearful eyes.

Mike startled, staring at her for a moment, puzzlement prickling across his arms. "How...?"

The girl just continued to stare silently.

He exhaled sharply, staring for a second longer. "My house is only a little farther. We're almost there."

Still silence.

"Ah man. My parents are gonna kill me... I should have been home over an hour ago. We need to hurry." Mike exhaled sharply, pushing the bike past and continuing on.

The girl again watched him pass before moving her feet and continuing behind him.

Chapter 7

As Mike approached his house, he readied himself for the looming conversation, and his parents' shock when he showed up with a little girl that looked like she just crawled out of the woods. The lights in his house were on and he could see his dad just finishing something up in the kitchen. He stopped, turning to the girl. "All right," he said, turning back to the house. "This is my house. My mom's still at work but my dad'll know what to do. You're gonna be okay now."

He turned and continued up the driveway.

When he opened the door, he could hear his dad lightly humming from down the hall.

He stepped in, holding the door for the girl as she made her way inside. "Dad?" he called out.

There was a shuffle down the hall and then a moment later his father entered the living room. "Hey Mike," he said as he finished wiping his hands on a towel. "How was your day?" His dad paused, glancing at his watch. "You should have been home over an hour ago." He glanced at him disappointedly. "You're lucky your mom's not home yet..."

Mike paused, puzzled that his dad hadn't immediately asked why there was a girl with him.

"Yeah. Sorry Dad." He paused. "Um..."

"You OK?" his dad asked, concern moving to his words. "Did something happen? You seem a little shaken up."

Mike stared for a moment and then turned to where the girl had been standing. Again, he was punched in the gut with shock as the space she was in was now completely empty. Somehow, she had vanished into thin air. "What the heck?" he whispered, moving to the door to glance out.

"You okay, Mike?"

Mike's gaze worked across the empty yard. Then he closed the door and turned back to his dad. "Uh. Dad. There was this girl..."

Mike's dad stared, his eyebrows slowly rising up his forehead. "Girl?"

"Yeah. She was right here.... I found her when I was riding home. She was on the side of the road. I think she was lost or abandoned. I don't, I don't know." Again, he turned to open the door and looked outside quickly. "She was right here."

The look on Mike's father's face slowly shifted from puzzlement to concern. "Found her?" he asked, hesitating on the thought.

"Yeah," Mike replied. "Mr. Brimhall pulled up while we were walking, and she disappeared. And she was just right here. But now she's gone again."

His dad stood there, slowly folding his arms in front of him as his demeanor shifted. "Mike," he started, a serious tone slipping into the conversation. "I have to ask this, as your father. But you and your friends aren't experimenting with anything, are you? Anything I should be aware of? You know, things you shouldn't?"

Mike stared at him, surprised. "Experimenting? You mean like drugs...?" His face scrunched. "No!"

He couldn't believe his dad was asking him that. He knew what his opinion on drugs were. He'd always been against them. None of his friends did drugs. Yeah, some of the people they hung around smoked pot and had tried acid a couple times, but never him or Jeff, or Todd, or John. He knew Denise had smoked pot once or twice, but she wasn't a stoner. But more than that he was struggling to wrap his mind around the fact that the little girl, who had just been standing next to him inside, was gone.

"OK," his dad continued. "Cause you're acting pretty weird right now."

Mike stammered for an explanation. "But she was right here…"

He could tell that there was no way his dad was going to believe him, and if he kept going further that it would get brought up to his mom, and then they'd have to sit down and have *the talk*, and right then, that was the last thing he wanted. So instead, he opted for the smartest choice in his favor. "Never mind," he said, his words falling out dejectedly.

His dad stared at him for another moment, sizing him up and studying him. Mike almost expected him to step closer and sniff his hair for smoke. Then he loosened up, his arms unfolding. "Look. Why don't you go wash up and get ready for bed? It looks like you've had a long day…" He paused, glancing at Mike's arm. "And what did you do to your elbow?"

Mike looked down, turning his arm out to get a better look. "Oh yeah. That… The guys convinced me to jump the creek in the field by Todd's house yesterday."

His dad nodded with a smirk. "Doesn't exactly look like you landed it…"

"I did!" Mike snapped "I rode it for about twenty feet before I fell."

His dad nodded again in agreement. "Well, I guess that counts."

"That's what I said," Mike replied, upset that the others had weaseled their way out of the bet with a technicality.

"Well. Go on."

Mike nodded, stepping towards his room.

He made his way past and started down the hallway to his room when his dad called out one more time.

"Mike."

He stopped, turning around.

"You're *sure* you're not messing around with anything? Cause I really don't wanna have to bring this up with your mother. *Neither* of us wanna have *that* talk…"

Mike exhaled heavily. "I'm sure Dad. I promise."

"All right then," his dad replied, still watching him. "Go on."

Mike turned and continued towards his room. *How did she disappear? She was right there. There was no way I could have imagined that…* He was confused, his brow pressed together in a wrinkle of doubt. He had just spent the last forty minutes walking down the road with her. He could see every line in her face, every speckle of dirt and those piercing green eyes behind the frightened gaze crystal clear in his memory. There was no way he had imagined it. No way.

The light in his room flickered to life as he stepped in. His twin bed was against the wall, sheets still in the same position he had pushed them to that morning. His mom hated that he left his bed undone, but he barely had enough time to eat, watch TV and get ready in the mornings as it was. His video game controller sat on the bed next to the book about a killer clown that lived in the sewer and fed on children. His mom hadn't been too thrilled about the book, but it was an argument his dad had helped him win. He was old enough to not let a book scare him. Heck, most of the games he played were scarier than that, but he didn't tell her that.

He turned and closed the door, pausing for a moment before turning back to the room. His dad had to think he was going crazy, and at that moment he was even beginning to entertain the thought himself. She *had* been there.

As he turned back, cold, pain-filled eyes stared back at him from behind dirt crusted lids three feet away.

Mike *yelped* loudly, stepping back, his back slamming heavily against the door as he did.

"How?" he stammered, struggling to make sense of the girl's reappearance and not understanding how it was that she had somehow managed to get past him and his father, who he had been facing the entire time, but had gotten into his room unnoticed. Slowly it began to sink in.

Now *he* stood there, wide-eyed and unblinking, his panicked gaze locked to the girl who stared back, the unshifting expression of sadness still heavy on her face.

A moment later there was a knock at his door.

Mike startled again, turning quickly at the sound.

"Mike?" the voice from the other side called out. "Are you OK?"

Mike stared at the door for a moment before quickly glancing back at the girl. Then he turned and opened the door, just a crack. "Yeah," he answered. "Sorry Dad. I thought I saw a spider."

Outside Mike's dad edged over, straining to get a peek inside the room. Mike felt pressure as his dad pushed to open it.

Mike pressed back for a split second and then resolved to the fact his dad was coming in rather he liked it or not, and that attempting to keep him out would only make his current situation much worse. So, he took a step back and let his dad step in. He hadn't even realized that his heart was pounding, and his breaths were coming short and quick.

Mike's dad gazed around the room, scanning it himself for anything out of the ordinary, or paraphernalia that could explain his son's strange behavior. "Are you *sure* you're OK?" he asked, his gaze finally settling back on his son.

Mike stared for a moment, now well past the shock of his dad not being able to see the little girl standing plainly behind him. "Yeah," he said, glancing behind. "Seriously dad. I thought there was a spider, I freaked out. Sorry."

His dad gave him a suspicious look before turning with a *hmph* and making his way back towards the living room.

Mike shut the door and turned to the girl. "No," he whispered. "No, no. Uh-uh. No way..."

The girl looked back at him, her expression unchanged. Then things started to make sense, or as much sense as the insane thoughts he couldn't believe he was having could.

Slowly he stepped towards her, his hand rising up as he moved to touch the girl's arm. As his fingers brushed past her skin, everything he had ever been taught to believe about life after death and spirits was turned upside down. He watched as his hand moved right through her arm, *phasing* through it. He didn't feel anything, no cold, no strange sensation, no tingling. Nothing. It was as if he had simply waved his hand through one of those hologram projectors you see in the mall kiosks that spell the time out in red. A trick of light and steam.

The realization sent Mike reeling. He stumbled backwards, again landing heavily against the door after tripping over a pair of shoes and falling to his rear. "Oh my god!" he said, staring at her. "You're a ghost. You're a ghost, and I brought you home. Oh crap. Oh crap..."

Fear and panic rushed through him. The worry of what his father was going to think was a distant memory, hidden far behind the current fear of what stood before him. "So, I guess that explains why you can't talk," he said, his nervous system beginning to settle. Then the cloud of fear begun to dissipate, a nervous excitement replacing it. "Oh man," he said, still staring up at her from the seated position against the door. "Jeff's gonna freak." Fear gave way to a thin tremble of excitement.

Then a loud knock sounded just above his head.

"Mike! Open up!"

Mike jumped to his feet and spun to grab the handle. "Yeah Dad."

He turned the knob and let the door open.

Again his dad scanned the room, his uncomfortable gaze locking to him. "Look," he said, still glancing quickly past him. "You're not acting like yourself and I'm getting a really weird feeling. Are you sure you're all right? I mean, if you need to talk to your mom or I about anything, anything, you know you can, right?"

"I know dad," he replied.

"Cause. You know, sometimes grownups talk to themselves too. We just try to be a little more discreet about it."

"Um, yeah. I was uh, I was figuring out how to beat uh, a level in the game I'm playing. Just a little pep talk."

His dad stared at him for a moment before glancing back into the room. "Well, whatever this is, I just want you to know, you can talk to us."

"Thanks Dad," Mike replied, waiting for the opportunity to close the door.

Then with one last quick glance his dad reached out and pulled the door closed.

Mike spun around, conscious of how loud his voice was. The little girl stood silently, staring. "Oh my god," he said, his hands balling to fists. "They're never gonna believe this..."

Chapter 8

Mike flew into the field the next morning, his tires spinning possibly faster than he'd ever gotten them to go. His muscles ached, fueled by short bursts of oxygen from his burning lungs. He was covered in sweat and even the quick breeze rushing past did nothing to cool the hot moisture falling beneath his soaked shirt. He hadn't stopped pedaling from the moment he left his house, and the normal, forty-minute ride had quickly passed in just over twenty. His mind reeled with the night's events, and he went over and over the different ways which he was going to present the story to the others, knowing that they were going to tell him he was crazy and that he didn't need to make things up to be cool. Of all the options he offered himself, the only one he kept coming back to was simply telling them everything as it had happened and being as straight forward as possible. Likely they still wouldn't believe him, but he still had to tell.

When he had woken up that morning the little girl had again disappeared. He had called out to her a few times, not too loud mind you, he didn't need a repeat conversation with his dad, and his mom was home, so... He had gotten dressed quickly, shouted to his parents and rushed out the door. The only time he'd stopped momentarily was at the spot on the road where he had found her, but she was nowhere to be seen. After that he pedaled, not taking a moment to even breathe, until his tires touched dirt.

As he rushed forward, he saw Jeff, Todd and John sitting in the folding chairs at their spot. Denise was probably running late as usual. Even he had woken up later that he had desired.

He kept pedaling, putting the last of his steam into a short burst across the hundred-yard field.

Then he skidded to a stop and dropped his bike to the dirt, his dramatic entrance pulling puzzled glances from the others as the plume of dust left from his appearance wafted over them.

"Oh my god!" he belted out, his bike tires still spinning wildly behind him as the dust cloud continued forward. "You guys are never gonna believe this!"

He was out of breath and his Hypercolor shirt was now a completely different color than it had been in his dresser drawer a half hour prior.

"What?" John smiled. "Why it took you so long to get here, or that you showered after getting dressed this morning...?"

Jeff coughed, lifting his hands to fan away the dust still drifting past.

"Dude!" Mike said, struggling to catch his breath while at the same time ignoring John's marmy response. "I was riding home last night. There was this little girl. I brought her home. Dude... She's a freaking ghost!"

Now he had their full attention. Each of them shared a quick glance before turning their attention back to him. A small grin started splaying across John's cheeks.

"You mean *that* little girl?" Todd asked, his gaze moving past him as he pointed his finger to a spot just behind where Mike stood.

Mike turned around to see the little girl standing just a few feet behind him. She looked exactly as she had when he had found her, the dirt smears and thin flakes of dried blood exactly intact.

"Yes!" he said, turning back to the others. "Wait…" He paused. "You can see her?" He paused. "How did you—" His words cut short as it all started making sense.

Again, there was a rapid exchange of puzzled glances.

Jeff glanced past him to where the girl stood. "Of course we can see her. She's standing right there."

"Wait," John asked, his eyes narrowing. "What do you mean *found* her?"

"Dude…," Jeff added, a thin waver of concern in his voice. "I didn't see her walk up… Did you…?"

"I'm telling you," Mike barked. "She's a ghost." He paused, taking a deep breath and exhaling as he wiped the thick layer of sweat from beneath his hat. "I was riding home, and she was on the side of the road." Again, he looked at each of his friends individually. "I'm trying to tell you, she's a ghost."

"Really?" John asked as he set down his cola and rose from his chair. "You can just tell us you have a girlfriend. We'll understand. Even if she is only in the fourth grade." He paused, glancing at the girl, his eyebrows scrunching together. "And looks like she just crawled out of a storm drain…?"

"Dude," Mike insisted. "I'm serious. I brought her home with me and my dad walked right into my room and couldn't see her. She was standing right behind me. Nothing. He didn't even know she was there."

"Wait," Todd continued, his eyes now locked to her. "Can we just go back to how it was that she just…?" His face was warped in confusion.

Jeff smiled, now completely intrigued by the scenario. "No way…" It had caught his attention more than the others.

41

Jeff had always been intrigued by the supernatural. He had a library comprised of werewolf and vampire novels, knew everything there was to know about all the urban tales and all the famous serial killers. He'd even gone so far as to get himself suspended for a week the year prior for doing an essay on John Wayne Gacy, submitting it to the class complete with grisly backstory and crime scene photographs.

Mike knew there was only one way to show them what he was saying. "All right," he said, his breaths starting to level out. "You gotta promise not to freak out, all right."

The others exchanged glances again, but this time there were no smart-aleck remarks. Each of them hung on bated breath.

"Watch," he said, turning and taking two steps towards the girl. "Sorry," he whispered as he stopped just in front of her. "I have to show them, or they won't believe me."

The girl looked deep into his eyes.

The others watched as he slowly lifted his hand in the air, extending his arm out towards the girl. Then Mike took a deep breath and moved his hand downwards and through her forearm.

"AAhhh!" Jeff yelped, jumping back. "Holy shit!"

John's jaw dropped. "What the fuck!? No way!"

A smile worked its way to Todd's face. "Holy crap," he said slowly, his voice barely above a whisper. "Do that again!"

Mike turned to face the others. "Dude, she's not some freaking circus trick, OK?"

"Dude," Todd replied. "I thought ghosts were supposed to be all, you know, like transparent or something. See through. Or like, gross and covered in blood and ooze..."

"Yeah," Mike replied. "Imagine how I felt when I got home, and she just appeared in my bedroom. That's what I thought too, but I guess not."

"No way," Jeff said, stepping closer. "Hold up..."

Mike turned his attention to his friend. "What?"

Jeff was staring directly at the girl. "I know this is gonna sound strange, but I think I recognize her." He stared for a second longer. "What's your name?"

"She can't speak," Mike said after a moment, the girl looking to him for the answer.

"Maybe she could write her name?"

Mike glanced at John. "I tried that."

"Damn."

"Well, there's gotta be some way to communicate with her," Jeff said, finally ripping his gaze away. "I mean. Can she hear us, or understand what we're saying?"

"I don't know," Mike replied. "I think so. I mean, she understood when I told her to follow me home..."

"What about a Ouija board?" Todd asked from behind.

Jeff shot him an irritated glance. "Dude. Those are for *summoning* spirits. As you can see, somebody already did that."

Jeff turned his gaze back to the girl for a moment. Then he glanced at the others. "Look. I swear I recognize her." He paused, staring at her for another moment. Then he glanced back between the others. "I'm gonna head to the library for a minute. Don't go anywhere." And as quickly as he had formed the words he was darting to his bike.

"Don't tell anyone!" Mike shouted as Jeff mounted his bike.

Jeff stopped, turning his puzzled gaze on him. "Dude... Really? What do you think I'm gonna say? Hey, Mike found some dead chick and brought her home, and now she's hanging out with us..."

As he was speaking Denise came riding up on her bike. She set it down, glancing at the group who were uncharacteristically serious. In the commotion none of them even noticed her approaching.

"Just saying," Mike replied.

"Hey Denise," Jeff said as he put his foot on the pedal and pushed off, riding down the trail towards the street. "I'll be right back," he called out as he rode away.

Denise watched Jeff ride off frantically and then turned to the others. "So... What's this all about? And who's the little girl?"

Chapter 9

Mike spent the next half an hour retelling how he had left the day before and found the girl while riding down the highway. He told them about his interaction with his dad, and how she disappeared and reappeared. He told everything in vivid detail. The entire time the four had their attention locked to him. Denise however stood staring at him like he was attempting to convince her that Santa and the Easter Bunny were real.

"—and now she's following me," he said, finishing his tale. "I think maybe she needs our help or something. I mean, there has to be a reason she's here, right? Ghosts don't just appear, right?"

Denise glanced at the girl who was still standing in the same spot. "I don't know. I never really believed in *ghosts*, or spirits."

"Neither did I," he replied, holding his hand out towards the girl. "But..."

Denise stared at him for a moment, still trying to figure everything out. "Why you?" she asked after a moment. "Of all the people that she must have had pass by her, why did she pick you?"

Mike paused, glancing at the girl for a moment. "I don't know. But I can't lose the feeling she needs help. Every time I look at her it's like I can see in her face that she's in pain. I don't... I just know she needs our help." He also realized how calmly Denise was taking all of it. She had been the one he had assumed would be freaked out the most.

"Do you think she knows she's dead?" Todd asked.

"I don't know," Mike replied. "She isn't exactly saying much."

"What if?" Denise started, pausing as she glanced at the girl. "No offense." Her gaze turned back to the others. "What if she's like, a vengeful spirit, or a poltergeist, or something? Dude, you let her into your house..."

"Dude," Mike replied quickly. "I'm pretty sure she would have done something already, like attacked me on the road, or torn my house apart. And I didn't exactly let her into my house. I just went into my bedroom, and she was there."

"You told her to follow you," Todd replied softly.

Mike shot him a frustrated look.

Denise stared at Mike. She had only ridden up a short time ago and in that time, she had seen and heard things that an hour prior, would have laughed about and walked away. Ghosts were in stories, and movies. Dead people didn't come back to life, spirits didn't come back to haunt, fairies were in tales and there were no dragons or wizards. Now she realized she might just have to rethink a lot of things. The enormity of it all continued to build. Then she turned around and shook her head. "This is crazy."

"I know..."

There was a moment of silence between the group.

Denise turned back around. "Well, what are you gonna do?" she asked after a moment.

Mike stayed quiet, pondering the question himself. "I don't know," he replied, glancing at the ground for a moment before lifting his gaze. "I figured maybe we could try and find out why she's here, or what happened to her. We have to figure out what to do with her." He paused, glancing at the girl. "Jeff says he thinks he might recognize her."

"Wait," Denise replied sharply. "Figure out what to do with her? Mike, she's not a puppy. I don't think it's as simple as that. I mean." She lowered her voice. "She's a ghost. And as much as it sucks to say it, that means that little girl is dead." She scoffed, shaking her head. "I can't believe we're even having this conversation. Twenty minutes ago, I didn't even believe in ghosts..."

"Well, what could I do? I couldn't leave her there. I didn't know she was a ghost when I found her." He exhaled heavily. "I just... I can't explain it, but I really think she needs us to help her. I can feel it. I..." He sighed, his head dropping down as he pressed his eyes closed.

"Us," Denise asked, staring at him. "You mean you. She didn't show up at *my* house, or Jeff's, or John's. She showed up at yours. This isn't *our* responsibility."

Mike took off his hat and ran his fingers through his hair. He was frustrated by her response, but she was right. The girl was following him, so that meant she was his responsibility. But this was something he didn't exactly think he could do on his own. At that moment he was overwhelmed, intimidated and afraid, and he needed their help. But the problem that kept stabbing into him was that he didn't know what it was that she needed, or what help his friends could even be. How do you help someone who can't tell you what they need?

"Hey guys."

Mike lifted his gaze to see Todd pointing across the field.

As he turned his head he saw Jeff riding quickly towards them, a piece of white paper waving in his hand like a raised flag of surrender.

The group watched him approach.

"I knew it!" he said excitedly as he dropped his bike to the ground and stepped towards them huffing and out of breath. He was holding the piece of paper out in front of him, a big smile on his face. "I *knew* I recognized her."

The others stepped closer, all craning their necks to get a look.

Jeff handed the paper to Mike. "So, I was scanning this website of missing persons the other night and decided to search Cedar City. That's when I came across this."

"You were scanning a website for missing persons...?" John asked hesitantly. "You *do* realize you just said that like it's a *perfectly normal thing*, right?"

Jeff smirked at John, dismissing him quickly. "Her name's Maggie Lorris. She was twelve years old when she went missing." He paused, letting the others read the page. "Guys... That was twenty years ago."

"What?" John said, still not believing Jeff. "Let me see that."

John snatched the piece of paper out of Mike's hand and held it up between himself and the girl, glancing back and forth between the two for a moment. On the paper was a black and white picture of Maggie. She was smiling. Above it was her name and beneath; *Missing June 10th, 1975.* John read the caption below out loud. "Maggie Lorris. Abducted from Pine Lanes Bowling Alley on June 10th, 1975. Last seen getting into an early model red ford mustang." He lowered the paper, still staring at the girl. "Holy shit..."

"Dude," Jeff repeated. I told you I recognized her."

"OK, if this is true then we have to go to the police," Denise said, the reality of the situation hitting her full force.

"And tell them what?" Jeff blurted. "That our friend found the ghost of a little girl who went missing twenty years ago and now she's following him around? Oh, but by the way, we're apparently the only ones that can see her..."

"Well, if she went missing, and she's still here. Then maybe—"

Jeff looked at Mike, excitement glowing on his face. "Maybe she was murdered, and her spirit can't rest until the killer's been brought to justice."

John shook his head, looking away as if he'd been waiting for Jeff to take the conversation in that direction. "And here we go..."

Denise looked at him for a moment before glancing at Maggie. "Ugh..." She shook her head. "As much as I really, really hate that I'm going to say this, and I know I'm gonna regret it later... Jeff might actually be right."

"Of course I'm right," Jeff continued. "When a person dies a horrifically tragic death, their spirit can't cross over to the other side. And some cultures believe that unless their body is put to rest, they are stuck here, wandering the earth for all eternity." He paused. "Come on. You all saw the Crow."

"That was a movie dumbass," John said, again shaking his head.

"But it's gotta be based off of an idea that came from somewhere."

"Dude," John replied flatly. "The Crow's based off of a fucking comic book dude," John replied flatly.

"But where did *they* get the idea?"

John brought his hand up, slapping his palm against his forehead.

"Look," Mike said, pulling their attention to him. "Maybe we should figure out where she used to live." He reached out and took the piece of paper from John, turning to Maggie and holding it up. "Is this you? Are you Maggie Lorris?"

The girl shifted her gaze from him to the paper. Then slowly her head nodded up and down.

"See, I told you," Jeff said matter-of-factly.

John watched unamused, turning his focus back to Mike. "I thought you said she couldn't communicate."

"I said she couldn't talk or write. Look. Like I said, maybe we should figure out where she used to live. Get a little more information. I mean. We're the only ones that can see her, it's gotta be for a reason."

John still couldn't believe what was happening, or that the others were actually entertaining the idea of going on a stupid Hardy Boys adventure. So much for a lazy summer spent swimming in ponds and hiking in the mountains. "Yeah, but we don't *know* that. You said your dad was the only one that's been near her other than us, and that Joe guy. Then you brought her straight here, so we don't know if it's just us, or maybe it was your dad that couldn't."

"Hey losers!"

The group turned their gaze to the approaching voice.

"Just great," Jeff said quietly. "It's Greg..." He scoffed. "Perfect timing..."

They watched as an older teen wearing shredded jeans and a Whitesnake t-shirt strolled towards them. He had a shoulder length mess of dishwater blond hair and a mischievous look in his eye. "Hey weirdo," he said, sneering at Jeff. "Been busted for looking at any snuff videos lately?"

Jeff tightened. "Hey man. That was only once, OK? And I told you, it was for a school project. I just, hadn't told the teacher about the project yet."

This brought a smile to John's lips.

"Yeah," the bully replied. "Whatever perv."

The older teen came to a stop directly next to where Maggie stood. His gaze slithered over the group while he calculated who would be the easiest target to harass next.

"Hey Greg?" Mike asked.

Denise and Todd glanced at him, both shooting him a look that said *don't*.

Greg's eyes shifted to him, narrowing slightly.

"Do you recognize her?"

Mike lifted his hand and pointed directly at Maggie.

The kid turned his gaze in the direction Mike was pointing and traced his finger to the other side of the field. "Who?" he asked, irritation flooding his response.

Mike looked at John, squinting as he cocked his head to the side in victory. "Never mind," he said, looking back at the other. "It's nothing." He raised his eyebrows and cocked his head to the side, mouthing the word see.

The older boy scanned the group again, a confused look working its way across his face. "You guys are fucking weird."

The others watched in amusement as he kicked a large dirt clod in their direction and scoffed as he turned to walk past. "Have fun playing with your dollies or whatever the fuck it is you do out here," he called back without looking. "Freaks."

"Nice to see you too Greg," Mike said, watching him leave. "*Douchebag*."

The group watched him walk away, and when he was finally out of ear shot and when Mike couldn't contain it anymore spun to the others. "See! We *are* the only ones that can see her. That means she came to us for a reason."

"You," John said, still watching the older teen making his way out of the field. "She came to you."

"Well then why can you guys see her too?" Mike asked. He was growing tired of hearing them push her appearance on him. "Huh?"

"Maybe cause we're all friends?" Todd said, glancing at Maggie for a moment. The fact that there was a ghost standing a few feet away still gave him the heebie-jeebies, but at least the initial fear had dissipated, slightly.

Mike looked at Todd for a moment. "Whatever the reason, we need to figure out why she's here. I really think she needs our help."

"OK mike," Denise said, resolving herself to the fact that this was the direction they were heading. "Then what do you suggest?"

"Jeff," Mike started, his plan formulating as he spoke. "Can you do that thing that you do and find out as much information about her as possible? Address, police information, things like that."

Jeff nodded, a smile growing on his face. "Easy."

"Denise," Mike continued, turning to her. "Your dad works at the school. Could you ask him if he knew Maggie, and find out if she had any friends that we could talk to?"

Denise shifted nervously. "Uh, sure. But what do I say when he starts asking questions?"

"Tell him it's for a project we're doing. Extracurricular summer credits."

Denise smirked at him. "Uh, he works at the school genius. Pretty sure he'd smell that bullshit a mile away. He's the one that has to *okay* the extra credit assignments."

"I don't know," Mike answered. "Make something up. Tell him we're helping Jeff with one of his creepy projects."

Denise nodded. "*That*, he might actually believe."

Jeff furrowed his brow, glancing between the two of them. He held his tongue because he knew it was likely true. It was a reputation that followed him. He was used to it.

"I'm gonna head back to my place. I promised my dad I'd help him in the yard today. But we should meet here tomorrow at nine?"

"I've got a scout meeting at nine," Jeff replied. "Can we do eleven?"

"I've got a scout meeting at nine," John mimicked mockingly. "Can we do eleven?" He paused, shaking his head. "Fag."

"Hey dude," Jeff snapped. "At least I'm doing something for my future."

"Yeah," John replied. "Cause tying knots and jerking off your scout leader's gonna give you a real big advantage later."

Jeff frowned. "You know what dude, you're a dick."

"Just saying..."

Jeff exhaled sharply, turning his attention to Mike. "I'll see what I can find."

Denise nodded. "I'll ask around too. Maybe somebody knows something." Her gaze turned to John. "And asshole. I happen to like girls too, so you wanna knock it off with the gay bashing. It's getting a little old."

"Well excuse me princess," John remarked sarcastically.

"You're such a prick," she said, shaking her head in disgust.

"All right," Mike said, satisfied that everyone was on board. "I'm gonna take off. I'll see you guys here tomorrow."

He turned to Maggie. "I guess it's safe to assume you'll be coming with me."

She stared back blankly, her gaze drifting towards the others. Some of the panic behind her eyes was now gone, replaced with a thin confusion. Something behind them told Mike that she knew about as much of what was happening as they did. There was no comfort to be found in that thought.

Mike made his way to his bike and picked it up. Then he climbed over and pedaled away. Behind him the others followed suit, each making their way home for the day as they dispersed in separate directions. Another day of their vacation slipped past, the birds chirping in the field behind completely uncaring of the direction the group's summer had just been taken.

Chapter 10

"Mom?"

"Yeah sweetie?"

"Do you believe in ghosts?"

Jeff's mom lifted her gaze from the macramé she was working on, her hands stopping in place. She had grown accustomed, even accepted that her son was into some strange things and had, *odd* habits. "Uh. Wow." She scrunched her eyebrows together, pondering the question. "I suppose I believe in Jesus, and heaven, so... Yeah. I guess that means I have to believe that there is something after we die. I suppose *ghosts* would fall under that category."

Jeff lifted his hand, closely inspecting his fingernails. "Do you think they're like..., something we could ever see?"

His mom gave a puzzled smirk. "Well, I don't think it exactly works that way." She paused. "I think that we all have a spirit inside us, and that when we die, that spirit goes to either heaven or hell. I'm not sure that it can stay like that."

"Oh," he replied.

"Why the sudden fascination with ghosts?" she asked, setting the row of braids into her lap. "Is this for another of your *projects*?

"No!" he snapped, realizing his reaction was abrupt and trying to cover it as quickly as possible. "My friends and I got into a really big conversation today about it. I just was wondering what you thought."

"Well," she said. "I believe there can be ghosts I suppose. But I definitely don't think *we* can see them."

"OK," Jeff said, turning to walk away. "Thanks Mom."

"Of course, sweetie," she said, the puzzled look returning to her face as she lifted the small rope object again.

Jeff made his way down the hall and opened the door leading to the basement. A few years prior he had asked his mom if he could move his room down there and she hadn't found a reason to argue it, so now that was his room, and his old room had become her new craft room. The deal had worked out well for both of them. Though initially she had been worried about the lack of sunlight, he reminded her that he was mostly outside all day anyways, so she didn't have much to argue about the fact. He liked the quiet and it was way bigger than his old room used to be. Sure, he shared it with the washer and dryer, and if his mom forgot to put the heater on in winter, he'd wake up to seeing his own breath and would have to go all the way upstairs to adjust the thermostat. Other than that, he loved it. He had his own mini fridge; his computer desk was set up the way he liked, and all his anime scrolls and posters covered the walls. He even had three lava lamps that casted colorful glows across the cement surfaces. He loved his room.

He reached the bottom of the stairs and flipped the light on, making his way over to the desk. He tapped the keyboard of his computer, bringing it to life. He reached into his fridge and pulled out a Dr. Pepper, sliding his chair to the desk and cracking the can with a hiss. Then he held his hands out in front of him and cracked his knuckles, homing in on the grey screen before.

Chapter 11

The rest of the day had passed by with Mike finishing up his chores and showing Maggie the world of video games, which consisted of her sitting on the bed next to him while he played. She didn't show any interest and her lack of enthusiasm did nothing to detract from his enjoyment. But regardless of her presence, he still had to do something to pass the time, and she wasn't exactly the greatest conversationalist. So, he'd resorted to his normal routines. He still struggled to get past the dirtiness of her clothes, and the scrapes and bruises, and on more than one occasion felt the need to reach over and brush off the bed where she sat. But after a while he came to understand that though she was there, she really wasn't *there.* Not in the sense that the dirt on her clothes would transfer to his bed. It was still something he was struggling to get used to. Mike had been playing for most of the late afternoon into evening and it wasn't until his dad had called out that dinner was ready that he turned off the console and made his way out to the dining room. He was trying his hardest to act normally but found it increasingly difficult when every time he looked up Maggie was standing just a few feet away, her gaze slowly working between them. His dad was still eyeing him suspiciously and he could feel his mom starting to tune in on it.

"So how was your day?" his dad asked, the tone almost inquisitive, a noticeable difference from the usual conversation starter.

"It was good," Mike replied, trying to play off not noticing Maggie looking around the kitchen. "We just hung out at our spot. Jeff's doing this project on a girl that went missing in the seventies. We're gonna help him out with it."

"He's a strange one that kid," his dad replied, glancing at his wife. "Anything else exciting?"

Mike shook his head. "No. That was pretty much it."

"Well," his dad said, loosening up a bit. "Thanks for helping me finish up the yard. I appreciate you not forgetting this time, and not having to remind you."

"You're welcome."

Mike's mom chimed in, her question holding so many undertones that Mike didn't even know which one to worry about first. "So, how's your little friend Denise doing?"

Mike readied himself. "She's good."

Instantly he picked up on the innuendo in her voice. He knew what was coming next...

His mom smiled. "You know. You too look really cute together."

"Mom!" he snapped.

"Debora," his dad said with a grin. "Leave the boy alone."

"I'm just saying. I think you two would make a cute couple."

Mike shook his head and exhaled sharply. "Ew. That's gross. She's basically like one of the guys. And besides, she kinda likes girls..."

His mom's demeanor shifted immediately. "You mean, likes, likes?"

"Yeah mom..." he replied.

Mike's dad set down his fork and wiped his mouth with a napkin, shooting his wife a glance Mike hadn't seen before and then quickly changed the topic. "So, I've gotta shoot out to the quarry tomorrow to check the water levels. You wanna ride with your old man?"

Mike paused. He knew his dad liked it when they spent time together and hated having to make an excuse not to go, but the dead little girl standing a few feet away didn't leave him much in the way of options. "I'm really sorry dad. I want to, but we all promised Jeff we'd help him work on this project. We're all meeting him at eleven after he finishes his scout meeting."

His dad smirked. "Scout meeting? Isn't he a little old to still be in scouts?"

"Yeah," Mike replied with a sigh. "That's what we've been saying. But his mom wants him to see it the whole way through. She says it'll build character or something like that."

His dad chuckled. "It'll build character all right, when he's getting his ass kicked for still wearing a scout uniform at sixteen."

"Jim!" his mom barked, setting her fork down on her plate.

"Just saying sweetheart. There's a lot cooler things he could be doing. I mean the kid's already a walking prophylactic."

Mike looked at his dad puzzled. "What's a pro-fa-lac-tick?"

His mother shot his dad a look that this time, he *was* very familiar with.

His dad took a deep breath and exhaled slowly. "It just means he's not very... cool. That's all."

"Oh," Mike replied, storing the word in his memory banks for future use. "Well," he said, trying not to glance at Maggie. "I'm kind of full. Is it okay if I go back to my game?"

His dad nodded. "Yeah. Put your plate in the sink, and don't forget to brush your teeth. I don't want you falling asleep with the controller in your hand again and not waking up until morning without having taken care of your basic hygiene."

"OK Dad."

Mike didn't see his dad flinch, or notice his mother kick his shin under the table as he walked his plate towards the sink.

He deposited his plate in the sink and ran a bit of water over it before turning and making his way towards his room. As he got a few feet past the table his dad called out, stopping him.

"Aren't you forgetting something?"

Mike turned. "Oh. Sorry."

He stepped back, leaning down to give his mom a kiss. "Night mom."

"Good night sweetie," she replied. "Don't stay up too late."

"I won't."

Mike turned and made his way back into his room, closing the door behind him.

Then he turned to Maggie, whispering quietly. "Could you try not to walk around so much?" he asked. "My dad already thinks I'm on drugs, and if I keep looking at something that he thinks isn't there…" He sighed, shaking his head. Then he reached out and pushed the power button on the console and picked up the controller as he climbed onto his bed.

Chapter 12

The group was in the field chatting amongst each other when a rooster tail of dust pulled them from the heated discussion they were having.

"No way! Lestat could have taken Louis out in a heartbeat if he wanted. He was way older than him."

Todd scoffed loudly. "Dude. Louis took out an entire den of vampires. And you heard what Armand said, they were all just as old as Lestat."

"He never said that. He said *he* was, not the others. Lestat was just lucky that Claudia was the one that tried to."

"Guys."

Todd and John stared at each other for a moment before looking at Denise.

"Here come's Evel Knievel..." John grinned.

Todd chuckled himself at John's remark.

A moment later Mike came skidding to a stop.

"Looks like you beat him."

Mike paused. "Who?" Then he looked behind him to see Jeff flying towards them full speed.

"Huh," Mike said, turning to bump fists with the guys and smiling at Denise. "Didn't see him."

Then Jeff slid to a stop and dropped his bike. "So, I did some searching," he said hurriedly, completely skipping the usual greeting. "I found out where Maggie lived. It's just outside of town. 49 Cedar Drive. Her mom died a few years after she disappeared, and her dad's been living there alone ever since."

Mike bobbed his head up and down. "OK."

"I talked to my mom," Denise added. "She says she remembers Maggie disappearing, and that there was one girl she always hung around, Brandy Whiting. She says she's a manager over at the Town and Country now."

"The diner on fourth?"

Denise glanced at Mike. "Yeah."

Now they were getting somewhere. Mike could feel a nervous excitement building in him. "OK," he said. "Well. We should probably go check out her house first. Maybe her dad'll have some information that could help. Then we should go see her friend."

Denise looked concerned. Getting the information was easy but putting it to use. She didn't want to open old wounds that had surely healed by now. She didn't want to see the faces of those that knew the girl when they came strolling up out of nowhere asking questions. She could only imagine the pain that her parents and friends had felt. But at the same time... "Who's gonna go? I don't think we should all show up to her dad's house together asking questions. It might be a little much. You know... He lost his daughter. And not to be gross, but we're about to pull that scab off."

The others looked between each other. They hadn't thought about that. Till that moment it had been purely an adventure; a quest to find One-Eyed Willy's treasure, to collect the Tri-Force and save the kingdom. It had been fun and exciting. Now it was serious. Now... now it was real. This was a real little girl, and a real father who had felt the pain of her death. Things slowly took on a somber tone.

"I'll go," Mike replied. "I'll take Todd with me."

John puffed up. "Why Todd?"

Mike looked at John, surprised that he would even ask a question like that after what Denise had just said.

"Because, you're a loud mouth, you're insensitive and you swear too much...?"

"So!?"

"Dude... We're going to talk to this guy about his daughter who died twenty years ago. It's probably gonna get a little emotional, and I don't want you messing things up because you can't keep your mouth shut or decide to say some smartass comment."

"That's fucked up."

"Case in point," Jeff said with a shake of his head.

John smirked, settling for the response and knowing it was probably true.

"Denise," Mike said, putting his attention back to her. "You wanna take Jeff with you and go talk to her friend?"

Denise nodded. "Yeah."

John's mouth opened slightly as his arms came up, palms lifted. "And what am I supposed to do? Stand here with my thumb in my ass waiting for you guys to get back? The fuck?"

Mike snapped his gaze to him. "No. You're gonna go to the police station and ask them if they have any information on a missing persons case from 1975 involving a young girl named Maggie Lorris."

John paused, a worried hesitation moving across his face. "Hold up... The police station...?"

"Yeah. The police station."

John took a deep breath, his cheeks puffing up as he exhaled loudly. "Fuck that! You're not sending me into the lion's den..."

Mike stared at him for a split second. "Dude, just do it, okay?" Then he glanced to the others. "Meet us back here at three?"

There was a unanimous nod of agreement.

Then he turned to Todd, tapping him in the chest. "All right. Let's go talk to Maggie's dad."

John watched the others leave, still steaming about the task assigned to him. He'd never had any run-ins with law enforcement, but he hated what they stood for, laws and authority. They were oppression, pure and simple. He watched T.V. and read about how cops treated people in the big cities, especially when it came to minorities, and though all of his friends were white, he felt an obligation to hate them even more for it. And now they wanted him to just walk into the station, open arms and ask about a girl who'd been dead for twenty years...? They weren't gonna hear the end of that any time soon. This one he would be filing away under favors next time he needed something.

Chapter 13

The azure sky overhead was tufted with silver-lined white. Birds sang their midday songs and the smell of freshly cut grass and summer flowers danced in the air. A soft clink of metal chimed out; the small bell Todd had attached to the bottom of his bike clinking lightly as he jumped off the curb behind Mike into the street. All around them summer suggested slow days; backs laid in soft grass with gazes locked to the endless sky and feet pressed against the cool grass. The warm air offered listless afternoons and care-free bouts of lazy enjoyment. But on the street, Mike and Todd did their best to fend off the enticing temptations and focused on their task at hand; finding out exactly who Maggie had been, before someone made her a ghost.

"So, what are we supposed to say when we get there?" Todd asked as he pulled up next to Mike and matched his speed.

"I'm not sure," Mike replied, scanning the road ahead. "That's what I was just trying to figure out."

Todd swerved his bike, avoiding a large rock that was in his path. "What if we tell him we're doing a school project on people that have gone missing in Cedar, and that Maggie came up?"

"We already thought about that," Mike said, glancing to him quickly and then back to the street. "It's summer break remember?"

"Yeah," Todd replied, his small bell chiming as he rode over a bump. "But the guy's gotta be like eighty years old by now. He's definitely not gonna know the school schedule.

65

And even if he asks, we'll just make something up. It's not like the guy's gonna check up on our story."

Mike smirked. His friend wasn't wrong. "Good point. Just let me do the talking when we get there."

Todd nodded, looking up to see the address at the end of the block. He was more than okay with that. Mike was way more outspoken than he was. He hated the term shy. He just preferred not talking to people he didn't know.

"That's the house," Mike said, glancing at the numbers painted on the curb.

They both slowed down, hopping off their bikes without stopping and pushing them towards the yard.

"Like I said—" Mike started, reminding Todd one last time to just stay quiet.

"Check it out," Todd said, interrupting him mid-sentence.

Mike turned, glancing at the house to see an older man exit the front door and start across the yard towards an old pickup truck parked in the driveway.

"That's gotta be him," Todd said, watching as the man climbed in the truck and started the engine.

"Damn," Mike said, watching as the truck backed out of the driveway and started down the street.

"Now what?" Todd asked.

"Well. Looks like we're gonna have to wait."

The next hour went by slowly, neither of the boys really doing much talking. They waited for the man to return, each lost in their own daydreams. Todd was intertwining two long weeds together, making what the kids referred to as a boondoggle. Mike went over the pending conversation again and again, formulating the least painful way to broach the subject. Though, no matter how he spun it, the fact that they were there to talk about the man's daughter who went missing twenty years prior and was never found. There was no way the conversation wasn't going to be awkward, or anything but painful for the man. He sat there trying to formulate any other way they could get the information they needed, any option but the one they were having to take, when the sound of an old engine coming up the street lifted his gaze.

Todd dropped the rectangular art piece he had been weaving to the ground and glanced at Mike. An uneasy nervousness worked its way into both of their guts as they watched the truck pull into the driveway and come to a stop. The older man stepped out, cursing as a metal object clattered to the ground at his feet. The boys watched as the man ran one hand through the thin sliver hair atop his head and then slowly bent over and picked up the silver item. He unscrewed the top and put it to his lips, tilting his head back to take a large swig. Then he screwed the top back on, grabbed two bags of groceries from the bed of the truck and made his way around and towards the house.

The man's back curved gently to the left and his steps were small and limped. He wore faded blue jeans that seemed to hang loosely over his fragile frame and had a dark blue t-shirt tucked into them. His tennis shoes shuffled against the ground as he closed the space between the truck and the house, and they could see that even in the short walk he was beginning to lose his breath.

Mike tapped Todd's arm and rose to his feet. "Come on."

Todd stood up, grabbing his bike and started after Mike.

As they came across the yard Mike called out politely. "Excuse me, Sir?"

The man turned, glancing suspiciously between the pair. "Whatever you're selling I ain't buyin, and I already got a subscription to the paper, so..."

"Actually," Mike replied, coming to a stop a few feet away from the older gentleman. "We were hoping it would be okay if we asked you some questions about a girl that used to live here. Maggie Lorris."

Instantly the man's demeanor shifted. Mike could see what was left of the short breaths the man was taking visibly leave the man's lungs. A nervous silence fluttered past as long forgotten memories were painfully drug to the surface. *So much for taking the gentle approach...*

He stared at the boys for a moment as he slowly composed himself. He glanced up and down the street as if expecting another group to come rushing forward. Then he turned his gaze back to the pair. "I suppose it couldn't hurt anything." He paused, looking between each of them. "Name's Alan. Maggie was my daughter." Then he paused, glancing down for a breath before looking back up to meet their gazes. "I suppose we should probably go on and talk inside."

Mike and Todd exchanged a quick glance.

"Thank you," Mike replied, following the man as he started towards the front door.

"Go ahead and park your bikes on the porch," the man said as he opened the front door. "They'll be safe there."

"Can we give you a hand?" Mike asked, seeing how the plastic sagged in the man's frail grip.

"Oh, I got it," he responded, not turning to look at them. "Ain't crippled yet."

Mike pushed his bike to the porch and set it against the stairs. Todd leaned his against Mike's and then they both made their way up the stairs.

As they stepped in the first thing Mike noticed was how dark the house was. All the curtains were drawn and there was an odor of old cloth and paper that hung in the air, the kind of smell that hung around his grandmother's linen closet.

The man made his way towards the kitchen, calling out behind him as he did. "Go ahead and make yourselves comfortable. I just gotta put this stuff away fore' it goes bad."

Mike tapped Todd's arm and nodded towards the couch.

As they sat down, they could see the amount of clutter that had built up over the years. The table closest to the door was piled with old mail, bills and advertisements, old newspapers. It was obvious that the man had been living alone for quite some time and that company wasn't something that he experienced often.

"Dude," Todd leaned over, his nose wrinkled tightly and whispered, "It smells like a nursing home..."

Mike looked at him, his eyebrows raising up as he splayed his hands out slightly. "Dude, he's like ninety."

Todd gave an exaggerated shudder. "Ugh..."

Mike replied with a look that told him to knock it off.

Todd gave one last small shudder and then turned his attention to glancing around the room.

A minute later Maggie's dad stepped out of the kitchen and made his way towards a brown houndstooth patterned recliner next to the couch. He sat down and pulled the flask from his pocket, unscrewing the cap and taking another swig before refastening it and setting it on the coffee table in from of them.

Mike glanced at the flask.

"Sorry," the man said. "Forgot my manners. Ain't often I have company these days. You boys want somethin' to drink?"

Todd opened his mouth to reply but Mike cut him short. "No, thank you. We're fine."

The man looked between them for a moment before settling back into this chair. "Suit yourself," he remarked, pausing for a moment. "Well. You mentioned you had some questions?"

Mike shifted nervously. "Uh. Yeah. So. You're Maggie's father?"

"That's what I said," the man replied. "Was..."

"Uh." Mike still struggled for the best way to enter the conversation, settling on a straight-forward approach that Denise probably would have suggested against. "What can you tell us about her disappearance?"

Mike channeled his inner detective. He'd watched Ed Green interview countless suspects on Law and Order. Just keep it simple he told himself. Get as much info as possible and don't arouse any suspicion.

Maggie's dad glanced at the flask again but didn't reach for it. "I suppose you'll be wantin' to hear the whole story start to finish then?"

Mike glanced at Todd. He was expecting it to be a long drawn-out conversation with dozens of questions. He hadn't expected the reply to come so easily. Part of him wanted to sigh in relief but he maintained his inquisitive composure. "If you wouldn't mind, that would be great."

"All right," the man continued. "I've told it a hundred times, what's once more I guess?" Again, he glanced at the flask. Mike could see that just the feeling of it being there in sight brought the old man comfort. "It was late October," he started. "Maggie had gone to the bowling alley with her friends to celebrate her birthday early since it fell on a weekday." He paused, remembering. "Back then we didn't have to worry about child murders and kids getting abducted. It was safer than it is now with the internet and, drug parties and what not." He paused. "Anyways, I'd dropped her off and told her to be safe. And she'd told me she'd call when she was done, and I'd shoot down there and pick her up like I always did." He paused, taking a deep breath and again glancing at the flask. "But I never got that call. And that was the last time my wife and I ever saw our little girl…"

Mike watched as the man's memories flared sharply and his gaze lost itself to the wood grain of the coffee table for a moment. Then he inhaled sharply and continued.

"The police reports said that for whatever reason, she wound up going back out to the parking lot. Her friends said that there was some red car parked in the lot, a mustang… I don't know why, and I seriously doubt anybody will, but for some damned reason, she got into that car." He paused again. "They drove off and that was the last anybody heard from her or saw that car again." He nodded, glancing at the table again. "You know. For weeks I drove up and down old highway 56, hoping to find something, hoping to see her wandering the side of the road, making her way back home. But I never did. No one did. She never came home, and her body was never found." He paused again. "You know, for

71

almost three years after she disappeared, I'd go sit almost every night in that damn parking lot, waiting for that sum' bitch to come back." His gaze drifted off into the darkness of the room. "Just me, my rifle and a shovel…"

Mike glanced at Todd. He didn't say anything, but he found it odd that her dad referred to her body never being found like her being dead was the only possibility. But at the same time, he supposed the man had had twenty years to come to terms with it. Still, something about the way he said it didn't sit right.

"I still catch myself looking every time I drive down that highway…" The old man paused, this time reaching out and picking the flask up. He unscrewed the top and took another sip before setting it back down.

Mike glanced at the flask, noticing the small ornate initials engraved on the front.

"Well," the man continued. "Her mother, god rest her soul, passed away a couple years later, and I've been here ever since." He paused. "Police never did find her. Her picture was in every paper across Utah and on the back of milk boxes for months. Nothing. Whoever it was that she got into that car with. They got away with murder."

Mike stared at the man, waiting to see if he was going to continue. "Do you happen to remember what she was wearing the night she disappeared?"

The man glanced at the table for a moment, pulling the memory back to the surface. Then he glanced up at him nodding. "One of her dresses, I think. I know it was October, so she would have had her thick leggings on underneath. Don't remember what shoes."

"And nobody got a look at who was driving?"

"No. One of her friends was the one who saw her get into the car. But they didn't see em'. All she saw was that it was a red mustang."

Todd sat silently as Mike continued his questions.

"And the police ran a check on all the red mustangs in the city?"

"I would assume," her dad replied. "To be honest I'm not rightly sure of what they did. My wife and I were a mess for quite some time after. But I knew Chief Bauer pretty well, back when he was still the Chief. He did everything he could to find her. Hell. There was a state and nation-wide notice put out. They had a local search party. You name it. They never found anything."

Mike glanced at Todd who nodded. There wasn't much point in dragging the conversation any further. They were only there to get info, not to interrogate the man. And Mike could already see that the memories were bad enough. "Well. Thank you for your time. I hope we didn't bother you."

"Not at all," the man said, standing up. "Good to see somebody taking an interest in Maggie's old case."

Mike and Todd rose.

"Well, thank you again."

"Yeah," Todd added for the sake of being able to say he was part of the conversation. "Thanks."

The man started towards the front door, opening it for them as he approached.

Mike and Todd both stepped outside, making their way down the steps towards their bikes. Behind them the man watched them pick up the bicycles and push them across the yard before closing the door and disappearing back inside.

When the boys reached the sidewalk Mike glanced at his watch. "It's 2:30. We should head back and see what Denise and Jeff found out."

Todd nodded, climbing on his bike and pedaling off. Mike followed shortly behind. The man's face hung in front of him for the next three blocks, the musty smell of the house clinging to the inside of his nostrils. They'd gotten as much information as they could, but nothing that was gonna help them find her killer. There had to be a million red mustangs. How the heck were they supposed to find one, and one from twenty years prior...?

Chapter 14

Denise and Jeff stepped into the diner just after the lunch rush had finished up. They approached the host stand and waited for the younger girl to notice them.

"This is crazy," Jeff said, glancing around the restaurant looking for anyone he could imagine the woman looking like. "There's no way this woman's gonna remember what happened twenty years ago. She was twelve. I barely remember anything when I was that young."

Denise scowled at him. "Really...? That was *four* years ago. You can't remember four years ago...?"

Jeff exhaled sharply. "I'm just saying, I think this is a long shot."

"Well, we don't really have many other options do we?"

"Hi there."

Denise and Todd looked up to see a young girl approaching them.

"For two?"

"Actually," Denise replied. "We were wondering if there's a woman named Brandy that still works here?"

The hostess stopped, her face growing inquisitive. "Um. You mind if I ask what it's regarding?"

Jeff glanced at Denise.

"It's about a friend of hers that went missing twenty years ago," Denise replied, watching the girl's eyebrows scrunch together at the response. She realized as the words left her lips how strange that must have sounded. "We're doing a school project, on, uh, people that have gone missing here in Cedar..." She wouldn't have believed her if she had heard it, but the girl smirked again, nodding slightly. "OK...? Um. You wanna wait here and I'll see if she's available?"

"Sure, Thanks," Denise replied, glancing at Jeff who stood with his eyebrows lifted next to her.

"Smooth," he said, bobbing his head.

Denise lifted her hands slightly. "Dude... I..." She exhaled sharply and turned her gaze to the server area the hostess was making her way to. They watched as the girl walked back towards the server station. She had a brief conversation with a blonde woman in her mid-thirties that was rolling silverware, and they could see by the facial expressions that she was relaying the message just as awkwardly as Denise had delivered it. They spoke for a second before the woman turned to them with a confused look on her face. Then the hostess made her way back.

"She'll be right out," the hostess said as she walked back to them.

A few moments later the woman emerged from the back and walked towards them.

"Um. Hi. Kelly told me something about a missing friend. Is there something I can help you with?"

Jeff could see by the look on the woman's face that she had no idea what they were talking about. He almost let an *I told you* slip when Denise spoke up.

"Brandy Whiting?"

"Yeah... That's, me."

"Look. I know this may sound strange, but we're investigating the disappearance of a young girl named Maggie Lorris. We heard that the two of you may have been friends when you were younger."

As Denise spoke the color in the woman's cheeks faded away, a soft alabaster softly shifting the tone of her makeup.

"We were just wondering if we could ask you a few questions?"

The woman stared at them for a moment and then turned to the hostess who stood eavesdropping at the stand. "Kelly. Uh. Could you tell Evan to watch my tables? I'm gonna need to step out for a moment."

The girl nodded, turning to walk away as Brandy looked back to Denise.

"You uh, wanna step outside?"

A few minutes later the three were standing near the rear of the building. The waitress was fumbling with an unlit cigarette in her hand, a lighter held in the other. "I. I don't really remember much from that night. It was a really long time ago." The woman paused, glancing into the parking lot for a moment.

"Well, whatever you can tell us will help."

"What's this about anyways? Did they find something? I thought they gave up looking years ago."

Denise glanced at Jeff for a moment.

"They did," he said, jumping in to take the lead. "We're doing a school project, kind of an extra credit summer thing. We were just hoping to get some information about her. Where she was last seen, if she had any enemies, things like that."

"Enemies?" Brandy stared at Jeff for a moment. "Maggie was twelve... Nobody has enemies at twelve years old. Some sick fuck—" The woman stopped, her gaze working quickly between them. "I'm sorry," she said quickly, embarrassed for swearing in front of them. "It's just..." She lifted the back of her hand to her forehead and pressed her eyes closed tightly for a moment. "Sorry.

Denise jumped in, diffusing the situation as quickly as she could. "It's OK. We, don't mind." She paused, taking a small breath and exhaling sharply. "What he *meant* to say was, could there have possibly been anybody who may have had an interest in her. Anybody she could have been close to?"

Brandy exhaled slowly, shaking her head. Then she lifted the cigarette to her lips and lit it.

A thick cloud of smoke lifted into the air.

"We were at the bowling alley the night she went missing. We had been celebrating her birthday. It was a Saturday. I remember because her birthday was on a Monday that year and because of school we had it two days early. We were all bowling when Maggie said she'd be right back. None of us thought anything about it." She paused, taking another drag from her cigarette. "Sorry. It's just... I haven't thought about this in a really long time."

The pair stayed quiet.

"We'd seen her talking to some older guy near the bar... Well, older then. He was probably in his twenties. None of us thought anything about it. It was just some guy sitting at the bar. There were always people sitting at the bar. We figured maybe it was a family friend or something. I remember seeing her walk towards the front door a few minutes later. I don't know. I guess I had a funny feeling. I realized that the guy was gone and just thought it was a bit weird that she was going outside when everyone had already arrived. So, I followed her." She took another puff from her cigarette, watching as the smoke lifted up and dissipated. "By the time I got outside she was getting into that car."

"You didn't see who was driving?"

She looked at Jeff. "No. It was parked behind one of those big cement light poles. I couldn't see." She paused. "I was about to go towards her when the car started and then screeched out of the parking lot." The waitress's gaze dropped to the ground. "I remember watching the taillights fading away and just knowing, *somehow*, that was the last time I was ever going to see her." Again, she paused, her gaze lifting away from the concrete. "That's when I went inside and told one of the parents that were with us, and they called the police."

"Did the bowling alley have any cameras?"

"Yeah," she replied, looking at Jeff. "But apparently they weren't working, and they never got around to getting them fixed."

"Do you remember what the man at the bar looked like?" Denise asked, knowing it was a long shot.

"No. Dark hair, I think. He was wearing a hat. I never saw his face though."

Denise nodded.

"Look," Brandy said, dropping the cigarette to the ground and stepping on it. "I'm sorry I can't be more of a help, but I told the police everything I had seen the night it happened. I gotta get back inside."

"Thank you for talking with us," Denise said, seeing the distress now enveloping the poor woman.

"Yeah. I hope you find something that helps. Um. Yeah."

Jeff and Denise watched as the waitress turned and walked back towards the entrance.

"Well, that wasn't very helpful..."

"At least we tried," Denise said, her gaze moving back to the woman as she entered. "Let's head back. Maybe Mike and Todd found something out."

Chapter 15

The ride into town had taken John about twenty minutes. The time it took him to gather the courage to walk into the police station, nearly three times that long. He had stopped just in front, freezing when one of the officers had walked out of the entrance. "Fuck this...," he'd scoffed, turning and making his way to the park two blocks away. He had sat there watching traffic and coming up with the different lies he could use upon returning when he finally came to the realization; this was important for Mike, and as much as he hated what he had asked him to do, he knew Mike would do the same for him. So, he growled softly, slapping his hands against his legs and then stood, climbed on his bike and made his way back to the police station.

The air was cool as he stepped in. He expected it to be a bustle of police officers, all rushing to and fro, dozens of people struggling against handcuffs and the smell of coffee and donuts rising into the air. But the lobby was quiet and smelled clean.

There was a single officer sitting behind the large desk that ran nearly the width of the room. He could see dozens of wanted posters hanging on the walls behind him and the wall to his side was adorned with dozens of city plaques and certificates. Another wall had five rows of police officer pictures with their names engraved into tiny plaques beneath. He assumed it was the officers that worked there, or some type of cop memorial.

The desk sergeant looked up as he made his way across the room towards him.

As John stepped closer, he caught a faint whiff of coffee. He did all he could to stifle the grin.

"Um. Yeah. Hi," he began, placing his hands on the desk in front of him. "Um. My friends sent me in here to see if I could ask about a *missing persons case*, from twenty years ago."

The officer eyed him suspiciously. He could only imagine how uncomfortable he looked standing there...

"And what's this regarding?" the officer asked.

John smirked slightly. "A missing person...?"

The cop took a deep breath, licking his lips in frustration as he blinked slowly. "Yeah. I got that. What I'm asking, is what is the reason you're inquiring about this missing person?"

"Oh," John replied. "Um." He smirked again. "School project...?"

The officer exhaled sharply, staring at him for a moment. "OK." He shook his head slightly. "Well, what's the name?"

"Uh, Maggie. Maggie Lorris." He paused, watching as the officer continued to study him. It felt like at any moment the officer was going to stand up, tell him he was under arrest and handcuff him on some suspicion or another. But the man eventually lowered his gaze and typed something into the computer.

"What was the year?" the officer asked, glancing up at him.

"Um. It was, nineteen seventy-five."

The man glanced back down, typing something again. Then he looked back up. "Yeah. The case was never solved and was marked for closure in early seventy-seven. It looks like there were a few leads, but no suspects were ever brought into custody."

John stared at him, waiting for more.

"Is there something else I can help you with?" the officer asked.

"That's it?" John asked. "I mean. Could I get a list of names of the suspects?"

The puzzled look on the officer's face scrunched tighter. "Uh, no. That's private information."

John sighed heavily. He was trying, but he just had no idea what to ask. They should have sent Jeff. He would have been much better for this than he was.

"Look," the cop finally said after a tense moment. "The detective that worked the case is still in the department. If you'd like, I can see if he is available to sit down and talk with you about it—"

"No!" John burst, realizing just how loud it was as he did. "That's okay. Really. Thanks. You've been really helpful."

The officer settled back into his chair, one arm lowering to the padded armrest. The look on his face shifted from uncomfortable suspicion to pure confusion.

"So, there's nothing else then?" John asked, watching as the man stared at him as if he was a sandwich that had just grown legs and was walking away.

"No. There's nothing else." He paused. "Like I said. If you would like, I can schedule an interview with the detective who oversaw the case and maybe he can answer more of your questions. But other than that, there is nothing more I can offer you. Maybe try going to the courthouse and getting a subpoena..."

"A sup... A what?"

The man stared at him for a moment longer and then leaned forward, turning his gaze back to the computer screen before him. "Have a nice day."

John stared for a moment longer, realizing that the officer was not going to be lifting his gaze back anytime soon. "Yeah," he mumbled, turning around. "Thanks..."

John made his way outside and walked over to his bike. He shook his head at the entire ordeal and knew that this was a card he would be keeping close to his chest, for the next time he needed a *really* big favor. "Fuckin cops," he grumbled to himself... Then he pulled his bike off the rack, climbed over and started pedaling down Main towards their spot.

Chapter 16

"Did you find the house!?"

Jeff hadn't even waited for Mike and Todd to set their bikes down before rushing them, the anxiety laced question bursting forth.

"Yeah," Mike replied as his bike clanked to the dirt. "We talked with her dad, but he doesn't know much more than we do. Just that he dropped her off at the bowling alley and that sometime that night she got into a red mustang and was never seen again." Mike paused as Todd let his bike drop to the ground behind him. "What about you guys? Did you find anything?"

"We went to the diner," Denise answered before Jeff could start. "The lady my dad had told me about, Brandy. She still worked there, so Jeff and I chatted with her for a little bit. She didn't remember a lot, but she did tell us that Maggie had been talking with some guy that was sitting at the bar that night, but that was about it." She paused, looking at Jeff for a moment. "I felt really bad bringing it up. You could see that just thinking about it was still painful."

"She didn't have anything else?"

Jeff chimed in. "She didn't know anything."

"What about you?" Mike asked, looking at John.

John smirked and shook his head. "Same thing. Cops don't remember and the case has been closed for years. All the files are in storage somewhere and without a court order they're not pulling them out to review any time soon." He paused. "Still can't believe you had me go there."

"Oh, get over it," Mike snapped.

John scoffed again.

"OK. Jeff, is there any way you could find out who had a red mustang registered to them at the time of her disappearance in the county?"

Jeff nodded. "It'll take some work, but if it's in the database I should be able to find something."

"OK. I'm gonna shoot out to the bowling alley and ask around. Maybe somebody there remembers something."

Denise looked at him softly. "Mike. It was twenty years ago."

"Yeah, and?"

"I really doubt that it's the same people working there now that were there then."

"Your dad still works at the school."

"Yeah. I know Mike, but he's the superintendent."

Mike was beginning to feel the serrated edge of frustration. He knew he was clutching at straws, but he wasn't going to give up and anything that could possibly help was worth looking at. If they asked a hundred questions and got even one answer back, that was more than they would have known giving up, and that was one thing he was not going to do. "I don't know about you guys," he said. "But I'm pretty sure that whoever it was that she was talking to at the bar is the one that took her."

"Dude," John chimed in. "The cops already went over all this twenty years ago when it happened. And they didn't find anything out then. How the hell do you expect us to find anything out now?"

"Look," Mike snapped back, the frustration reaching a boiling point. "We gotta try *something* OK? She didn't just appear for no reason. She needs our help."

"And why are you so hell bent on this whole her needing help thing? How the hell do you know she's not some lost spirit, or ghost that just doesn't want to cross over to the other side?"

Mike turned to where she was standing and held out his hand. For a moment he realized he hadn't actually entertained that thought. Then he shook his head quickly, abandoning the notion. "Does she look like she's just hanging around? Huh? Does she look like she wants to be here?"

John looked at Maggie who shifted her gaze to meet his for a moment.

"No," Mike continued. "She looks sad, and frightened, and lost. And it's obvious at this point that we're the only ones that can help her. So…"

John took a deep breath and exhaled loudly. "And here I thought I was gonna have a nice relaxing summer, not be babysitting some dead chick…"

Denise cringed. "You are such an asshole… Oh my god…"

"Right," Jeff said, shaking his head. "Jesus, dude…"

"What?" John asked, oblivious to the insult he had just delivered.

"Look," Mike said a second later. "I gotta go home. I'll see you guys tomorrow." He turned to Denise. "I'll call the bowling alley and ask, but you're probably right. Most of the people that work there aren't that old." He paused, glancing at the others. "Later guys." Then he made his way to his bike and picked it up before glancing at Maggie. "Let's go."

The group watched as he rode off, Maggie walking slowly in the direction he rode off in before fading away in the same manner as a mirage when approached.

"Way to go John," Jeff said, shooting a dirty look at him.

"What the fuck? What did I do?"

Todd scoffed as he started towards his bike. "Same thing as always dude. Same thing as always..."

Denise and Jeff both turned and walked towards their bikes.

Behind them John lifted his arms into the air. "Seriously?" He barked. "What the hell?"

Chapter 17

"Hey Dad," Denise said as she stepped in to the small two-bedroom house they shared. Her mom had passed away when she was young and her and her father had lived by themselves since then. The others had joked that since her dad was single and Jeff's mom was divorced, that they should hook up. That was a notion that Denise had quickly and very loudly shared her opposition to. Jeff's mom was kind of..., heavy... Though she would never say that to his face. Her dad was still relatively young, just over forty, and in her opinion still pretty good looking. He was handsome, and fit. She knew that the only reason he hadn't started dating was because she still lived at home, though many times she had told him he should and that she wouldn't mind. He told her he just wasn't ready, but she knew it was because he still felt that he had to focus completely on being a dad and taking care of her. Those were just a few reasons that she loved him so much and that they had a friendship and bond that was stronger than any she could have imagined.

"Hey Chipmunk," her dad replied from the kitchen. "How was your day?"

"Oh," she replied, making her way across the living room. "You know. Hung out with the guys."

"How are they doing?" he asked as she stepped into the kitchen.

She made her way over and gave him a hug, and then turned to open the fridge. "They're good. John's still an asshole and Jeff's got us all working together on that missing person project I was asking you about..."

Her dad raised his eyebrows as he cocked his head to the side. Then he scoffed lightly before taking a sip from the beer bottle that had been sitting on the counter, his hand wrapped around it. "I still don't know how you got wrapped up with them...?"

Denise pulled a soda from the fridge and turned, popping the top with a soft *hiss*. She shook her head as well. "Me neither..."

"That Jeff's a weird one..."

"Tell me about it," she smiled. "But they're all good guys. And, well, they accept me for who I am."

"A rabid chipmunk...?"

"You know what I mean."

Her dad smiled. "I know." He paused. "I'm sorry people can't be more open-minded."

"It's fine," she replied. "I'm used to it..."

Denise had realized that she liked girls when she was much younger, that she was attracted to them. But unfortunately, she lived in Southern Utah, and as open and free as places like California we were at that time, Cedar City wasn't one of them. Sure, they weren't as crazy as some of the places she had heard of in the south, or like Kansas, but still. Cedar City was a Mormon town. They had their own ways and beliefs and were very strict about them. Being a lesbian wasn't exactly one of their accepted qualities. So as far as who she had come out to, it was pretty much just her dad and the guys. And that was one of the reasons they were such good friends, both her father and the others. Because they didn't care.

She remembered back on the first time she had gotten up the courage to tell them that she liked girls. She had been worried, nearly paralyzed with the fear of it. They had all gotten to be really good friends, and she was so worried that they were going to stop talking to her, or not want to be around her. But when she told them, Mike had smiled and simply said, *welcome to the club*, and John had said something along the lines of, *nice, threesomes!* Of course he did... Her dad on the other hand had sat her down and told her that he accepted her no matter what, and that she should never let anyone dictate or decide her life. God had made her exactly how he wanted her to be. Then he had told her that he would never put up with anyone treating her badly because of it, and that if she ever had a problem in school to let him know and he would deal with it immediately. In the end she just decided it best to not tell too many people. Not at least until she was in college. High school was hard enough already...

"Do you mind if I ask you a few more questions about Maggie Lorris?" she asked, taking another sip from the can.

"No," her dad replied. "Of course not. I mean. I don't exactly know *that* much. It was like twenty years ago, so..."

"Well. We found Brandy. She still works at the diner. Thank you for that."

He nodded with a small grin.

"Was there anybody else that she hung out with, or friends that she had?"

"Sorry sweetheart," he replied. "I really couldn't say. I just remember her one friend. And I only remember that because she had been a big part of the investigation."

"Well. What about the bowling alley she disappeared from? Do you think anybody that worked there then still does?"

He smiled, setting his beer down on the counter. "Well. I suppose we could drive out there and ask."

Her gaze moved to the beer bottle.

"I just opened it," he replied. "It'll be here when I get back."

"Are you sure?"

"Sweetheart, I'm the school superintendent, and the person who pushed to have the D.A.R.E. program integrated into the system. Trust me, if I had even finished that beer, we'd be calling the bowling alley." He paused, reaching out to put his hand on her shoulder. "Besides. It's been a while since I've beaten you on the lanes..."

"You cheated," she replied, brushing his hand away playfully. "You changed the score when I went to the bathroom."

"I did nothing of the like," he replied, lifting his nose to the ceiling.

"Suuuure dad. Right..."

He smiled and turned to put his beer back in the fridge. "Let me just throw some shoes on and I'm good to go."

"OK," Denise replied. "I'm gonna change real quick. I've been out in the sun all day in these clothes." She wrinkled her nose and squinted.

"Then you better go change your fur."

She smiled and turned, making her way to her room and changing.

Twenty minutes later they were driving through town on the way to the Alpine Lanes.

"So I just gotta ask," her dad asked as they drove past a popular restaurant hangout built in an old train car. "How did Jeff, decide on this Lorris girl?"

Denise exhaled heavily as the burger spot flashed by. "Um. I don't know, honestly. He just kind of showed up really excited about it the other day. We weren't really doing anything else so..."

"You guys are still hanging out in that field then...?"

"Yep. It's dirty and full of weeds, but. It's ours."

He shook his head, not understanding, but accepting. He'd had some strange places himself when he was a kid.

A short time later they were stepping out of the car and making their way through the same parking lot that Maggie had been abducted. There was a strange feeling that accompanied it for Denise, and as she looked over to the light pole Brandy had mentioned, her mind conjured all manner of horrible visions. The stalking predator, the red car illuminated from above, the lure of candy, the screams.

She shook the pictures away and continued behind her dad to the main doors.

When they entered there weren't a lot of people yet. It was still early and on a weekday. Though she was on summer vacation, the general group of people that patroned the lanes were older and still had their nine to fives. They hadn't begun to filter in yet, but the clock read six thirty-five, so she assumed they would soon.

They walked up to the counter and to her surprise, her dad was the one to ask.

"I know this may sound random," he asked the older man who was waiting for them to order their lane and shoes. "But there wouldn't happen to be anyone that still works here that also worked here back in seventy-five, would there?"

The older man gave him a puzzled look and then nodded. "Well, I guess I'd be the only one to match that description. How can I help you?"

Denise's dad smiled and then tapped her on the arm. "Well?" he asked. "Don't you have some questions for the man?"

She looked at him, slightly shocked. For a moment she had assumed that he was going to handle the entire conversation. "Uh, yeah," she replied, turning her attention to the older gentleman. "Uh. My friends and I are doing a project on a young girl who went missing here twenty years ago."

"The Lorris girl," the man replied much to her surprise.

"Uh, yeah," she replied, struggling to compose herself.

"Well," the man began. "I'm not sure there's much more I can tell you than I did the police back then, but I'd be obliged to offer what I can." He paused, glancing between her and her father. "What would you like to know?"

"Well. I was wondering if you happened to remember a man who was sitting at the bar that night? He was in his twenties or thirties and was wearing a hat?"

"Well. That's the problem," he replied. "We have a lot of folks that come through here. Being as we're the closest source of liquor to all the communities out here, it's hard to say. I do remember something about that." He paused, thinking. "Could have been the Maitland boy..." He paused again. "No. That wouldn't be right. He went off to college out in Florida in seventy-three. Maybe the Cowles boy. He used to hang out here a lot back then."

"Cowles?" Denise asked.

The man nodded. "Yeah. His daddy owned an auto shop outside Cedar. Could have been him." He paused. "But again.

I'm sure I would have given all this information to the police who was investigating the case. So, if they didn't happen on anything..."

"Well, what about cameras?" her dad asked, glancing up at the camera pointing down at them.

"Oh," the old man replied. "Yeah. They'd went out a few years prior to that." He shrugged. "Never really made much sense gettin' em' fixed. In all my time here, we'd only had one fight." He paused. "I got em fixed a couple years back when some bikers started frequenting and scarin' off the regulars. But they went on about their way a short time later." He glanced up at the camera himself. "Doubt I'll ever have a use for em' again."

"So, there's nothing else you can remember about the night?" Denise asked."

"Nothin' in particular. Sorry I can't be bigger help."

"No," Denise replied politely. "You've been perfect."

The man smiled. "I've been called a lot of things in my time. Not sure *perfect* is one of em'."

A large smile drew itself across Denise's face.

"Well," her dad chimed happily. "I guess since we're here, we'll take three games and two pairs of shoes."

"That be three games each or three total?"

"Three each," he replied. "Six total."

"All righty. Sizes?"

"Eight for me." He turned to Denise. "What size shoes do Chipmunks wear again?"

"Five Dad," she replied, turning to the man. "Five please."

"Okie dokie," he said, turning to make his way to the shoes.

"Well," her dad said, turning to look at the spanning lanes. "Did this help at least a little?"

"Yeah," Denise replied, turning to do the same. "Thanks Dad."

"Of course," he replied. "Now let's just see if you remember how to throw a ball."

"I'll just make sure to go to the bathroom *before* we start playing."

Her dad smiled. "Still no clue what you're talking about...."

"Uh-huh..."

The man returned with their shoes, and they made their way to their assigned lane. They spent a few minutes picking out their right combination of balls. By then a few of the local patrons had begun to filter in. The next two hours moved by with Denise and her dad laughing and teasing each other. By the time they made their way back out to the parking lot it was nearly full, the local league having shown up just a short time before. Denise looked past the light pole, again feeling the cold caress, knowing the history it brought. Then she pulled her gaze away and got into the car.

As they pulled out onto the highway the lanes drifted away. Dozens of people threw their custom balls down freshly oiled lanes, laughing and chatting away. Beer flowed and burgers and nachos were devoured. The lanes were a bustling monument to community and friendship. But beneath it all lurked a sad secret, a forgotten tale of a young girl who the lanes were the last to see.

Chapter 18

Jeff sat at his desk, the dull, green hacker glow of the computer monitor casting an ominous shadow across his face. Empty cans of soda and candy bar wrappers scattered his desk, remnants of the sugar-filled fuel that propelled him through his search. His brow was dropped low and there was what could almost be construed as a scowl on his face. He was focused, searching, doing what he prided himself on being the best at.

On the screen in front of him words flashed into existence as his fingers raced across the keys. *Red Ford Mustangs, Iron County, 1975.*

In a flash the next screen was littered with websites, all showing the keywords beneath in italics, a vast list of blue possibilities. He scrolled down and clicked on one. *Vehicle Search Portal.* A few moments later a single column popped up on the screen with a handful of vehicles listed. It appeared that there weren't exactly that many of that make and model listed in the city during the time that Maggie went missing, so he went one by one as the rest loaded.

"Are you using the internet again!?"

Jeff turned his head, yelling up the stairs to where his mom stood at the top. "Yeah mom! It's important."

"Well hurry up," she barked back. "I've gotta make a phone call."

"I told you we needed two lines mom!" he yelled back.

"Then maybe you should get a job and then you can pay for your own line yourself." There was a pause while she waited for a response. When Jeff offered none, she finished by shouting, "Just hurry up. It's expensive right now."

"All right mom!" he yelled back, turning his attention back to the screen. "Jeez..."

He scrolled another two names down, holding the mouse button and dragging it down the large pad on his desk. Then he stopped.

Jeff stared at the screen for a moment, his eyes working back and forth on the vehicle. Same model, same year. But this one was listed as non-operable in seventy-three, two years prior, and the color listed was blue. He scanned the name attached. *Donald Cowles*.

For the next few moments he stared, feeling the flesh on his arms starting to rise. Then he opened another tab and typed the man's name and the city listed in the WebCrawler browser. At the top of the page was a listing for a DC Auto body. Jeff stared, a nervous tingle growing upwards. "No F'ing way..." A smile crept across his lips. "Gotcha..."

Across town Mike had just stepped into his living room. His mom and dad were sitting on the couch watching television, their hands intertwined between them. A beer rested in his father's free hand and a glass of red wine on the end table next to his mom. As he stepped in, they both looked away from the T.V. Maybe they felt his question before he even answered, or maybe it was the awkward look of concern on his face that had grabbed their attention. Either way, they both sat quietly, waiting for him to speak.

"Do you guys remember anything about a little girl named Maggie Lorris? She disappeared about twenty years ago?"

His mom and dad looked at each other briefly, then both gazes moved back to him.

"Yeah," his dad replied, a squint flashing through his eyes. "I think I remember something about that." He turned to his wife. "That's that little girl that was abducted from the bowling alley when we were at junior college right?"

His mom nodded, her expression shifting. "Yeah. I remember that. So sad…"

His dad turned back to him. "What brings this up?"

Mike took a deep breath, quickly forming the best response that would keep him from getting turned over to mental health. "Um. Jeff's doing a research project on her, and I was just trying to gather any information I could."

"Isn't that a little dark for a subject?" his mom asked concerned.

Mike's dad raised his eyebrows and exhaled heavily. "The kid's not exactly playing with a full deck Deb."

"Jim!" she exclaimed, though she felt the same way about him. He had always kind of given her the heebie-jeebies, and if it weren't for the fact that Mike liked him so much, she probably would have told him to distance himself from him long ago. There was just something a little off with that one, the kind of kid a mother felt happy hers hadn't turned out to be.

"It's kind of true mom," Mike interjected. "Everybody knows it. We always joke that he's gonna be the guy that ends up working in a graveyard at night."

His dad smiled. "Or an amazing detective…"

Mike nodded, glancing down the hall towards his room. "Well. I just thought I'd ask. Thanks anyways." And with that he made his way down the hall and into the safety of his room.

He no sooner closed the door and turned around than he saw Maggie standing there. "We're gonna keep looking," he said quietly. "Somebody has to know something." He paused, exhaling while staring at her. "I wish you could just tell us…"

Maggie stared back, her gaze piercing through him with a wave of sadness.

He really did wish they had some way to communicate. He had asked her dozens of questions, but only a few times had she responded with a nod. When it came to asking specific details, like where she had been, who she had been with when she died, where they had taken her. She just stared back through dead eyes; her face sunk in sadness. And it seemed after a long attempt at interrogation that even she wasn't aware of many of the details surrounding her own death and disappearance. He couldn't explain how he knew; he just did. It was up to them to find out. So, with that, he turned and powered on his video game system and flopped heavily onto his bed.

Chapter 19

The sun was still rising above the horizon when Jeff dropped his bike and was dashing to Mike's front door before it even hit the ground. He had stayed awake most of the night prior in anticipation of telling Mike what he had found. Now he couldn't get to the door fast enough.

A series of knocks and three doorbell rings later, Mike's dad swung the door open, sleep-filled anger clouding his eyes. "What the *hell* is the emergency?" he asked, crooking his neck to peer behind the frantic youth.

"Hey Mr. Tanner," Jeff replied, his eyes wide. "Is Mike up?"

Mike's dad stared at him for a moment, disbelief slowly pushing the sleep back. "Well, if he wasn't, I'm sure he is now... Kinda hard *not* to be with you ringing the hell out of the doorbell like that..."

"Sorry," Jeff remarked instinctively. "It's *really* important."

Jim stared at him for a moment carefully choosing his responsible adult reply. Then when he realized nothing but sarcasm was to come forth, he exhaled slowly, leaned his head back and called out. "Mike. Jeff's here. Says it's important." He shot a quick glance back to Jeff before continuing. "Apparently he's forgotten how to use a phone..."

Jeff stood there fidgeting, completely responseless.

Then after a moment Mike's dad stepped back and opened the door wider. "Well. Don't just stand there. You've already woken up half the neighborhood. Better come in before they start throwing things..."

"Oh," Jeff replied quickly. "Thanks Mr. Tanner."

Jeff stepped into the house, taking four of them exactly before coming to a stop directly in the middle of the living room.

Jim walked past him towards the kitchen, and the awaiting coffee pot that had started auto-brewing only a few minutes prior. He shook his head and scoffed silently to himself.

A few moments later Mike stepped into the room.

"Dude..." he said before glancing to his dad. "Sorry dad."

"It's fine," Jim replied while filling his cup. "Though you might wanna explain to Jeff here that he really only has to ring the bell once. It's not broken, and we can hear it just fine. Only the police knock like that..." He paused, grumbling. "Or the Jehovah's Witness..."

"Sorry Mr. Tanner," Jeff replied with a tinge of embarrassment.

"Yeah. Sorry dad."

And with that Mike's dad made his way past and disappeared down the hall, a vapor trail of coffee in his wake.

"Dude," Mike snapped softly. "What the hell man?"

From behind he heard his dad call out to his mom. *"Nothing Deb. Just Jeff, manic as always..."*

Jeff paid no attention, just snapped his gaze back to Mike and dove right in. "Dude! I found him!"

Mike shook his head, still half asleep. "Found who?" Then he paused, glancing out the window. "What time is it?"

"Just past six," Jeff replied quickly. "Dude. I found him!"

Mike yawned. "Found who?" he repeated.

"The owner of the mustang!"

And just like that, Mike was fully awake. "Wait, what? You're serious!?"

"Yeah dude, we got him." Then he paused for a moment. "I mean... I'm pretty sure."

Mike's expression shifted.

"I mean, it's not the same color *exactly*, but it's the same make and model, and it's the only one that was registered in Cedar at the time of the abduction."

"OK. Then what color *is* it?"

Jeff shifted again. "The car listed is blue, but here's the thing. The guy it's registered to owns a body shop. DC Auto down on Third Street." He paused for a moment, waiting for some sign of recognition. "You know, that old junkyard at the edge of town." He paused, giving it another moment to sink in. "If anyone could have changed the color of the car and re-registered it, that would be the guy."

Mike took a deep breath, exhaling slowly to stifle another yawn that was creeping out. "I guess it makes sense."

"It makes total sense."

"Shit..." Mike replied, glancing at the floor for a moment.

"Yeah. Shit..."

Now things began to sink in. "Dude," Mike replied, all sleepiness on his face now gone. "We gotta tell the others."

"Uh, yeah," Jeff quipped. "Why do you think I'm here at six in the morning?"

"All right," Mike replied. "You call them while I get ready. Tell em to meet us at the spot. I'll be ready in five." Mike paused. "Why *didn't* you call...? You literally just rode a half an hour to get here. And now you gotta turn around and ride right back...?"

Jeff thought about it, shrugging. "I don't know. It just felt like the thing to do. Didn't wanna wake your parents up."

Mike smirked. "Well, you didn't do a very good job of that..."

"Yeah..." Jeff said, his face pulling back in apology.

"It's cool... Just make the calls while I get ready."

Jeff nodded, already making his way to the phone.

"Hey dad," Mike shouted as he made his way down the hall. "I gotta shoot out. It's kind of important. It's about our project."

"All right," Mike's dad shouted from his parent's room. *"Be home by dinner. And make sure to eat lunch, I left you five dollars on the table."*

"Thanks Dad," Mike called back. "I will."

Ten minutes later the breeze was blowing past as Mike and Jeff pedaled as fast as they could down the highway towards their spot. Overhead the sun was just beginning to caress the concrete beneath them, spreading its warmth to the air that whipped past.

"Why the hell do you have to live so far out?" Jeff asked, panting heavily.

"It's not my fault. I didn't pick our house."

"Well, it sucks."

"Hey dude," Mike replied. "You're not the one that has to ride it twice a day." He pedaled a few moments longer. "I can't get my driving permit until next year. I swear I'm never gonna ride a bike again after that..."

The next few minutes went by wordlessly. Each of them focused on falling into a pedaling pattern, keeping their breaths steady as the blacktop whipped by.

"So, you're sure about this?" Mike shouted a short time later to Jeff who was riding a few feet ahead.

"Yeah," Jeff replied, not looking back. "First, I did a public search of any mustangs registered in Iron County. Then I cross-referenced with the DMV and local automotive auctions. Then I took that and checked it against people and shops with parts for sale including body parts from classic mustangs that were red."

"Jesus, dude," Mike replied.

"Yeah," Jeff continued. "It took me a while. But the only thing I came back with was a blue one. So, I checked the name it was registered to and then looked that name up and saw that he owns the auto shop and scrapyard in town. His dad owned it at the time of Maggie's disappearance. But apparently, he took over some time after and still runs it. It's listed under his name now."

"Damn dude," Mike chuckled. "Maybe my dad *was* right. Maybe you *should* be a detective."

"Your dad said that?" Jeff asked, now glancing back.

"Yeah," Mike smiled. "But my parents still think you're a nut job."

Jeff smirked. "Huh..."

Jeff nodded, pleased with himself as his eyes flicked in the direction of a red truck driving past. Every flicker of that color now commanded his attention. He put his focus back onto the pavement and pedaled faster.

Mike slowed, Jeff slowing his bike ahead of him.

"What's up?" Jeff asked, his eyes moving to Mike's bike as he inspected for a flat tire or skipped chain.

Mike looked off to the side of the road where the gravel turned to dirt and weeds, and that to trees. "This is where I found her."

"Whoa," Jeff replied, his eyes moving to the woods. "She was just standing there?"

"Yeah," Mike replied, pointing out. "She was right there." He paused. "She just watched me ride up and stood there staring."

"She does that a lot huh?"

"Yeah," Mike sighed. "I wish she could say something."

"I'm not really sure I'd wanna hear what she had to say...," Jeff replied.

"Yeah," Mike added after a moment. "Me neither..."

They both eyed the space for a moment longer, and then Mike dropped his foot on the pedal and started off, Jeff moving to catch up.

A short while later the pair were riding up the block to John's house.

They dropped their bikes in his yard and crossed the lawn, approaching the door and giving the bell a ring. It was a few moments before it opened and John stood there in his boxers, a suspicious look on his face.

"Dude," Jeff barked, standing there irritated. "Don't you ever answer the phone?"

John rubbed his eyes, glancing at Mike. "What time is it?"

"It's seven," Jeff replied quickly. "Now get dressed and come on. We found the guy who owns the car."

"What?" he smirked, turning his attention to Mike. "Is he serious?"

Mike nodded. "Yeah. Apparently so."

"Well shit, why the hell didn't you just open with that?" He turned his head back into the house and shouted something in French.

Jeff glanced at Mike and shook his head.

"What?" John asked, giving them an accusatory look.

"Nothing *oui oiu*," Jeff chuckled, the joy of John's nickname giving him pleasure every time he used it.

John shot a look at Jeff like a dagger. "You're an asshole, you know that..." Then he turned and slammed the door in their face.

Jeff smiled at Mike who turned around and sat down on the steps. His gaze moved to the grass. He was being bombarded by a hundred questions and concerns. What if it wasn't the car? What if it wasn't the guy? What if they got somebody in trouble because they were all playing police? A dozen other questions went off in his mind. Then he had to ask the question that had been burrowing outwards for the last three minutes. "You really think it's the guy?"

"Yes," Jeff replied flatly. "The guy's a total creepo. Like, *Silence of the Lambs* creepo."

Mike turned his head towards Jeff who was rubbing a nipple with his finger. "And how the hell do you know this?"

"Dude," Jeff started. "So, a couple months ago my mom had to replace the alternator on our car. She decided to save some cash and instead of going out and buying one from the store, she decided to drag us to the junk yard to find a used one. The same junk yard the guy owns. Well, while we were there, I kept getting this really creepy vibe off the guy. I'm telling you..." He paused, rubbing his nipples again while moving his hips. "It puts the lotion on the skin...."

Mike shook his head and at the same time the door behind them opened up and John stepped out.

"This better be good," John said, walking past them towards his bike that was propped against the side of the house. "Seven o' clock in the morning...," he scoffed as he grabbed his bike and swung it around to mount. "Well?" he asked, looking at Jeff and Mike who had just stood. "Can we go?"

Jeff grinned, glancing back at him. "Oh, oui monsieur!"

"Dude..."

Mike tapped Jeff's arm and smiled. "That was good." Then he walked over to his bike and picked it up. He swung his leg over, dropped his foot on the pedal and pushed off.

By the time they arrived at the field they could see Denise already standing at the spot. As they got closer they could see the look on her face saying that it was way too early and that she had been waiting there for far too long.

Mike rode up first, dropping his bike and stepping towards her. "Hey Denise," he said as Jeff and John followed suit.

"Morning," she grumbled. "This was his idea, wasn't it?" she asked, tossing her head in Jeff's direction.

Mike lifted his eyebrows in silent response.

"Well, it better be good," she said, glancing at Jeff and John who stepped up. "It's early, it's cold and I just got my period."

"Eww!" John remarked as he stepped up. "TMI dude!"

"Wow," Denise replied, "I'm surprised you even know enough about girls to know what a period is."

"Whatever," John defended. "I've had girlfriends..."

"Sorry dude," Jeff chuckled. "But Carrie Jergens and a sock doesn't count."

Mike even laughed at that one.

Before John could retort Denise nodded to the opposite end of the field where Todd had come flying in at, a large rooster-tail of dust behind him.

John shook his head, purposely stepping past Jeff so he could jab his shoulder into him as he made his way to his chair.

"Ow," Jeff barked. "Dick."

"Least I got one," John said, dropping into the fold out seat.

A few moments later Todd came skidding to a stop and dropped his bike into the weeds.

"Hey guys," he said as he stepped up. "Denise."

"Todd," she replied.

"Where's Maggie?" he asked as he nodded at the others.

"I told her to stay at my place," Mike replied. "I'm not exactly sure how the whole ghost thing works, and I knew we were gonna be moving fast today. Didn't want her to get lost."

"Uh, I'd say that's the least of her worries," John replied, eliciting a less than pleased look from the others. "What?"

"So, you said something about knowing who it was that killed her?"

Jeff turned to Todd. "Yeah. His name's Donald Cowles. He runs the scrapyard shop at the edge of town."

"I know that place," Todd replied quickly. "My dad goes there sometimes."

"Wait," Denise interjected. "Donald Cowles...?"

"Yeah," Jeff replied, his face scrunching with intrigue. "Why?"

"Well, my dad and I went to the bowling alley yesterday and talked with the guy who runs it. We asked if he remembered who the person sitting at the bar had been that Maggie was talking to that night." She paused, lifting her eyebrows. "One of the people he said it might have been was named, Donald Cowles..."

"No way," Jeff replied. "Get the hell out of here."

"Seriously."

"Wait," John remarked. "You actually told your dad about Maggie and this *ghost hunt*?"

She turned her eyes to him. "No dumbass, I told him that were researching the old case. He just happened to wanna drive out to the bowling alley." She paused. "You're welcome jerk..."

"Oh," he replied flatly.

"Anyways," Jeff continued. "Donald Cowles was the only person in Iron County that had a mustang registered at the time Maggie went missing. The car that took her was red, but the one this Cowles guy had registered was blue. But the guy runs an auto shop. They paint cars there. It wouldn't exactly be too difficult for him to change the color and reregister it. And the thing that really caught my attention was that in their database the car was listed as inoperable." He paused. "Again, the guy owns an auto shop, so why didn't he just fix it...?"

"All right Sherlock," John snickered, actually finding himself mildly surprised that Jeff had found the information.

"Look," Mike said. "We just need to go there and..." He turned to Jeff. "What's that thing called when cops hang out and watch a place?"

"A stakeout," Jeff replied quickly.

"Yeah," Mike continued. "We just need to go there and stake the place out. Who knows? The car might still be there."

John scoffed lightly. "After twenty years...?"

"Dude," Mike snapped. "It's a junkyard. That's what they do. You wanna *not* be such a negative Nancy for once?"

"Sorry," John growled. "Jeez." He paused. "Did you get your period too?"

"I swear to god!" Denise snapped, as Todd reached out and grabbed her arm, pulling it back.

"Look!" Jeff barked, grabbing their attention. "I'd go myself, but I can't today. I have a scout meeting in a few hours and then I have to go with my parents to St. George. My mom's scheduled some family retreat thing. She's trying to bring us closer together or some crap like that."

John carefully filed that one away for further use and replied uncharacteristically conversational. "Yeah… My parents are forcing me to get a job for the summer. Something about responsibility or some shit like that…" He shook his head. "I have an interview at the paper today at one."

"At the paper?" Mike asked, the entire notion of John holding any form of responsibility bordering humor and astonishment.

"Yeah…" John replied flatly.

"Hmph."

Jeff took his turn. "You're gonna have to get up every day at five and go door to door with one of those stupid pouches on?" He chuckled loudly. "Oh, this is gonna be good."

"Whatever man," John replied smartly. "It wasn't my choice, my dad's making me. And at least I'm not the one going door to door selling cookies."

"That's the girl scouts, dick," Jeff snapped.

"Oh," John smiled. "I thought that's what you were in…"

111

"Dude, fuck off."

"Guys!" Mike said just below a shout. "Seriously. Jeez. I'll go, okay? I'll keep an eye on him since it seems to be that much of a damn hassle for everyone else."

"What about Denise?" John asked, oblivious to the obvious.

"Dude," Mike said, shocked. "The dude kidnapped and murdered a little girl, and you wanna send Denise in there?"

It clicked.

"Guess you got a point there."

"Besides," Mike added. "She said she wasn't feeling well."

"She said she was on her period, not that she was dying."

"I swear to Christ John!" Denise said, stepping towards him with her fist balled.

Todd reached out again and held her back.

"You are such a fucking prick!" she barked, jerking her hand back.

"What?" John shook his head. He didn't understand why she was so agro all of a sudden. He'd joked about it in the past with her. *'Whatever,'* he thought, turning his attention to Todd who had pretty much stayed quiet during the entire conversation. "Well, what about you? Or are you busy too?"

"I said I'd go," Mike replied, already knowing where it was headed.

"Yeah," Todd replied. "Church thing..."

John shook his head. "Fuckin' Mormons..."

"Hey man," Todd replied calmly, not feeding into his friend's bullshit. "My parents are Mormon, not me. Feel free to take my place if you want. I don't wanna be there."

John smiled genuinely. "You know what my parents would do to me if I became a Mormon?"

"Stop letting the priest molest you?" Todd smiled back.

John lifted his finger to reply and then paused, a big grin growing across his face. "That was good." He stuck his fist out and Todd reached out, pounding it with his. "Learning you are," he added in his best Yoda impression.

"If you two are done flirting," Jeff said, "I've gotta take off." He turned to Mike. "Head to the shop and see what you can find. Let's all meet back here tomorrow morning."

"Yeah," Mike replied. "Sure."

The others said their goodbyes and the group parted ways. Mike watched Todd get on his bike and ride away behind John. Jeff headed off in the other direction.

"Sorry about him," he said, turning to Denise who was picking her bike up. "He just..."

"I'm used to it. He's an idiot."

"Yeah, but—"

"It's fine," she replied, cutting his attempt at making up for John's inability to have a normal, functioning social interaction. "He's got a tiny penis, and he makes up for it by acting like a big one."

Mike laughed. He wasn't expecting that one.

"One day he's gonna say the wrong thing to the wrong person and he's gonna seriously get his ass kicked. I think that'll be the day he finally figures it out." She paused, nodding. "Actually, I'm pretty sure that's *exactly* what he needs."

"Yeah..." Mike replied, glancing towards the opposite end of the field. "I think you're probably right."

"Look," Mike said, turning his attention back to his friend. "If there's anything I can do…"

"Oh my god…" Denise groaned, lifting her gaze to the sky for a moment. "It's just, my period. Every girl has them, and we have been since the beginning of time. No one has ever died because of it, it just sucks. OK? God you guys…"

"Sorry," Mike said, cringing back. "Just offering to help."

Denise exhaled heavily. "It's fine."

Mike nodded.

"Hey," she said, turning towards him, her demeanor shifting. "Be careful yeah? If that guy really did do what Jeff says…" She paused, watching as Mike slowly nodded. "Just… Be careful."

"I will."

"All right," Denise said, moving her hand to her stomach. "I gotta get out of here. I'm gonna go punch something."

Mike smiled, watching as she lifted her leg over her bike and started pedaling off with a backwards wave.

"All right," Mike whispered to himself. "Let's go stake out a junk yard…"

Mike lifted his bike and climbed atop. With one forward push he was pedaling down the dirt trail towards the main street. He had no idea what he was supposed to do, or what he was supposed to be looking for, other than a red, or blue mustang. But what he did know was that Denise was right. If this was the guy, he wasn't going to be too happy with someone snooping around or asking questions, especially about the car or Maggie. So, he had to be careful, play it safe and not make things too obvious. Just how exactly he was supposed to do that? He had no idea. So, for now he just focused on the cool breeze, and the thought of Maggie sitting on his bed waiting for him to get home.

Chapter 20

A vapor of uncertainty accompanied Mike as he turned off of Main Street onto Third. Traffic was just starting to build, the local community on their way to work, an early morning bustle that was still shaking off the chill from the night before with coffee and Thunder 91, the university station. Summer hadn't truly arrived yet and the mountain still blew its cool breath down into the valley, so most of the windows driving past were up, the occasional one cracked, a thin stream of cigarette smoke billowing out.

Mike felt the brunt of the cold air full force and pulled one hand off the handlebars, balling it into a fist and exhaling warm air into it. But the chilly morning was the last thing on his mind. Twenty years ago, someone had abducted and killed an innocent young girl, and now he was about to go face to face with the person he and his friends believed may have done it. Beneath his shirt his stomach was balled tightly in a knot. A phrase he had heard his father use more often than not came to mind. *This is way beyond my paygrade...*

Mike shook off the worry and pushed on, navigating the main street's sidewalk, intent on not getting struck by a car backing out. That was his biggest fear, someone reversing quickly out of their driveway without looking. It had happened to John last summer and sent him to the hospital with a dislocated shoulder and sprained wrist, putting a rather large dent in his summer vacation. So now, whenever Mike was forced to ride on the sidewalk, he did it with a heightened sense of awareness.

A short while later the businesses at the edge of town fell behind and the large fence that indicated the edges of the junk yard fell into view, a browning span of sheet metal pockmarked with rust and aging graffiti that ran six blocks in length. Most of the traffic had already peeled off, the main section of town hosting the stream of cars, the outskirts only industrial, feed supply stores and an animal shelter. So now Mike was back in the street and riding at normal speed. He continued down the block, nearing closer to the auto shop and slowed his bike. His gaze moved along the large fence and up to the loosely coiled razor wire that ran across the top. *So much for hopping it*, he thought as he brought his bike to a stop. Not that he would. His parents would murder him if he went to jail for breaking and entering or trespassing, and he'd seen enough films that showed the effects of razor wire, and it wasn't something he had any desire to come in contact with. So, he slowed his bike to a stop and stood there, surveying the perimeter, his gaze working its way towards the small parking lot at the entrance and the shack-like building that constituted the scrap yard's office. Then his eyes moved to the large sign overhead. DC Automotive and Scrapyard.

He pedaled forward to get a better view of the entrance. The parking lot was empty, and he could see that there was an iron gate that blocked the entrance to the shack. It was padlocked shut. That meant that no one had arrived yet. Not surprising, it was still really early, and businesses like this didn't generally open until later. Then it hit him. It was Sunday...

Mike groaned, dropping his head and shaking it. How could he not have realized that...? Todd's church thing should have given that away. But it was early, and summer vacation, so none of them really paid attention to what day of the week it was when they were on break.

Mike grumbled again in frustration and started to turn his bike around when the sound of a car engine caught his ear. He turned his head and looked back down the street in the direction he had just come from moments before. A few blocks away an older car that looked like a hybrid of a car and a pickup truck pulled out onto the street. Mike edged his bike out of the way and watched as the car drove past. The man inside very adequately matched the decrepit vehicle he drove, late forties, dirty trucker hat and soiled flannel. He wore an exceptionally unpleasant scowl and carried a suspicious gaze that slithered over Mike as he drove past before turning into the scrapyard parking lot. The man in the car was absolutely a product of his environment, and the feeling Mike felt in his wake gave him the willies. *That had to be him...*

Mike moved his bike across the street and bent down, pretending to check his tires, while at the same time, keeping a watchful eye on the man who stepped out of the banged up El Camino and made his way to the gate, where he unlocked it, opened it slightly and then disappeared into the small building.

Mike stared, one hand resting on his front tire, the other holding the bike steady. He waited for movement, for some inclination that the man was going to open shop. A slow building excitement worked into him as he eased into his detective role.

For the next ten minutes he stayed kneeled next to his bike, waiting, watching, observing. Then a restless boredom only afforded by youth edged in and he folded out the kickstand and took a seat on the curb. He pulled out his pocketknife and started cleaning the dirt beneath his fingernails. As he did, he thought about the little girl. Why

118

had she chosen him? Was there something more to it? How many people had driven past her standing there at the edge of the road, helpless, scared? Dead. At the last thought Mike took a deep breath and folded his knife, putting it back into his pocket. He forced his thoughts to a lighter place, thinking about the girl he sat behind in his creative writing class. Camille Traveler. A warm feeling came over him. He had the biggest crush on her. Her smile, the way she dressed, slightly preppy but just a little bit of country in her. The way her hair smelled as it brushed past him every day in third period. Jeff and Todd teased him about it and Denise had told him just to talk to her, but there was no way he could. She was in all the clubs, had been crowned queen at Junior Prom. She was way out of his league. That, and she was very Mormon, which meant there was no way he was ever gonna get a shot. Like John he had been raised Catholic and knew well enough, Mormons dated Mormons, that was it. But that didn't keep his heart from fluttering in his chest every time he saw her or stop the nervous sweat from breaking out across his palms.

He sat there, a thin tremble of nervousness edging in just at the thought of his first high-school crush, when anxious boredom brought him to his feet. He was just about to start his way across the street when the man stepped out of the shop with a small bag in his hand. Mike stopped, quickly moving his hands to the break cable on his bike, pretending to adjust it. He glanced up to see the man stop near the front gate, his gaze slithering across the street to where Mike stood. The man eyed him suspiciously for a moment, his gaze narrowing. Mike dropped his gaze and started tugging lightly on a brake cable again, checking to make sure it was attached properly. He could feel eyes burning into him, but he kept his gaze lowered and continued pretending.

Then the man turned and locked the gate before returning to his car and driving away.

Mike watched as the car turned a corner and disappeared. Then he stood, waiting another couple moments before hopping on his bike and pedaling to the front of the shop. The gate was again secured, and there was no way to see inside the scrapyard. He glanced back down the road where the car had disappeared to. "Damn...," he whispered. Then he turned his bike and pedaled back in the direction of town.

Chapter 21

That evening Mike sat in the chair in his living room, one leg draped over the arm, the phone receiver crooked between his cheek and his shoulder, his fingers fidgeting at the edge of his fingernails. "Yeah," he said, flinching as he tugged a small hangnail off. "I watched him show up, grab a bag of something and then leave."

Across town Jeff sat on his bed, phone in one hand and the other jammed into a bag of potato chips. Next to the chips was an open can of soda and a video game controller. "OK," he replied. "Well, what did you see?

Mike's voice filtered through the receiver. "Nothing. Just that. The guy showed up, unlocked the place, went inside, and came out with a bag. Then he left." He paused. "You were right about one thing. I got a really creepy vibe from him."

Jeff shoved a small stack of chips into his mouth and continued. "Told you. Did you get a look inside?"

Mike shifted in his chair, listening to the sound of his friend crunching chips in his ear. "Nah. The place was locked up, and there's a fence around it. It's got razor wire across the top dude. The only way to see what's in there is to actually go in. And none of us thought about the fact that it's Sunday, so everything's closed." He paused, the crunching sound getting lighter before renewing full strength again as his friend shoveled more chips into his mouth. "I was surprised that the guy even showed up."

"Damn," Jeff said over the phone. "What's your plan?"

Mike cocked his head slightly, his gaze dropping from the muted TV in front of him. "I think I have an idea. Let me figure it out and I'll tell you tomorrow."

"Cool," Jeff replied, renewing the crunching. "Wait," he said, pulling his hand away from the chip bag. "You're not gonna try breaking in there are you?"

"No!" Mike burst from the other end. "Dude! Do you know what my parents would do to me if I got caught trying to break into some place? They'd freaking kill me or send me to some stupid boy's camp."

"Hey man," Jeff replied while reaching out to pick up the soda. "Just asking. I know how you get sometimes."

"No dude. I don't get like *that*."

"All right man," Jeff said, raising the soda to his lips. "Keep your panties on." Then he took a large gulp and burped into the receiver.

Mike shook his head. "Really dude...?"

"What?" Jeff replied, feigning innocence.

Mike exhaled sharply. "Look," he continued, "I have an idea, but I gotta go. I'll see you in the morning all right?"

"OK," Jeff replied from the other end.

Mike reached out and dropped the handset back onto the receiver. Then he leaned back in his chair and let his gaze move to the empty kitchen.

Chapter 22

The next morning Mike turned his bike onto the dirt path leading into the field. He could see John and Jeff already engaged in another of their heated arguments, Todd standing next to them with a concerned look on his face. He could hear Jeff shouting from where he was, so he put on the gas and pedaled towards them even quicker.

"Look!" Jeff shouted, leaning in to emphasize his words. "I'm telling you. If he killed her, then he scrapped the car. Dude, he works at a junk yard!"

"Dude," John barked back. "Nobody's gonna scrap a classic mustang, murder or not. You just don't do that!"

Mike pulled up, dropping his bike to the ground and glancing at Todd who lifted his eyebrows and shrugged.

"I'm telling you dude," Jeff continued. "You're wrong!"

Mike took the split second of silence to jump in. "So... What's going on?"

John turned his gaze to Mike, who could see the anger coursing behind. "Dumbass here thinks that the guy scrapped the car. But I keep telling him that *nobody* would destroy a classic car like that, *especially* a mustang. It just wouldn't happen." He looked at Mike in near desperation.

"The Mustang's a classic muscle car dude," Todd chimed in. "He's kind of got a point. They don't make em' like that anymore..."

"Oh what!?" Jeff barked; his vigor renewed by Todd now taking sides with John. "You think he's just gonna keep it around, like, *hey, here's the evidence you need to bust and convict me of murder? Anybody wanna come put me in prison?*" He was only a couple notches down from yelling at this point.

"Guys!" Mike said, stepping between them. "Chill! We don't even know if it's the right guy. Or if there even *is* a car. We don't know shit. You're standing here yelling at each other over a bunch of stupid assumptions. Just stop."

The others stopped, his words sinking in.

"What we need to do is continue following the only lead we have." He paused. "And if you guys would shut up for a minute, I think I just might have a way that we can get in there and look around without raising any suspicions."

Jeff and John glanced at each other, each of them taking a deep breath and exhaling sharply, signaling that the bickering had ceased. They did this quite frequently...

Mike looked around for a moment, realizing their group was a person short. "Where's Denise?"

"She had something that came up last minute with her dad," Jeff replied. "She said she'd meet up with us later." He paused, glancing behind Mike. "Where's Maggie?"

Mike shrugged. "She was at my place when I left. She kind of comes and goes as she pleases."

As he finished his sentence Maggie stepped out from behind him, materializing as his words trailed off.

"Jesus!" John startled, taking a step back. "Fuck."

Mike spun, startling himself to see Maggie standing there. He took a second to regain his composure. "Yeah. Still not used to that myself..."

Maggie's gaze shifted between them, settling back on Mike.

"That shit is fuckin creepy dude," John said, his eyes locked to the little girl.

"Dude, would you shut up already," Jeff snorted.

A slightly queasy look flashed across John's face. "Well, it is…" He shuddered. "Ugh…"

"Look," Mike said, pulling the conversation back to focus. "The only way one of us is gonna get into the scrapyard is if we're looking for car parts, or if we work there. And since none of us obviously own a car, or know anything about them… "

"I do," Todd said softly.

The three of them turned their gaze to Todd who fidgeted for a moment.

"Yeah," John answered after a moment. "Matchbox and RC don't count."

Todd shifted, his hand moving back to his neck, his face disappointed.

"I'm gonna go there today and try and get a job," Mike continued. "Even if it's just sweeping up around the guy's shop. At least that way I can get in and take a look around."

"Dude!" Jeff burst out, startling John who was still staring at Maggie. "That's genius!"

"Yeah," John said, slowly pulling his gaze away from her, "Except for the part where you get chopped up and stuffed in the trunk of some rusted out car. Or have you forgotten that the guy's a freaking murderer…?"

"You have any better ideas?"

John growled. "You still don't even know if it's the guy. Just because he had a mustang. That's like saying that everyone who wore a hat that day could have been the killer."

"Dude…" Jeff growled, irritation moving back into his words. "He had the *only* mustang registered in the county at the time."

"And here's another thing," John added. "Why is it that you are so sure that whoever abducted her is from around here? They could have been from another city, or even another state. What if they were like a hobo or something, or some serial killer that got off on killing little girls? We have no idea. It could have been a million different people. Look at Ted Bundy dude. He killed girls in dozens of states."

"It wasn't dozens dude," Jeff remarked. "It was like four. OK. Colorado, Utah, Florida and Washington..."

"I'm just saying dude. It could have been somebody like that."

Jeff continued, ignoring John's stupid remarks, replying instead with more educated assumptions. "Dude. She was abducted from a bowling alley. Either the guy was hanging out there, which makes him a local, or he followed her there and waited for the opportunity to lure her outside and into his car. Either way, that pretty much indicates that he is from around here. How many people come from out of town to hit Alpine Lanes...? It's not exactly the fanciest bowling alley in the state." He paused, narrowing his focus to Mike. "That guy I found had a mustang and worked at an auto body shop at the time. Now he's driving another classic car, and you said it's also red. It's too perfect, I'm telling you."

"Look," Mike said, Jeff's reasoning actually making sense to him. "I'm gonna go there and try and get a job. Even if I have to do it for free, as *volunteer work* or something. That way at least I can get in there and have a look around. Then we'll know for sure if he still has the car or not. Or if there even is a car."

"Well, what if it's parked at his house?" John replied.

"Dude," Jeff snapped. "He's not gonna keep the car he used to abduct his victim just parked in the driveway.

"Just saying," John snorted. "There's a possibility…"

"That's why I'm gonna go get a job there," Mike replied.

"It's crazy, you know that…" John continued.

"Crazier than a dead girl following me around?"

John smirked. "Point taken…" Then he sighed heavily and shook his head. "Why couldn't we have just had a normal summer like everyone else, with bike rides and sunburns from hanging out at the pool?"

"At least we won't forget about this one," Todd said, bringing nods from the others.

He was right. They could have had a normal, boring summer like they always had, but this one was going to stick with them for the rest of their lives. In a sense, it was becoming a better summer than any of them could have imagined. The only question was, would they all make it out of it unscathed? That was the one question that continued to linger in the back of Mike's mind. And at that thought, he turned to Maggie. "You don't have to go if you don't want. If it is the guy, it might be painful for you. So, you can wait for me here if you want, or head to my house."

Maggie stared back blankly, the faint hint of sorrow not fading from her gaze.

"All right," Mike said, turning to the others. "Here we go."

"Mike," Jeff said, bringing his face back around. "Be careful."

"Yeah man," John added with a nod from Todd. "Watch your ass in there."

Mike nodded. "Yeah." Then turned and picked up his bike, riding away.

"I hope he knows what he's doing," John said, watching his friend ride off.

"Me too," Jeff added. "Me too."

Chapter 23

It was nearly an hour later when Mike walked into the auto shop. Fear pressed in from all sides, smothering him. His hands shook and he could feel the sweat building beneath his shirt. The cold grip of apprehension pulled at him, begging him to turn around and leave, to go back to the safety of his friends and the quickly warming summer day. But as his feet slowed, he thought of Maggie, and the fear and pain she must have felt being abducted, the unimaginable horror she must have endured at the hands of her captor. The sadness she wore on her face flashed past, the ceaseless plea delivered behind confused eyes. That was all it took for him to take a deep breath, ball his fists and step through the door.

As Mike entered the dimly lit room his eyes darted wildly from one side to the other. No one was inside, but that did little to alleviate the tension still growing. Cluttering the space were dozens of spare parts, some new in dust-covered packages, some scattered in plastic bins around the edges of the walls. The heavy smell of oil and grease permeated the air, coating his nostrils, and he could feel the machine shop grit grinding beneath his shoes as he stepped. There was a dirty stillness about the shop that smothered him in unease.

As he stepped up to the counter, he leaned over to get a glimpse through the open doorway to the yard behind. It was lined with rows of old abandoned vehicles, some on lifts, their bottoms exposed, some with their hoods and trunks open, some missing doors and windows. It was a metal graveyard, a large and packed with the rusting corpses of hundreds of forgotten cars.

Mike lifted his hand, hovering it above the bell sitting atop the counter and paused. He knew that once he dropped the weight, there was no turning back. He could easily turn and run, or say that he had made a mistake, but that's something he would have to live with, and he had no idea if Maggie was watching, and the only reason he was there, was for her. So, with one last breath, he brought his hand down.

The bell rang once, echoing in the room and breaking the silent stillness that enveloped him. He felt himself flinch.

An endless moment passed; the tension continued to build silently in the room. He could feel his heart pounding beneath his ribs and the sweat on his palms now left them wrinkled and clammy. Then as he was lifting his hand to give it a second ring a shape emerged through the back door.

"What can I do you for?" the man asked in a thick country drawl as he stepped in, using a blue shop towel to wipe the loose grime from his hands.

Mike watched the man step up to the counter. It was the same one that had shown up the other day, the one he had watched come and go. He was wearing the same clothes, dirty, grease-smeared blue jeans and a red and black flannel shirt. The dirt on his hands looked as if it was part of him, staining that had been with him his entire life. The air about him smelled of cheap aftershave, cigarettes and motor grease.

Mike stared at him for a moment longer, pulling his gaze away from the man's hands and locking eyes with the cold stare being returned. "Um," he staggered, now struggling to retain the tiny portion of courage he had mustered moments ago. "I was wondering, if you had any work?" He paused, watching the man finished wiping his hands. "I'm trying to save up for the summer." It was the best he could come up with under the pressure. He had crafted an entire spiel on the way over, how he was planning on becoming an automotive mechanic and needed experience, and how he had compared all the shops in town and decided that this would be the best fit, and how he was a hard worker and didn't have any problems getting his hands dirty. But at that moment, staring down the barrel of the man's gaze, it was all but forgotten.

The man eyed him a moment longer before sniffling and tossing the towel on the counter. "Nah," he replied, a country drawl lilting his words. "Kind of a one-man job round here."

Mike paused. He hadn't been ready for if the man said no. Until that moment he had only concerned himself with what he was going to do once he got the job. His mind raced. "Um. What about volunteers?"

The man narrowed his gaze, studying him with further intent.

Mike fumbled through the pitch that was slowly coming back to him in bits and pieces. "I, wanna be a mechanic when I get out of school, and my parents told me I should start trying to get experience. Even if it's for free, at least I could start somewhere." He paused, watching for a change in the man's demeanor which was as unmoving as the bucketful of empty beer cans next to him. "I could sweep up around the shop for you, or help organize." He paused again. Still no response. "I don't need any money. My parents give me an allowance. I just need experience, and you're the last mechanic shop. I'd really appreciate it." He cursed himself for saying he was the last. It made it sound like he had tried all the others first and gotten turned down. He winced inwardly, a reaction that went unseen by the other.

The man stared at him for a moment longer, his gaze narrowing even further. Mike could see him running calculations and tasks in his head. Finally, after what could have been a lifetime, the man cleared his throat and looked around the shop. "Volunteer work," he smirked, his eyes grazing the dirty shelves. "Sure, I guess. Why not? So long as it's okay with your folks. I guess I *could* use a spare hand around here."

Mike exhaled heavily, holding his posture as straight as possible to keep the man from seeing his obvious relief. He was worried that the sweat he could feel growing on his scalp would give his nervousness away.

"It's kinda hard keepin' this place clean and runnin' at the same time." The man's eyes moved to the corner where the bucket of cans was. "Why don't you go ahead and grab the broom and dustpan over there and give the office a good sweep. So long as you don't mess that up, I suppose I could find other things for you to do around here." He paused, his gaze moving back to Mike. "But don't expect no easy meal ticket here. Volunteer or not, I expect you to work like you mean it. Ain't gon' be no slacking on my watch. I won't put up with it." He raised his finger, pointing sternly at him. "Don't you forget it was *you* who come askin' me, not the other way around, you got that?"

Mike nodded. "Yes sir."

"Good," the man replied, reaching out for the dirty towel. "Then go on. Get to work."

Mike nodded, moving towards the broom.

"Name's Don by the way," the man added.

Mike stopped, turning to him. "I'm Mike."

"All right then. Get to sweepin'."

The next few hours drug by. Mike had swept the entire room, or *office* as the man had referred to it. He had emptied the bucket of cans and an overflowing can that was tucked hidden away under the desk. Even though he hadn't touched much other than the broom, dustpan and a few shelves, he felt filthy. He could feel the dust clinging to the inside of his nostrils and his throat was dry. There was a single water container in the shop, but it was empty.

He had just set the broom down when the man walked in from the back. Mike watched him wipe his hands again, *a pointless act* he thought before tossing the towel back on the desk and glancing around the shop. He gave an approving smirk and then turned to Mike. "I'm gonna go grab a bite to eat. Can I trust you to keep an eye on things while I'm gone?"

That was *it*! The opportunity he had been waiting for, hoping for. It was all that he could do to keep from exclaiming loudly. "Yes sir,' he replied calmly.

"All right," the man replied. "I'm trusting you."

"Yes sir," Mike repeated.

"Supposn' you're hungry too?"

Mike nodded. "Yes sir."

The man exhaled heavily while pulling his wallet out. He opened it and glanced inside, then put it back into his pocket with a disappointed scowl before looking back to Mike. "All right. I'll grab you a burger on the way back. Should be about twenty minutes, give or take." He paused, glancing back to the floor. "Since you're done sweeping, why don't you go ahead and tackle the bathroom while I'm gone." A thin smile worked across his lips. "That should work up an appetite. Been a while since that one's been done."

Mike nodded again, glancing towards the closed door with a sign that read *shitter* on it. "Yes sir."

The man nodded. "And you can stop callin' me *sir*. Makes me feel old." He paused. "It's just Don."

"Yes s—" Mike started, catching himself. "OK."

"All right then. Don't cause no trouble. I'll be back in a few." With that he turned and made his way out to the parking lot.

Mike stood there, waiting for the sound of the car's engine to start and for the man to drive away. The moment the car faded into the distance he set down the broom and made his way through the back door into the actual yard.

Inside the car the man glanced into the rearview mirror, a funny feeling bringing his foot off the gas pedal and onto the brake. The car slowed as he kept his gaze on the shop. Then he turned the wheel and started back around.

The sun washed across Mike as oil splattered dirt replaced the scuffed linoleum of the office. The sun blazed down on him, the brightness of it forcing him to bring his hands up to shield his eyes for a moment as they adjusted. As the scrapyard came into focus, he saw the aisle of derelict vehicles lined out before him, row after row of cars, parts dotting the ground between. A dirty palate of reddish browns and corroded blues, faded green and yellow, and dull silver spread out to the end of the yard hundreds of feet away.

Slowly his hands came down as his eyes focused on the sight before him. He looked from left to right, overwhelmed at where to start. Then he narrowed his focus and started straight forward.

As he walked the ten-foot-wide path, emblem after emblem passed by; Buick, Cadillac, Ford, Dodge, Chrysler, a dozen other companies he had never heard of, from cars to trucks to the mash of vehicles in between. The odd thought hit him that at one point in time, every one of these vehicles had been new, driven off a lot somewhere by a happy person about to feel the wind in their hair and soft touch of new leather and upholstery. Long gone was any semblance of new car smell in this place. No. Now they sat forgotten, rusting sentinels in a metallic graveyard, littered with steel skeletons.

Mike kept walking, his mind coming back to focus. His eyes now scanned the car logos, but with intent. A horse in full run, a stallion, a *mustang*. That was what he was looking for now.

Scattered every few vehicles were crates with spare parts overflowing from them. Nuts and bolts, pistons and valves, every manner of part that could be heaved from within lay in piles.

Behind him he didn't hear the car pull back into the driveway, or the sound of a door slamming heavily.

He kept moving, making his way towards the end of the aisle. When he reached it, he looked right, then left. That's when his eyes caught something out of place, a color and shape that didn't quite fit with the rest. All the cars and trucks he had passed sat out in the sun, barren, exposed to the elements. But this one was different, this one was covered, a large faded blue tarp tucked around it and tied loosely around the wheels to keep it in place. Slowly Mike started towards it, the tarp moving gently in the breeze. The rest of the cars surrounding it faded from his focus.

Mike inched closer, the hair on his arm slowly rising upwards. His heart began to race, the moisture in his mouth evaporating with every breath. He floated another few steps, stopping just before the covered car. His gaze worked across the crosshatched pattern of blue and the shape beneath it. Then slowly he edged forward, leaning down to take one corner of the tarp in his fingers. Gently he lifted.

"Hey!"

Before he spun around, he caught a flash of an emblem on one of the hubcaps. A horse running at full gallop.

"What are you doing back here?"

Mike watched as Don continued towards him, anger on his face.

"I don't want you snooping around back here, ya hear? *Last* thing I need is you messin' around, and getting hurt, and you parents comin' here with *lawyers* trying to sue me."

"S.., sorry," Mike stammered.

"You just stick with doing what you're told, and we won't have any problems. You got that?"

Mike nodded, almost glancing back at the car but catching himself at the last moment. "Yes sir. Uh, Don. Got it."

"All right then," Don continued, glancing at the covered car. "Well, the reason I come back was to see if'n you drank soda pop." He paused, waiting for Mike to pick up on the question. Then when he realized the kid was a deer in headlights, simplified the question. "You drink soda, yes or no?"

"Uh, yes," Mike replied, still nervous about getting caught. He could have messed everything up right then because he got impatient. He wouldn't make that mistake again. "I do."

"All right then. Figured I'd find out 'fore I went and wasted my money on it." He paused. "Don't drink it myself, too much sugar and my teeth ain't none too good these days. Ain't really got the spare cash if you know what I mean to go spendin' on no dentist." He glanced around to the junk yard to emphasize his point. "Don't like em none too much no how."

Mike nodded. He didn't like the dentist either, but now was not the time to discuss such unpleasantries.

"All right then," Don said, nodding his head back to the office. "Enough yappin'. Back to work."

Mike lowered his gaze and quickly started back to the building.

Behind him Don's gaze moved up and down the aisle before settling on the covered car. It lingered for a moment before slithering back to Mike who was almost at the office. "Fuckin kids," he hissed, shaking his head and starting after.

It was another few hours before Mike said his goodbyes and jumped on his bike to head home. His feet were tired and filthy. He hadn't imagined how much work it was going to be. He'd swept and mopped the entire office, swept and cleaned the entire bathroom, the toilet included, which ran a shudder through him as he thought of it. He'd emptied most of the shelves and dusted them, slowing towards the end as he realized that if he worked too efficiently, he would soon be out of work, and that would defeat the entire purpose for him being there. Besides, at the end of the day, he *was* working for free.

It was about a half hour later that Mike pulled up to the Top Spot. He took small comfort in knowing that of all the places in town people his age hung out, this was the one place that was an unspoken *sacred* ground, the one location that all the different cliques of kids from all groups could gather without any problems. Most of the time anyways. You had the cool kids and jocks wearing their letterman jackets, with their popular, super pretty girlfriends. You had the science nerds tethered to the books they always had with them, and the stoners with their AC/DC and Metallica t-shirts and acid washed jeans. Lastly, you had the hicks... That was the biggest group, comprised of the local rednecks and rodeo club members all clad in their dark green rodeo team dusters, cowboy hats and boots, and their shining badge worn bright in silver and gold in the form of an over-sized belt buckle. This was the group that Mike and his friends had the most frequent run-ins with. The jocks generally left them alone, and the nerds pretty much minded their own business, the stoners as well. They had their own thing going. But the hicks... It always seemed that wherever Mike and his friends turned, there was a pickup truck loaded with ignorant assholes always prepared to sling insults their way or looking to fight. But only three at a time. They were pussies when they were on their own or pretended to be cool trying to hang with the other cliques. It wasn't odd to see one of the cowboys hanging out behind the vocational building smoking weed with the stoners or chatting it up with a group of jocks. In their own way they were also kind of the cool kids at school. But just because there were so many that it was hard to keep them separated.

Mike eyed one truck in particular as he placed his bike on the rack and made his way in. Lee Taylor. *Sheep fucker* he muttered silently in his mind as he pulled the door open to the smell of greasy burgers and video game noise.

No sooner than he had stepped in than he was greeted by his friends.

"Yo Mike!" Jeff shouted as he entered, scooting further into their usual bench to make room for him.

Mike made his way over and took his place at the table which was near the video arcade section of the business. The cooler kids hung out near the front, but they were too busy stroking each other's egos to bother with the games.

"So, how'd it go?" Jeff asked before he had even finished sliding in.

Mike nodded with a smile. "I'm in."

"Yes!" Jeff exclaimed, slamming both hands down heavily on the orange tabletop.

"Yeah," Mike continued, watching the excitement grow on Todd and John's face as well. "I got the job."

"Did you have to blow him?" John asked, elbowing Todd lightly, who smiled.

"No, dick," Mike replied. "I told him I wanted to be a mechanic and that my parents told me to get work experience."

"And he hired you?" Jeff asked. "Just like that?"

Mike shrugged. "I told him that I'd volunteer and that he didn't have to pay me."

"He blew him," John smirked with a nod.

"Whatever dude," Mike replied, ignoring it. "So, what's been going on here?"

"Well," Jeff answered, glancing at the arcade machines. "Dumbass over there dropped his last five bucks trying to reclaim the high score on Killer Instinct again."

Mike grinned. John had spent the last twenty minutes trying to knock whoever it was that held first place out for quite some time. Every time he did, they came in and raised it up a couple thousand. John was convinced that they were fucking with him.

"Fucking AAZ," John muttered. "I'm gonna find them one day, you watch. Then I'm gonna break their fingers so they can't play anymore."

"Jesus, dude," Jeff scowled. "It's just a game."

"No, Jeff. It's not just a game, it's principal."

"Anyways," Jeff continued with a quick shake of his head. "Did you find anything?"

Just as Mike was about to answer Denise walked in.

Jeff raised his hand in the air and scooted in further, giving Mike room to do the same.

"Gentlemen," Denise said, stopping and covering her mouth with dramatic effect. "I'm sorry, did I say *gentlemen*? Definitely the wrong table for that..."

"Oh, ha ha," John said, shaking his head with a small grin.

Denise slid in saying hi to the others.

"So?" she asked. She'd been waiting all day.

"Mike got the job," Jeff said, leaning forward so he could see her.

"Oh shit!" she burst, lowering her voice instantly. "That's awesome!"

"Yeah," Jeff agreed excitedly. "And he was just about to tell us what he found out."

All eyes shifted to him.

"Well?" Denise said, lightly elbowing him in the side. "Come on. Spill it."

Mike exhaled sharply, the day flashing past again. "Um, so yeah. I got the job. I actually spent most of the day cleaning the guy's shop." He paused again. The bathroom... Worse than room 237... He shook off the image of the bathroom, and the red and orange lined hallway at the Overlook and looked between the others. "I found a car at the back of the lot. It was under a big tarp, but I got a quick look before I got busted being back there." He stopped, glancing between the others.

"And!?" Jeff asked, his voice bordering panic.

Mike nodded. "I saw the logo on the tire. It's a mustang."

Jeff balled his fists, pumping them in front of him, his eyes squeezed tightly shut. "Yes!" he burst swinging his fists down but stopping them just short of the table. "See!" he exclaimed. "I freaking told you!"

"Calm down," John said flatly from across the table. "All he said was he found a mustang." He turned his gaze to Mike. "What color was it? What year? Did it have a license plate?"

Mike sighed, shaking his head lightly. "I didn't get a good look. The guy showed up and busted me while I was lifting the tarp. All I saw was the mustang logo on the tire."

"Oh shit," Todd said concerned. "What'd he do?"

"Nothing. Just sent me back to work and bought me lunch."

"So, you don't know if it's even the same model?" John prodded.

"No," Mike replied, glancing at the glass in front of him on the table. "I've gotta wait for him to leave me alone again. Then I can go back and get a better look. Hopefully he goes out for lunch again tomorrow. Then I'll take another look. This time I'll make sure he's gone before I do."

"But you said it's a mustang, right?" Jeff added, not letting it go.

"Yeah," Mike answered. "But like I said, I couldn't see what color it was, or the year. All I saw was the tire."

"Maybe we should go to the police now," Denise said, pulling all eyes to her quickly.

"And tell them what?" John asked, his eyebrows rising upwards. "That we've been trying to solve the murder of a little girl that happened twenty years ago, because her ghost keeps following our friend around, and that we found a car that possibly matches the description of the one that was used to abduct her? Oh, and we're not really sure if it's even the same car because our friend who is working undercover for the man we think killed her, couldn't get the color or year, or any information on the car." He scoffed. "Yeah. That'd go over well."

Denise opened her mouth. She already knew what she wanted to say but opted for a more productive response. "OK. Then what *are* we gonna do?" Her original response played on repeat in her head. *Asshole...*

"I was thinking about that today," Mike said, glancing past the others to Maggie who now stood just outside the diner, her gaze working between the others that lingered in and around the restaurant.

"Here," Mike said, nudging Denise with his hip. "Let's see something."

Denise stood up, moving for Mike who started outside. Then she glanced at the others and quickly turned to follow, the guys getting up and chasing after.

Mike made his way to where Maggie was standing, stopping just in front of her. "Hey Maggie," he started, not taking into consideration how he must have looked to anyone who would have looked out at that moment to see him standing there talking to a window, his friends huddled around him. "Um. I'm really sorry to ask you this, and to be honest, I'm still not even sure if you can hear me or understand what I'm saying, but I kind of have to." He paused, staring into her cold gaze. "Do you remember where you were when you died?"

Maggie's gaze wandered from his, her head turning in the direction of the mountain, in the direction of the highway he had found her on.

"Ho–ly shit," John remarked quietly. "She really does know what you're saying."

Maggie's eyes shifted to John for a moment before lowering to the ground.

"Hey," Mike said, reaching out his hands to place on her shoulders, then stopping as he remembered that they would have faded right through anyways. "Can you show us? Could you take us there?"

Maggie lifted her gaze, nodding lightly.

The excitement that should have accompanied her reply was lost somewhere in the solemn sadness of her gaze.

"It'll be OK," he said, lowering his head a little to reach her gaze. "We'll be there with you. We won't let anything happen to you, I promise." He turned his head to the others. "Right guys?"

Everybody nodded and mumbled their agreements.

"Not that anything worse could really happen to her," John said in a sarcastic whisper.

This time Denise did hit him. She balled her fist tightly and slammed it into his shoulder as hard as she could.

"OW!" he barked, staggering backwards as his other hand came up to his shoulder. "What the fuck!?"

Denise stared at him, the look in her eyes simmering him down almost immediately. "I was just saying... Jesus. I can't feel my arm now, thanks."

Mike turned back to Maggie. "Do you think you could do that?"

Maggie slowly looked between the others and then back to him. Then in a slow, steady motion she nodded once.

"All right," Mike said, turning to the others. "Look. We just need to follow Maggie to wherever it is that she died. Once we get there, we'll look for clues, anything that can help us figure out what happened."

"Mike," Denise said softly. "We don't know where that is. It could be a hundred miles from here for all we know. We have no idea how long she was out there before you found her, or if that is even close to where she was—" She paused, glancing at Maggie for a second, her voice lowering to a whisper. "Where she was killed."

Mike nodded, his gaze dropping to the ground for a moment as his mind raced with ideas. Then he lifted his gaze and locked it to hers. "Stay here," he said, "I'll be back."

"Where are you going?" John asked.

"To make a phone call," Mike said, turning and making his way quickly past the bathrooms to the payphone on the corner of the building.

The others watched as he fished a quarter out of his pocket and dropped it into the slot.

"What is he up to?" Todd asked, watching him carefully.

"I'm not sure," Jeff replied quietly. "But I have a feeling I know…"

A moment later Mike hung up the phone and started back.

"All right," he said as he stepped up. "As far as my parents are concerned, I'm staying at Todd's place tonight. Just in case she's farther than we expected."

The others looked between each other, slightly frantic.

"You can't go alone man," Jeff replied, a concerned look awash his face.

"Well, are any of you coming with me?"

The others exchanged glances again, all realizing that for them to spend the night, their parents would have to talk to each other, and that would screw up the entire plan.

"Yeah," Mike continued. "Didn't think so."

"Be careful man," Jeff said, wishing he could talk his friend out of going, but knowing damn well that would be a fool's errand. He knew Mike too well for that one.

"Here," Todd said, reaching into his pocket.

Mike watched as he pulled a pocketknife out, and handed it over.

"It was my dad's. Try not to lose it. He'll kill me." He paused. "Seriously, he will."

Mike nodded, taking the knife and putting it in his pocket. "I won't. Thanks dude."

"I can't believe you're doing this?" John said. "You're either really brave, or really stupid."

"Guess we'll see," Mike said, turning to Maggie. "You ready?"

Maggie stood blankly, her gaze locked to him.

"All right." He turned to the others. "If I'm not back by tomorrow..."

"Be careful," Denise added. "And don't do anything stupid."

"I won't."

Mike turned to grab his bike when everything stopped. Sound faded away and nothing but the soft touch of wind brushed past him. Stepping out of a car twenty feet away was the girl of his dreams, his endless waking crush; Camille Traveler.

Mike watched as she closed the car door and started towards him. All he could do was stare.

"Hey Mike," she said as she walked past, the smell of lavender and warm sunshine wafting off of her.

"...H... hi," Mike stammered back, watching as she went inside and was greeted by a large group of friends.

Then a stiff fist to the shoulder pulled him back to the moment.

"Dude!" John barked, pulling his hand back. "Close your fucking mouth. Jesus..."

Todd laughed and Jeff smiled, shaking his head.

Mike moved his hand to his shoulder that was just beginning to throb. "What the fuck dude...?" he asked, rubbing it.

"You're hopeless," Denise smiled. "Adorable, but hopeless..."

Mike shook his head, shooting John a dirty look before turning and making his way to his bike. Then he pulled it off the rack, lifted his leg over and pushed off, pedaling away in the direction of the old highway.

"One day that guy's gotta grow the balls to just talk to her," Jeff said, watching as Mike pedaled away.

"One day he'll actually just grow balls," John said with a grin.

"You know," Denise said, smirking at them. "That's not cool. It's not easy talking to someone you have a crush on. Actually, liking someone and just wanting to hump their leg is different." She turned her gaze admirably towards Mike who was a good distance away. "One day you might get it."

"Shit," John said with a smile. "You'd have a better chance getting with Camille Traveler than Mike ever would..."

Denise turned and smiled coyly. "Who knows, maybe I'll try." She lifted her eyebrows and winked with a soft *click* of her tongue and then turned, making her way back inside.

Jeff chuckled and followed behind her, catching the door just as it swung shut.

"Fuckin carpet muncher," John said with furrowed brows and a shake of his head.

"She's probably right though," Todd said with a smirk.

John returned the smirk and shrugged in agreement. "Come on," he said, tapping Todd on the arm. "I gotta go beat this fuckin AAZ asshole..."

The pair turned and made their way back inside, the musical chaos of the machines lined against the wall pouring out as the door opened with the greasy smell of corndogs and hamburgers in the air.

Outside Mike was already well on his way towards where he had first met Maggie, his only thoughts on what he was going to do when he got there. How was she supposed to lead him to where she was killed? He had asked her before and the look she had given gave no indication that she even knew or remembered. But again, like he had said before, if he didn't at least try, he would never know. So, he exhaled sharply and pressed harder on the pedals, moving his bike quicker down the shoulder of the road.

Chapter 24

The sun had dropped to the edge of the horizon, a thin evening chill now whispering across the breeze. Mike pushed his bike along the edge of the highway, Maggie just in front. As he walked his gaze drifted through the trees. He heard it far before it passed and felt a ripple of nerves prickle as a car approached from behind. He edged his bike closer to the shoulder, watching as Maggie stepped further off the road, a look of fear moving to her eyes. Something about the road terrified her. There was a normal look of sadness in her eyes, something that mirrored a silent torment, but whenever a car passed the look morphed to fear. Mike thought about it for a moment and then glanced behind to see the car approaching.

He stopped a few seconds later, moving further onto the shoulder as the car drove past. He was generally pretty careful to give cars room to pass, but something about Maggie's reaction suggested he give a wider berth than usual.

The car blasted past, going well over the speed limit.

"Slow down!" Mike shouted. "Asshole..."

After the car passed he looked back to Maggie who stood silently, her gaze locked to him. "I still can't understand why someone would want to kill a twelve-year-old girl," he said, knowing the only response would come in the form of that hollow gaze. He glanced at the ground for a moment before looking back at her. Sadness moved inside him. "I'm really sorry," he said, emotion welling. "We're gonna find whoever did this to you. I promise."

Maggie looked at him for a moment before dropping her gaze to the ground and turning to continue on. Mike watched her take the next few steps before shaking his head and continuing after.

It was a short time later that Mike began to wish one of the others had agreed to accompany him. The sky overhead was quickly growing dark, the handful of early stars overhead barely visible. The fields on both sides were pitch black and empty save for the lone hoot of a distant owl. He shuddered, zipping his hoodie up to his neck. Up ahead he saw a large expanse where the trees pressed closer into the road. They had been walking for a good two hours at that point and were nearing the large rolling hills that surrounded that side of the valley. Beyond that were a handful of tiny communities and multiple mining operations, some still in use, some long abandoned. Mike realized they weren't far from the road that led to the pit. For a second, he reminisced, thinking about the few days prior and what that place held for him and his friends. Then he pulled himself from his thoughts and looked up. Twenty feet ahead Maggie had stopped. She stood with her back to him, her gaze turned towards the ground.

Mike approached.

"Is this it?" he asked, coming to a stop a few feet away.

Maggie slowly turned, locking her gaze to his and then lifted her arm, her finger pointing downwards at the space between them.

"This is where you were killed?" he asked, slightly confused.

Mike realized as he looked around that they were almost in the identical spot that he had found her the first time. They had wandered in a really big circle back to the highway.

He looked around. The road was empty in both directions, no lights, no sign of approaching vehicles. On both sides of the road were trees that went back hundreds of feet on one side, and all the way up the hill on the other. There was nothing around. *How did you end up here?* He pondered the thought as he set his bike down and pulled a small flashlight from his back pocket.

The light moved past Maggie, the light illuminating her face. Slowly her gaze shifted to the road.

THE FREEZING OCTOBER air bit at Maggie's dress, the one that had days prior been neatly pressed and clean, the one that now hung limply around her, strips of cloth torn away exposing her pale, bruised skin. Scratches ran up her legs past the mud and dirt that enveloped her feet and calves. Her hair was matted, and she struggled against the bitter cold wrapping around her. Her heart pounded from a combination of fear, starvation and the cold air slicing past. The pavement beneath her stabbed into her feet as she took her first bare steps out onto the main road. Tiny stones jabbed into her flesh with each step, and the coldness cut into her heels. She was cold, and tired, her entire body still aching from the violence it had endured the past three nights. But she had escaped, and now she stood on the side of the road, afraid and alone.

She turned onto the two-lane road and started in the direction she hoped would lead to home, or at least someone who would get her there. She had managed to escape the man who had taken her, but she was far from free. Then a distant light caught her eyes and her gaze lifted.

Down the road, headlights quickly approached. They swerved slightly, bobbing between the two lines that made up its lane. Maggie stopped, the light beginning to illuminate her face, the tear lines that cut through the dirt from her eyes to her chin now fully visible.

She tensed, the car getting closer. Then in horror she realized that the car wasn't slowing, and that it had started to veer straight for her. Slowly she brought her hands up to shield the crushing impact.

The last thing she remembered was the blinding light of the headlights and the piercing screech of rubber locking to pavement as the driver realized she was there.

Mike was shining his light around the shoulder of the road, looking for any clue as to what could have happened. He didn't notice Maggie staring down the road, or the tears that had begun to roll down her cheeks. He was focused on finding some kind of clue, and knew that what he was doing was wishful at best. But as he had said before, until the last few days, a lot of things he thought before were now *ass over tits* as John so eloquently phrased quite often. Mike shook his head and then turned back to Maggie. "You're sure this is where it happened?" He knew the ridiculousness of the question. If anyone was sure, it would be her, but he found himself compelled to ask. Slowly she turned back to him, nodding. He could see the tears on her face. That said it all for him. "Why?" he asked, his gaze moving to the ground. "Why here? We're right on the highway. Anybody could have driven past and caught them. Why would they kill you here?

It doesn't make sense..." He sighed heavily, shaking his head. "If only you could talk," he said, turning his flashlight and gaze back to the shoulder of the road.

As the beam of light washed across the ground something shined back, a tiny flicker, just enough to catch his eye.

He squinted, honing the light back onto the object that had reflected.

Then he slowly edged forward, his gaze not moving from the spot for fear that whatever it was would disappear and be gone forever.

Mike used his foot to brush away the dirt concealing the small object buried beneath. Then he froze, his eyes opening wide. "No way..."

He bent down, brushing the last of the dirt away, and stared at the object lying half-covered in the soil. It was a small pendant, the silver chain it was attached to still buried in the earth.

He reached down, taking hold of the necklace and carefully lifted it out of the ground. Dirt fell away as he let the chain links slide through his fingers until he was holding the pendant. The light flickered off. It was a small silver M. "Holy shit," he whispered, slowly moving his gaze back to Maggie. "Was this yours?"

Maggie's gaze moved from him to the necklace. As she stared her hand came up to her chest, right where the pendant would have sat. Then her gaze dropped to the ground.

"The M is for Maggie, isn't it?" Mike asked, watching her silent reaction. "This *was* yours..."

Maggie brought her gaze back to the pendant, her hand balling to a fist at her chest.

"YOU BE SAFE NOW, you hear," Maggie's dad said as she opened the door to the truck. "And call me when you're done, I'll pick you up."

"OK," Maggie said with a smile, stepping out and closing the door behind her.

As the truck pulled away Maggie saw one of her friends running towards her.

"Maggie!" her friend said, coming to a stop just in front of her as her gaze locked to the shining pendant hanging around Maggie's neck. "Oh wow!" she exclaimed. "It's so pretty!"

Maggie smiled, lifting it up to admire herself. "My mom gave it to me." She smiled, still watching the light twinkle off the tiny stones. "It's an early birthday present."

"Wow," her friend said with a grin. "Jealous!"

Maggie chuckled, letting the pendant fall back into place as her friend grabbed her arm and started leading her towards the bowling alley.

"Come on," her friend said. "Everyone's already here!"

Mike stood at the edge of the road, watching as Maggie's hand still hovered over the empty space below her neck. He watched as another tear worked its way down her cheek.

He struggled to put everything together. "So," he began, thinking out loud. "Somebody took you from the bowling alley, drove you out here to the side of the road and killed you? But why? Why go through all that trouble just to kill you? It just doesn't make sense..."

He turned back to the shoulder and scanned it again. Then he turned back to Maggie. "We should head back. I don't think it's too safe out here. It is kind of late and my parents would be pissed if anything happened to me. "Let's head back." He paused. "I'm gonna ride my bike. I'll see you at my place."

Maggie's gaze moved to the pendant one last time as Mike unzipped his hoodie and dropped it into his shirt pocket. "I've gotta show the others this," he said, zipping back up and stepping over his bike Then he put his foot on the pedal and started off.

Chapter 25

"Dude," Mike said into the phone. "I'm telling you, it's hers."

Mike had gotten home a short time ago, covering his arrival with a story about how Todd's parents had a last-minute thing they had to do and that the sleepover had been cancelled. He received his not riding home at night lecture and had eased out of it with a quick, *I know, I'm sorry. I won't do it again*. That was the last thing his parents said before he retired to his room, and they dove back into their game of Parcheesi.

"And you found it on the side of the road?"

"Yeah dude," Mike replied. "Pretty much in the exact spot that I found her."

There was a loud bang over the phone and Mike pulled the handset away from his ear. "What the hell dude...?"

"Sorry," Jeff's voice filtered through after a moment. "Fucking orcs..."

"Dude," Mike hissed. "Are you playing Warcraft or are you paying attention to what I'm saying. I'm telling you I found a necklace, and I'm pretty sure it belonged to her. This is huge..."

He heard Jeff sigh heavily. "Sorry man," he replied. "You're right."

There was a pause and Jeff's voice cracked through. "All right. I'm here." He paused for a moment. "So, if she was killed on the side of the road, then where's her body? Whoever killed her must have moved it. And why kill her on the side of the road? It doesn't make sense. There are dozens of roads that lead off into the hills or basically *all* of Cedar Mountain. Why there? It doesn't make sense."

Mike nodded, hearing another bout of laughter come from his parents' room. "That's exactly what I thought. But dude, she led me right there. And sure enough, that's where I found her necklace."

"If," Jeff interjected. "It *is* in fact, *her* necklace."

"Dude," Mike replied flatly. "Seriously...? It was buried in the dirt, and it's an M..."

"Still," Jeff replied.

"I think we should take it to the police," Mike said, holding the necklace out in front of him." He paused, looking at it.

There was a moment of silence. Then Jeff's voice came through the phone again. "You're not touching it are you?" he asked. "It's evidence from a crime scene."

Mike leaned back, his eyes getting wider. Then he cleared his throat and set the necklace down on the table next to him. "Uh. No. Of course not. It's in a plastic bag."

"OK," Jeff replied. "They might need to run forensics on it, check for fingerprints, or blood or stuff like that."

"Yeah," Mike lied. "No. It's totally in a bag."

"All right," Jeff said. "But didn't we already go over this? We can't go to the police yet because we have nothing to give them. Yeah, we have the necklace, but we have no proof that it belonged to her, and again, we can't exactly tell them that she's helping us..."

Mike nodded. "Then what are we gonna do?"

There was no reply.

"Jeff?" Mike asked.

"I'm thinking," Jeff snapped back. "Give me a sec."

Jeff dropped his gaze to the floor. In front of him the light from his computer screen illuminated the mess scattered across his desk. His foot tapped the bottom of his chair and he chewed at his bottom lip. Jeff slowly spun his chair, the phone cord wrapping loosely around him. "Look," he said after a moment. "Just keep looking around the auto shop. Try and get a better look at the car you found there. Like Todd said, it might be blue now, but that doesn't mean it always was. Try and get a closer look *without* getting busted. Until then keep that necklace safe. And Mike…"

"Yeah," Mike said after a moment of silence.

"Put the damn thing in a plastic bag yeah."

Across town Mike glanced down at the necklace. *How the hell does he know…?* "Yeah," he replied, listening as his parents began laughing again. "All right."

"Like I said," Jeff said from the other end. "It's evidence."

"Yeah," Mike replied. "I know." He paused as his dad called him from the other room. "Look, I gotta go. My parents want me to join in on this game night thing they're trying to start. Some *bring the family closer together* crap. I'll hit you up tomorrow."

"OK," Jeff replied. "Don't have too much fun."

"Right?" Mike said, rolling his eyes. "Later."

"Lates," Jeff said, hanging up.

Mike put the phone back on the receiver and stood up, calling out to his dad. "Be right there." Then he went into the kitchen and pulled a zip lock bag from a cupboard drawer and dropped the necklace into it, sealing the top and rolling it up. "Coming!" he called out, making his way towards his parent's room, pausing only to glance at Maggie as he tossed the bag onto his bed. He exhaled heavily and watched as her gaze settled on the plastic enclosed object. Then he turned and started down the hall.

Chapter 26

The next day Mike was sweeping at the shop. Somehow, no matter how much he cleaned, there was always another layer of dirt and clutter waiting for him when he arrived. That day had been no different.

He had arrived at nine in the morning and been put straight to work, and by the time that Don came in from the yard and offered to get their lunch, he was already covered in sweat and dust, with a thin streak of grease smeared across his forehead.

"I gotta shoot out for a bit," Don said, stepping in from the yard. "Got's somebody with a tractor they're lookin' to get rid of. Could turn out to be a pretty penny in it for me if I play my cards right. You go ahead and keep an eye on things till I get back. Shouldn't be more than a couple hours. They're over in Parowan. You can go ahead and take off when I get back."

Mike nodded, wiping his forehead with his sleeve. "OK."

Don glanced around the shop with a smirked nod. "Go ahead and finish sweeping up in here, and when you're done, I want you to go through those boxes over there." He nodded to a large stack of cardboard boxes with dates scrawled across them. They're full of old invoices. I need you to go ahead and straighten those out, make sure the dates match the boxes. But be careful. Don't want you loosin' any of 'em and the IRS coming back here and crawling up my ass."

"Careful with the boxes," Mike repeated. "Got it."

"All right then," Don said, turning to make his way outside.

Mike stood there, waiting for the Camino's engine to fire up and the sound to disappear. Then he waited another few minutes to make sure he wasn't gonna get caught by surprise again before setting the broom down and making his way out to the yard, and back to the tarp covered mustang.

He moved quickly down the aisle towards the back, turning the corner quickly and rushing to the car. As he approached, he stopped, cocking his ear towards the office and listened for a moment. Then he took a deep breath, exhaled slowly and bent down to pull the tarp up.

Beneath the faded blue was a late sixties model Mustang. It was blue, and through the dirty windows Mike could make out a burgundy interior. He flipped the tarp over the top and ran his fingers along the side, feeling the lines as he made his way towards the trunk. "This has to be it," he whispered as he eyed the vehicle. Then he paused, reaching into his pocket and pulling the knife out that Todd had given him the day prior. "Here we go," he whispered, leaning down and bringing the blade to the paint just beside the taillight.

He gently pulled the knife across it, the scratching sound much louder than he anticipated. Then his eyes locked to the small groove where the paint peeled away. Just beneath the sky blue was another color, this one brightly contrasting, the color of old cherry and faded fire hydrant.

"Oh, shit," Mike whispered, a chill running across his arms. "He was right..."

Mike knew how happy Jeff was going to be to hear that he had found the car, and that he was right about it being painted. But that was a quickly fleeting thought as he rose to his feet and moved to the passenger door and tried the handle.

Click.

The door opened with a creak, the last however many years of stagnant air wafting outwards.

Mike was hit with the smell of sun battered plastic and cloth, the fresh air swirling dust and particles into the air.

He snorted the air from his nostrils and pressed the lever to move the seat forward. It did with a soft *thump*. Then Mike leaned into the back and ran his fingers through the crevice of the bench seat.

Nothing.

He bent down to look under the seat.

Again nothing.

He tried the visor, under the front seats, everywhere. Not a thing. The car was completely empty, save for a set of keys in the glove box.

Mike stood, wiping his forehead again with his sleeve, and then turned to make his way to the back of the car again. He pushed the trunk button. It stood stiff, not budging beneath his finger. Then he made his way back and grabbed the keys from the glove box, returning to the trunk.

As the key slid into the keyhole all manner of frightening visions entered his mind; bodies folded up into bags, skeletons bound with bailing wire, piles of children's clothes and shoes. By the time he turned the key he was bordering on a panic attack.

Then there was a soft *click* and the trunk popped open a half an inch.

Mike took another deep breath and slowly pulled the trunk open, the hidden monsters inside coiling and crouched, ready to spring.

To his partial relief the trunk was empty. He was grateful he hadn't come across a grisly scene, but at the same time disappointed that there wasn't any solid evidence, like blood, or a piece of Maggie's dress. He sighed, leaning in to run his fingers along the edges. Then he stopped, his eyes growing wide.

He pulled his hand back and looked at the tiny object held between his fingers. It was a small earring, a tiny gold hummingbird with a single green stone as an eye.

"HEY!"

Mike spun, stepping back away from the car and almost tripping over a block of wood.

"What the *hell* did I say to you boy?"

Don stood there, fury written on his face. His hands were balled to fists and anger shot from his gaze.

Mike hadn't heard him return, had been too busy searching the car to pay attention. He hadn't heard The El Camino pull up, or the car door close, or Don calling out his name from in the office. He hadn't heard anything until the guy was already standing there.

"Was I not *God damned* clear about you snooping around back here?" Don barked. "Huh?"

"I…" Mike stammered, afraid and on the spot. "I'm sorry. I just… I just wanted to see what was under the tarp." As he spoke, he slowly dropped the earring into his back pocket.

"Well, it's pretty damned obvious you either got shit in your ears, or you're too stupid to be able to follow simple instructions." He paused, staring at him. "Either way you're done. You can go ahead and get the hell outta here. And forget about anymore work." He paused. "You won't be gettin' no references from me either."

162

Mike stared at him, fear building up.

"Well, what the hell are you still standing there for?" Don growled. "Get!"

Mike slunk past the man, quickly making his way towards the front. His heart pounded in his dry throat, and he could feel the man's greasy grip clawing at his back every step threatening to pull him back and lock him away forever in the black confines of the mustang's trunk.

Behind him Don turned his attention back to the car, carefully making his way around it. When he got to the rear he stopped, his gaze narrowing to the fresh scratch. Slowly his hand came out, his fingers working over the mark. Then his gaze lifted, a squint flashing past as he stared in the direction Mike had just disappeared to.

Chapter 27

Mike turned the earring over in his hand, watching as the light glinted off the green gem. His eyes were locked to the tiny object. The others in the group sat still, each of them still reeling from what they had been told moments before.

"It was in the trunk?" Todd asked, his hand coming up to his neck.

"Yeah," Mike replied, still peering down at it. "I'm telling you," he continued, "It belongs to her."

"Then we got him," Jeff said, his eyes watching Mike's hand turn the object over. "He's done..."

"An earring isn't going to prove anything," John said, his tone less cynical than usual. "It could have belonged to anyone."

"Her dad would know."

Mike pulled his gaze away from the earring, shifting it to Denise.

"He'd know," she repeated. "Trust me. We just need to go ask."

"What if we take it to her dad and he says that it is?"

"*Then* we go to the police," Jeff said, pulling everyone's attention to him. "*That* would be sufficient evidence." He paused. "I mean, we're still going to have a heck of a time explaining how we got it, or how we even figured out how it could have possibly been there in the first place, but it could be enough for them to go check the car. They'd have a warrant, better equipment. There could be blood, or hair, or something that you couldn't possibly have found."

Mike nodded. He was right. He had been under pressure and was only looking for obvious things. The police were trained to find evidence. He agreed, but part of him wanted to keep the entire thing to themselves, for them to be the one to find her killer and bring him to justice. But things were a little more realistic now. They had found her killer; they had proven that she had been in the car. But what were they gonna do, go arrest the guy? Make him confess? No. This wasn't the movies. All they would do was make things harder for the police. Jeff was right. It was time to hand it over. They had done all they could. But not before they found out about the earring. At least there was still *something* that they could do to dig further. Mike had come to realize that it wasn't about him, or the others. It was about Maggie, and finding whoever it was that had killed her that night. There was a reason she was still there, and something told him, if he could find out, maybe she would finally be able to rest.

Mike nodded. "Yeah." Then he looked between the others, letting his gaze settle on Maggie for a moment before pulling it back to Jeff. "Look. I'll go see her dad. I'll show him the earring and the necklace and see if they're for sure hers." He paused. "If they are, then we go to the police." He again let his gaze move between them. "But we need to be careful," he continued. "Don... The guy, caught me looking through the car. I might have messed everything up. If he's suspicious, he could do something with it. The cops might show up and it could be gone, so we gotta do this quick."

"Well then why you still sitting there with that stupid look on your face?" John asked with a grin. "Get the hell out of here."

"I'll go with you."

Mike looked across to Denise. "You sure? I mean—"

"Yeah," she said, cutting him short. "What, you were just gonna walk in there and tell him you found the necklace on the side of the road, and the earring in the trunk of a car you think was used to abduct her?" She paused, waiting for it to register. After a moment she sighed and explained. "Look. We show him the necklace. We tell him that her friend gave me the necklace and that we were wondering if it was hers. If he says yes, then we can pretty much assume that the earring is too."

"Huh," Jeff exhaled. "I hadn't even thought about that. Damn."

Mike nodded. She was right. How were they supposed to explain how they found the jewelry...? "She's right."

Denise smirked. "I usually am. Perks of being a girl."

"Well, it sure isn't the periods," John snickered next to her.

Denise stiffened, looking to the ground around her for something to pick up.

John chuckled, jumping to his feet and stepping back.

"John, I swear to God. One of these days they're gonna find *you* in a ditch somewhere."

He smiled. "Well at least now we know I'll be able to come back and haunt you. Then you'll be stuck with me forever..." He made his best ghost impersonation while moaning.

"Jesus, dude," Jeff replied.

Denise turned to Mike and stood up. "Can we go now?"

Mike glanced at John and shook his head. "Yeah." Then he looked at Jeff." Meet back here in two hours. We'll let you know what we find out."

"Oooohhhhh," John said, continuing his *ghost* moan as they walked towards their bikes.

Denise lifted her hand over her shoulder without looking back, saluting him with her middle finger.

"Yeah," John snorted. "You wish!"

"Denise exhaled slowly and even, bending down to pick up her bike. "Fuckin' idiot," she whispered as she lifted it up.

"Pretty much," Mike agreed, lifting his bike up and stepping over.

Then they both pushed off and made their way through the field in the direction of Maggie's house.

Chapter 28

The breeze drifted past, summer dancing around them on light wisps of warmth. Above, white tufts of cloud hung on a backdrop of light blue. It was perfect t-shirt weather as Mike liked to refer to it, that one month a year where he could retire his hoodie and jackets and spend day and night not worrying about if it was gonna be freezing on his ride home. Today, however, he rode under perfect skies, his mind light-years away from the weather, or the perfect conditions outside. A nervous tension swirled around him, tense and bitter. He knew what he was about to do, how returning to Maggie's house and showing her dad the jewelry was likely the last thing the man wanted or expected. He knew there was a possibility it could shatter him. He hated it. He hated that it was the only way for them to find out if they were in fact following the right lead. So, he put his head down and kept pedaling.

"I hate this," Mike said, not glancing at Denise who rode next to him. "It really sucks that we have to go back there. I just keep thinking how bad it has to suck for her dad, us showing up again and bringing back all the painful memories."

"Yeah," she replied. "But we kind of don't have a choice." She paused for a moment, swerving around a discarded fast-food bag. "Just try and think of it this way," she continued. "Imagine how happy and relieved he's gonna be knowing that the person who kidnapped and killed his daughter has been brought to justice. He's been waiting twenty years for that. And if us making him think about her helps catch the guy who did it. Then it's worth it."

"Yeah," Mike replied a moment later. "I guess you're right. But it still sucks, you know."

"Yeah," she replied. "I do. Why do you think I offered to come?"

Mike glanced over as she flashed a small comforting smile. She hadn't wanted him to go alone.

"Thanks," he smiled.

She smiled and turned her attention back to the street in front.

Three minutes later he and Denise were setting their bikes down on the man's front lawn. They exchanged a single glance, Denise telling him that she had been having almost the exact same thoughts with her uncomfortable gaze. He took a deep breath, sighing heavily and then they turned and made their way to the door.

Denise looked at Mike who stood there, his eyes locked to the door. Neither of them wanted to be there. Neither of them wanted to see the reaction that undoubtedly awaited them. Then Mike shook his head lightly and reached out, ringing the doorbell. "Here we go," he whispered, taking a single step back.

A moment later footsteps sounded inside, growing closer to the door. Then the lock *clicked,* and the door cracked open.

Mike looked up to see the old man's face peering out through the small gap.

The man glanced between them and then allowed the door to open fully. He sighed. "So, I'm guessing you're back cause you wanna know something else about my daughter?"

Mike glanced quickly to Denise, then back to the man. "Yes sir," he nodded. "If we could just have a minute."

The man glanced between them again and then stepped aside. "Well. Come on in. I'll put the kettle on."

A short time later Maggie's father returned from the kitchen with two cups in his hand.

He walked up, setting them on the coffee table before handing them out. "Hope you like instant," he said. "All I got."

"Yes sir," Mike said, reaching out to take the hot cup.

"Wasn't sure if you kids even drank coffee these days," he said, handing Denise a cup. "You know, in my time we were raised on it." He smirked. "I've been drinking it since I could stand." He paused, chuckling lightly. "And probably even before that knowing the amount my mama used to drink. Hell. I'm not sure I even have a memory of her without a mug in her hand." He paused, taking a small sip from his cup before setting it back down on the coffee table. "So," he said, getting right into it. "What's it about this time?"

Again, Mike glanced to Denise, before reaching into the small coin pocket in his pants and pulling the zip lock bag out. As he did, he stopped his hand pausing mid-motion.

Standing just off to the side of her father was Maggie. She stood there, the sadness in her gaze flowing outwards as she stared at him.

Maggie's dad eyed him for a moment, noticing that both of the kids were staring at something across the room. He turned his gaze, eyeing the space. The door to the bedroom stood open. "Something back there I can help you with?" he asked, his tone changing.

"No," Mike said, ripping his gaze back. He hadn't realized how long he had been staring. Maggie still stood there, a thin line of tears working down her cheeks as her gaze drifted around the room. "Sorry."

Mike slowly unfolded the bag before him.

Maggie's father watched in interest as Mike unfolded the plastic and fished out the item within. Then a painful recognition warped his face, a single tear forming almost instantly as both eyes welled up with moisture. Mike and Denise knew at that moment that what they had come to ask had just been answered.

Mike held his hand out, allowing her father to take the necklace up in his hands. He held it delicately, another tear forming as he stared into his open palm. "Where did you find this?" he asked, his words barely above a choked whisper.

"Brandy," Denise said quickly, glancing for the briefest of moments to Maggie who had locked her gaze back to her father.

The man's gaze didn't leave the necklace.

"We uh, we went to visit her," Mike continued. "We wanted to ask her about what happened the night Maggie went missing." He paused. "She was the one that gave us the necklace."

"Yeah," Mike agreed. "She had it this whole time."

Behind her father, Maggie had turned and was making her way slowly through the house, her gaze working over the pictures that hung on the wall, and the cluttered mess that made up the room.

The old man exhaled heavily, a deep shudder running through it. Then he slowly started to nod. "Maggie's mother gave this to her for what would have been her thirteenth birthday. It was an early birthday present." He smiled softly. "She was growing into such a beautiful young woman my wife had said, and she deserved to have a piece of jewelry that matched that beauty." He pulled his gaze from the necklace, looking up at them. "She was wearing this the night she disappeared. I remember, cause my wife had made a big stink about reminding her to wear it out. She wanted her to show it off to everyone." He paused, glancing back at the necklace. Then a suspicious look crossed his eyes. "If her friend found this at the bowling alley, why didn't she turn it over to the police?"

Mike and Denise glanced at each other quickly.

"Um," Mike began. "She uh, her friend said that—"

"She said it kept getting caught in Maggie's hair while she was bowling," Denise said, cutting in to save the conversation. "Maggie gave it to her to hold onto because there were no pockets in her dress, and she didn't want to lose it." She paused. "Maggie disappeared before she could give it back. I'm guessing she just forgot she had it during all the commotion." Denise looked past him. Maggie stood near a small bookshelf; her gaze locked to a picture of her family before she had died. Maggie smiled back from behind the dusty glass, her youthful glow peering out.

Alan nodded; her explanation sufficient enough to turn off any alarms. Then he turned the necklace over once in his hand, and then held it out. "Go ahead and give this back to her friend, won't you? I don't want it here. It'll only serve to hurt every time I see it." He paused "It's far too pretty to sit wasting away in a drawer."

Denise nodded, reaching out to take it. "Thank you," she said, folding the chain around it. "We'll let her know you wanted her to have it."

"That'll be fine," he replied, lifting his cup and taking a sip.

"There is one more thing," Mike said, watching as a squint flashed through the old man's eyes.

He reached into his pocket and pulled the earring out, holding it in his outstretched palm. "Do you recognize this?"

Alan glanced at Mike's palm, his eyes working over the small, jeweled earring. He set the cup down and leaned back, his gaze locked to Mike's hand. "I suppose she had that as well?" he said, his gaze rising to meet Mike's, suspicion edging back into it.

Mike swallowed hard, nodding.

"Hers as well," her father continued, glancing at Mike's hand one more time. This time however, he made no motion to reach out, or to take the item from them. "Her mother's actually. She had those on that night as well." His eyes narrowed.

Denise watched the man shift in his seat and felt the energy in the room shift. The friendliness her father had exuded when inviting them in was now gone, replaced with a cold firmness. In a blink they no longer felt welcome.

Mike began to shift in his seat, discomfort burning through him. He glanced to where Maggie had been and she was no longer there.

Denise noticed immediately and set her coffee cup back on the table. "Well," she said, tapping Mike's leg as she began to stand. "We're really sorry for taking up your time. You've been really helpful. Thank you." She glanced quickly at Mike. "I think we're gonna get going now, a lot to write you know."

"Yeah," the man replied in a tone both low and unfriendly as he slowly rose from his chair. "I think that'd be for the best."

Mike caught an air of malice in the man's tone. It brushed across the hairs on his arms, standing them up as it did.

"Before you go," he said, stopping the pair in their tracks. "What did you say her friend's name was again?"

Mike glanced to Denise.

"Oh," Denise said quickly. "Brandy. Brandy Whiting."

The man stared at her. Mike could see him playing the name over in his mind. "Yeah," he said after a moment. "I guess so. I remember Brandy. Sweet girl."

Denise tapped Mike on the arm. "We really should be going," she said.

Mike nodded. "Yeah," he replied, turning to start towards the door.

"I'll see you out," the man said, starting after them.

As Denise and Mike approached the door, Maggie's father stepped quickly in front of them, moving with a speed that startled the both of them. He reached out, placing his hand on the knob. They froze, watching as he slowly turned to them, his eyes narrowing.

Denise locked to his gaze, tensing as she did. There was something angry behind it, something hidden, and mean. It made every hair on her neck stand up, and it took everything in her not to grab hold of Mike's arm and cling tightly.

"I'd really appreciate it if you kids didn't come back here," he said, his gaze moving between the two of them. "I think I've said about all there is to say on the matter." His eyes narrowed on them. "My daughter's dead, and ain't nothing gonna bring her back. And I don't find myself enjoying having to revisit these old memories." He paused, looking between them again. "It took me a long time to forget about her," he said. "And I'd like to get back to forgettin'. I lived with that pain for long enough." He paused, watching for understanding in the kid's eyes. "Am I making myself clear on this? I don't want you comin' back here."

Mike nodded softly. "Yes sir."

The man looked to Denise who nodded quickly.

"Good," he said, turning the knob and pushing the door open as he stepped aside.

Mike ushered Denise through first and then quickly followed behind. It wasn't until they had picked up their bikes and were pushing them to the sidewalk that he chanced a look behind him. As he did, he saw the man standing in the window, watching them carefully as they left. Then Mike turned his head, planted his foot on the pedal and pushed down hard.

It was a good five minutes before either of them spoke, Mike finally breaking the silence.

"What the hell just happened?" he asked, watching as a car came to a stop at the intersection they were riding through.

"He's hiding something," Denise replied, glancing in both directions as they crossed. "Did you see the way he looked at you when you showed him the earring?" She paused, watching a man drop a bag of trash in a can as they passed. "It was like, I don't know... He was upset that we had found it."

"Yeah," Mike replied. "It feels like there's something he's not telling us."

"I think it's time to go to the police Mike. I don't care what the other guys think, we're in way over our heads." She stayed silent for a moment. Then added what they were both thinking. "This is starting to get dangerous."

"Yeah," he agreed a moment later. "I think I agree."

They rode the next half-block without speaking. Mike's head was a maelstrom of thoughts. Denise was right. This was starting to get way out of their league. It was to the point where he *was* worried one of them was gonna get hurt. Hell, for a moment he had worried that Maggie's dad wasn't gonna let them leave. And the guy at the auto shop. That was stupid. He had put himself alone with the man who they believed had already killed at least one person. He could have gotten added to that list, or worse. No. It was time to get help. "Let's get back to the spot," he said after a moment. "The others should still be there. We have to tell them what happened."

Denise didn't reply. She already knew what they were in for. She just picked up the speed, pulling ahead of Mike.

Overhead a thin layer of clouds gathered across the sky, blotting the sun out and casting a sheet of grey down on the street. A thin chill worked through the breeze, again reminding them that summer was fleeting, and the warmth would soon end. They made their way through the city, traffic passing by unaware as the pair continued riding in silence.

Chapter 29

"You gotta be shitting me," John burst, shaking his head. "You want me to go *back*?"

"Not just you," Mike said. "All of us. We *all* need to go there." He paused, turning his gaze to Jeff. "Denise is right. We're in *way* over our heads. It's too much..."

Jeff sighed heavily. He hated the thought of handing the investigation over to the police. They'd already had their chance and flubbed it years prior. He still believed whole-heartedly that the group could solve Maggie's murder by themselves. But also, Mike wasn't wrong. What if the crazy auto shop guy decided that they were getting too close? What if he decided to come after them and take care of the problem before everything came to light. Mike *had* gotten caught, so there was also the possibility that he would get rid of the car, and then there would be *no* evidence. He nodded, glancing at the ground for a split second before looking back up to Mike. "You're right. As much as I hate to say it, I agree. We should go to the police."

"This is stupid," John said, still upset that his friends were dragging him back to the police station. "The cop I talked to didn't even know anything about the case. I really doubt the cop who investigated originally is gonna remember anything about it."

Jeff looked at John and smiled, reaching out to slap him in the arm.

"Ow! What the fuck?" John barked.

"You're a genius," Jeff said, catching himself. "Though this is probably the first and last time you're ever gonna hear me say that..."

"Of course I am," John replied with a smirk. "Why...?"

"Dude...," Jeff said, shaking his head. "All we have to do is ask for the original investigating officer. They are sure to remember the case. I watch investigation shows all the time. They always remember the cases they couldn't solve. It haunts em. It's like, a cop's worst nightmare. And if we have evidence that could get the case reopened." He smiled, letting a single chuckle out. "It might just work."

The group looked between each other for a moment. It was Jeff who started towards his bike, prompting the others. "Well. Let's go get this case reopened."

John shook his head again. "I hate you guys..."

"Oh, shut up already," Denise remarked, starting towards her bike. "You've never even talked to a cop. You live in a nice neighborhood; your parents have money and you're on the freaking swim team for God's sake. Get off it already yeah?"

John scowled at her. "Yeah, well it doesn't mean I wanna go making friends with them either."

The others picked up their bikes and started through the field.

"Ah shit," John mumbled making his way to his bike. "Hold your horses, I'm coming," he shouted.

The kids made their way up Main Street into town. Jeff held the lead with Mike just behind. Todd and Denise followed up with John in the rear.

They passed the main park in town and cut through a shopping center parking lot that led to the back entrance of the police station.

As they turned the corner Jeff slowed down, hopping off his bike before coming to a stop.

He waited for the others to pull up and then nodded for them to move closer.

The group moved into a loose huddle.

"So, here's the plan," Jeff said, taking the lead. "We go in. We ask for the officer that was in charge of the Maggie Lorris investigation. When they get him, we show him the evidence, tell him we came across it while working on a school project for next year, some *get ahead of the curve* project or some shit. Then we try and get him to reopen the case."

"And what if they don't work here anymore?" John asked, still trying to slither his way out, knowing full well that the cop he'd spoken to had offered to schedule an appointment. "Or are off today?"

"Then we talk to whoever they worked with," Jeff replied. Most of the cops are my dad's age. They've been working there forever. Trust me, there's hardly any missing persons cases in Cedar. They'll remember…"

The others turned and made their way to a bike rack at the entrance and lined their bikes up. Then they turned and made their way into the police station.

Mike thought about what they were doing, about what the implications could be. He knew the police were gonna go back to Maggie's dad's house. He couldn't imagine the pain he would be subjected to again, having to reanswer all the old questions. He didn't care about Cowles, he deserved it. Mike looked forward to seeing him walk away in handcuffs. But Maggie's dad. They had already done so much. It was that single regret that tugged at him as he made his way towards the entrance.

Mike reached the door first, opening it and holding it for Denise. Slowly the others made their way into the station.

The officer at the front desk looked up, doing a double take before eyeing the group suspiciously as they approached.

"Hi," Jeff said as he stepped up. "We were hoping you could help us." He continued without giving the man time to respond. "We'd like to speak with whatever officer was in charge of a missing person's case in 1975, regarding a young girl named Maggie Lorris."

The desk officer worked his gaze between the group. It met with John's and held for a moment. He growled under his breath, holding eye contact with him before pulling it away and settling back on Jeff.

"We've come across new evidence that may help with the case," Jeff added in his best attempt to use *cop speak* as he referred to it.

The cop eyed them once more and then sighed, reaching out to pick up the phone.

Jeff watched intently as the man across the desk waited for the other end to pick up.

"Yeah, hey," he said, glancing at Jeff who was still staring at him. "I got a group of kids here. They're saying they may have evidence in a case from..." He looked at Jeff. "When did you say it was again?"

"Nineteen seventy-five," Jeff replied. "Maggie Lorris."

"A Maggie Lorris case," the cop said, turning his attention back to the desk in front of him. "Back in seventy-five." There was a pause, and then the cop smirked, looking up to Jeff. "Yeah. Same kid. But he brought his friends this time. All right. Yeah. I'll tell em to take a seat. Yep. OK." The officer hung up the phone. "Why don't you kids go have a seat over there," he said, nodding to a group of chairs in the lobby. "A detective will be with you shortly."

"Thanks," Jeff said, turning towards the seats and tapping Mike in the arm as he passed.

When they had all taken their seats Jeff leaned over to Mike. "Where's Maggie?"

"I don't know," Mike replied. "One second, she's there, the next she's gone. It's kind of her thing. She comes and goes, disappears and reappears. She's a freaking ghost dude..."

Jeff sighed heavily, letting his gaze move to the wanted posters on the wall.

"She kind of only appears when she wants to..."

John glanced up, again making awkward eye contact with the desk officer. Then he quickly lowered his gaze and slouched down a bit. "God, I hate you guys," he mumbled.

Mike shot him a dirty glance.

A moment later the door next to the main desk opened and a large African American man in khaki slacks, a tan shirt and dark blue tie stepped out.

The officer glanced at the desk officer who nodded to the group. "That'll be them," he said, turning his face back to the desk in front of him and whatever paperwork it was that he had been filling out.

The other officer nodded and turned towards them.

Mike watched as the cop approached. He was big, like football player big, and was in his late fifties. He wore a detective badge on his belt and a pistol on the other side. He had a shoulder holster that was currently vacant, but Mike recognized by the lighter grooves in it how well-worn it was.

"So, the desk sergeant tells me you kids may have some information on an old cold case we've got?" the man said as he approached, stopping just in front of them.

Jeff stood up, extending his hand. "Um. Yeah. Hi," he said, glancing at the others. Then he turned his gaze back to him. "My friends and I have been investigating the disappearance of Maggie Lorris that happened back in nineteen seventy-five and we came across evidence that might help to solve the case and wanted to turn it over to you. We were hoping that maybe you could reopen the case."

The man eyed the group with amusement and then reached out to shake Jeff's hand. "Well," he said, pulling his hand back. "I'm Detective Cordell." He paused. "Why don't we all head back to my office, and you can show me what you got?"

He turned and started towards the back, the others following him.

As they passed the desk the other officer looked up, watching them suspiciously as they passed.

John and Todd noticed, glancing at each other. "Guess he didn't get the last donut," Todd said as they made their way through the door.

John chuckled. "Right...?"

Jeff turned his head, shooting them a dirty look. If he heard the comment, he was sure the detective had, and the last thing he wanted was the cop to think they were dicking around and making things up. They needed to be focused and serious.

Detective Cordell opened the door to his office and stepped in, leaving it open behind him. Then he made his way around the desk and took a seat. "Sorry," he said.

"There're only two chairs. I don't usually do the group thing in here."

"It's OK," Jeff said, moving to take a seat.

Mike nodded to Denise who shook her head tightly. He shrugged and moved in to sit next to Jeff.

"So," the detective began. "I guess my first question would be, why is it that you're investigating the Lorris case? That case's been closed for two decades now."

Mike looked at Jeff who gave him a look telling him to take over the conversation.

"Well," Jeff said, turning his attention back to the detective. "We were given the option of doing a project for school, for next year. Extra credit. I came across the story in an old newspaper and we decided to do it on that." He paused. "It was either that or the old iron mines outside of town..."

"Fair enough," the detective replied. "Well. I suppose I should ask what type of evidence it is that you found, and how it is you believe may be pertinent to the case."

Jeff smiled inside. He liked the word pertinent and wished he had been the one to use it first. He was gonna file that one away for next time. "Uh, Mike?" he said, tapping Mike on the leg.

"Oh," Mike said, startling a bit. "Yeah." He reached into his pocket and pulled out the plastic bag. He unfolded it and slipped it across the desk. Then he reached back in and pulled the earring free and repeated the motion, sliding it just within reach of the detective. "Like my friend said," he mentioned, leaning back to his seat, "we've been investigating Maggie's disappearance. We found the necklace on the side of the road out on highway Fifty-Six. We also found what we believe is the red mustang that she was last seen being abducted with. It's at the DC auto body shop, in the back under a tarp. I found the earring in the trunk of the car." He paused, watching as the detective eyed each of the items carefully. He lifted his eyes at the last comment. "The car that took her was red, but the one at the shop is blue. Jeff, he checked, and it was registered as blue shortly after she disappeared. But I scratched off some of the paint, and the car's original color is red. The owner, Donald Cowles painted the car after she disappeared."

Denise jumped in, further attempting to coalesce the story. "We also spoke with her father. He confirmed that the jewelry *was* hers. And the man who still works at the bowling alley also said that it could have possibly been Donald Cowles that was seen talking to her the night she went missing."

The detective pulled his eyes away from the items on his desk. "Hold up a second," he said, a suspicious squint moving into his gaze. "Where again did you find these? And what were you doing at the bowling alley?"

Mike took a deep breath, sighing heavily. Here it came... "The necklace was buried in the dirt on the side of the road, out on old Fifty-Six near mile marker eighteen. The earring was in the trunk of the red mustang, that's now blue, at the DC scrapyard. Denise went to the bowling alley with her dad to ask if they remembered anything and talked with the older man there who said he remembered seeing her speaking to Donald Cowles. He also owns the scrap yard where I found the car."

The detective looked at them, confusion flashing past his face. "I'm not even gonna ask how it was that you *happened* to come across this necklace on the side of the road, or the absurd coincidence that it could actually happen to have belonged to her, or what in God's name you were doing breaking into a local business and snooping through their vehicles, which is illegal by the way and by your admission alone I could send all of you to juvie."

"I was working there," Mike interjected quickly, not seeing John and Todd edge closer to the door as he did, readying themselves to run if they had to. "I didn't break in. Don gave me a job cleaning up. I found the car while I was there."

The detective loosened up the slightest. "All right. I assume Mr. Cowles could confirm this?"

Mike nodded. "Yes sir." Now he began to feel nervous, a thin trickle of sweat tickling down his back.

"So, let's say it wasn't breaking and entering. It was still unsafe to be rummaging around in a scrap yard. You could have gotten cut and ended up with tetanus, or worse." He paused, exhaling sharply. "You said you showed these items to the Lorris girl's father and that he confirmed that they belonged to her?"

"Yes sir," Denise said, drawing his attention to her. "He confirmed that she was wearing these the night she went missing."

"So, then these *are* hers?"

"YES!" Jeff, Mike and Denise all said at the same time.

"OK," the detective said. "It's just habit. Always gotta triple check these things." He sighed, glancing at the items one more time before lifting his gaze again. "If you don't mind me asking, how did you manage to locate what you believe is the vehicle used in her abduction?" Now the kids had his attention.

Mike glanced at Jeff, holding his hand out.

Jeff swallowed quietly, taking a deep breath. "I cross-referenced the names of all the people who owned mustangs in Iron County in nineteen seventy-five. From that list I referenced those who no longer own one. One of the names that came up happened to be a man by the name of Donald Cowles. He originally had a red mustang registered, but two years prior to Maggie Lorris disappearing, it was listed as non-operable and later the color was changed to blue. It made too much sense. Auto body shop, car color change, just two years before Maggie went missing. And why was it listed as inoperable? The guy literally owns a place that fixes cars..." He paused, glancing at Mike for a moment. "So, Mike here, got a job volunteering at the shop. He managed to snoop around in the back and found the car under a tarp. That's when he scratched some of the paint off and realized that it had originally been red. It's also when he found the earring in the trunk."

Detective Cordell stared across the desk at Jeff, then slowly worked his gaze amongst the others. "Donald Cowles," he said after a moment, sighing heavily. "I'm well acquainted with that name... He was one of the prime suspects we investigated originally. He'd been brought in because he owned the exact car that had been used in the abduction. But like you already said, it had been listed as non-operable at the time, and the vehicle we had pulled him over in was completely different. Plus, the attendant working at the bowling alley hadn't been too sure if he was even there that night. He'd given us a long list of names and only a few of them had checked out." He paused, shaking his head as he again looked between them before settling back on Jeff. Then he chuckled, something completely unexpected by the group. "I don't exactly know how to say this. But. This is...

Wow." He shook his head, tapping his hands on his desk. "Why didn't you call us?"

Mike glanced at Jeff.

"We did the second Maggie's dad confirmed that the earring and necklace was hers."

You should have called us way before that. Do you have any idea what kind of potential dangers you kids put yourselves in? If the man you're claiming, is in fact the person that abducted the Lorris girl, weren't you at all the least bit worried he'd have no qualms doing the same thing to you? Imagined if you had gotten caught sneaking around?"

"We had to," Mike replied instantly. "You guys weren't looking anymore, and the case has been closed for years. Whoever did this. They think they got away with it." He paused, his hands now shaking. "She could still be wandering around out there, waiting for someone to catch whoever killed her. Or what if she isn't dead, and she's still being held captive somewhere?"

"Look," Cordell snapped, pulling his hands from his desk. "Our officers looked until we exhausted every single resource we had at that time. We had every officer on the force out looking for that girl, myself included. We combed the woods for weeks, covering every square inch of Cedar Mountain. We drove up and down every back road trail. We even had officers from neighboring counties out looking with us. I went back to that bowling alley over a hundred times myself just looking for clues. I walked the road leading away for miles. That girl disappeared." The detective paused, exhaling heavily. "And it wasn't for lack of trying that we didn't find her. She simply vanished..."

Mike felt bad. He hadn't realized that the detective had been so close to the case. But before he could offer an apology the detective continued.

"Just what *is* your fascination with this case?" he asked again. "And don't give me that *it's a school project* BS. Why are you really investigating it? That girl died well before any of you were born."

The group stayed silent, none of them knowing how to answer.

"We just wanna see whoever killed her, get caught," Mike answered after a moment. "It's not fair that they get to keep on living, and she had to die."

Detective Cordell slowly shook his head in silent agreement. "No. It's not." He paused. "But how are you so convinced that she was murdered?"

Mike lowered his gaze to the desk for a moment. Behind him the others glanced nervously at each other, a motion that didn't go unnoticed by the detective. Then he shrugged. "It's just a feeling," he replied. "She disappeared and was never found again. It's not like she ran away."

"No," the detective sighed a moment later. "It's not." He nodded slowly. "You're right. It's a feeling."

The room fell to silence. The group had nothing more they could offer, other than the truth, and exposing that would only serve to make mute the entire conversation. So, everyone simply held their tongue.

Then, after a few moments passed, Detective Cordell reached out and scooped up the plastic bag with necklace inside and used a pen to slide the earring off the desk inside it. Then he looked up at Mike. "I don't suppose you used gloves when you picked this evidence up and removed it did you?"

Mike shook his head.

"Told you!" Jeff said, elbowing Mike in the ribs.

Mike winced, glancing at Jeff.

"I did..." Jeff jabbed.

Then the detective pulled out a note pad and flipped it open. "So let me get this straight. The car you found is a mid-seventies model Ford Mustang, and it matches the description given of the car used to abduct Maggie Lorris back in seventy-five? And you said that you have located this car, albeit the color has now been modified to blue, at the DC Automotive and Salvage Yard, which is currently owned and operated by one Donald Cowles?"

"Yes sir," Mike replied, almost sensing the excitement pulsing off of Jeff.

"That is correct officer," Jeff added, making sure he was part of the conversation.

"It's detective," Cordell corrected. "Haven't been an *officer* for a very long time." He paused. "The Lorris case was one of my first as detective actually." He stopped, taking a split-second to reminisce. Then he shifted in his chair. "All right," he said, pushing his chair out and standing. "I'm gonna go ahead and shoot out to the auto shop and have a word with our old friend, Donald Cowles. But I need *you* to let *us* do our job from now on. If the vehicle you say is in fact on the lot, and we manage to recover it, then I'll look into having the case reopened. But for now, I need you to stay away from the scrapyard, and stop snooping around. That's what we get paid for. We're trained to properly deal with situations like this all right?"

Mike and Jeff nodded.

"And that goes for the rest of you as well," Cordell said, glancing to the three standing behind them. "Do I make myself clear?"

The other nodded, mumbling their agreement.

"All right," he said while starting around the desk. "Then why don't ya'll go ahead and head home, and I'll let you know if we find anything."

"Thank you," Mike said, turning to follow the detective towards the door.

"Mike scratched off some of the paint near the back right taillight," Jeff added, staying a part as long as possible. "You'll be able to see the original color beneath."

"I'm pretty sure I can figure out what the original color of the vehicle was," the detective said, rising from his chair. "Just look under the door panels," he added, humoring the kid. "Nobody ever thinks to paint there..."

"That's genius," Jeff replied, stepping aside as the detective reached out for the doorknob.

Cordell smiled, nodding as he held the door open for the kids to leave. Each of them nodded politely and thanked him, except for John. He walked out, eyes to the floor, only stealing a quick nervous glance as he left.

Cordell closed the door behind them and stood there, staring at the wood grains for a moment. He was baffled by what had just happened. He tried to bring reason to it, or form some explanation of how after all those years, a group of kids could have stumbled across enough evidence to reopen a case that had lurked at the edges of his conscious for the last two decades, a case he still thought about whenever he saw a young girl wearing a pink sundress.

After a moment he exhaled heavily and turned to make his way back to his desk. He didn't sit down, he stayed standing at the edge and reached out to pick up the phone. "Chief, it's Cordell. Look. You're not gonna believe this, but I think something may have just come up regarding the old Lorris case." He paused, listening. "Yeah. From seventy-five. Yep." He paused again. "I may have just gotten a potential lead on the vehicle used in her abduction. Yeah. No, it's pretty solid. No. Apparently it might have been recovered at the old scrapyard just outside of town. I'm gonna shoot out there and do some looking around." He paused again. "Yep. Same one. Oh yeah. He still runs it." He paused again, listening to the voice from the other end. "You got it Chief. Of course."

Cordell hung the phone up and reached into his desk drawer, pulling the small 38 snub-nosed pistol that filled the empty holster slung around his shoulder. Then he pulled his blazer off the back of his chair and slid it on as he made his way towards the door, glancing up to the ceiling as he did. "You're a funny man, you know that…"

Outside Todd pulled his bike from the rack and stepped over it.

"So, what now," John asked, doing the same.

"We should probably do what he says," Mike said. "There's nothing else we can do. It's their investigation now."

"Are you serious?" Jeff barked. "He's about to go bust this asshole and none of you guys wanna be there when he does?"

"He told us to go home," Mike replied, a slightly defeated tone hiding behind his words.

"Of course he did," John puffed. "He's a cop."

John didn't see the police officer walking past him on the way towards the station doors, or the dirty look that he gave.

Jeff lifted his hand and mouthed *sorry*. Then he looked back to Mike. "Come on man. Don't you wanna see the look on that guy's face when he realizes he's finally getting busted after all these years?" He paused, moving to put his hand on Mike's shoulder. "Seriously dude." He squeezed. "We're literally at the finish line. We have to see this through. I mean, come on…"

Mike dropped his gaze to the ground for a moment.

"We found the guy that killed her, dude," Jeff added. "We have to watch him go down…"

Mike lifted his head, locking his gaze to Jeff's as he began to slowly nod. "Yeah. All right."

"YES!" John barked, slapping his hands together loudly. "That, is what I am talking about!" He glanced at the police station one last time. "Now can we get the hell out of here? The smell of bacon's starting to make me sick."

Jeff shook his head, squeezing Mike's shoulder one last time before turning to grab his bike. "We did it," he said as he climbed atop. "Now let's see that bastard go down!"

Chapter 30

Detective Cordell pulled into the parking lot of the auto shop. Cowles' car was parked in the space nearest the gate. Cordell pulled into the space next to the car he knew all too well.

As he sat there his mind drifted back to twenty years prior, and the investigation. They had gathered a list of suspects, people of interest that stuck out amongst the others as ones capable, if not willing, to abduct a small girl. Donald Cowles' name had been on that list. Though he had only been twenty-five at the time, he had already been arrested a handful of times, assault, threatening violence and domestic abuse among the list of other charges that held him as one of the prime suspects. However, he had provided an alibi, one that had been substantiated. So that got his name crossed off the list. Now, as Cordell sat in his car, turning over the events in his mind, he wondered if maybe the kids were right. Maybe he just hadn't looked close enough. Because the car had been listed as inoperable, they had never bothered to inspect it closely. They had gone to the shop and Cowles had shown them the vehicle. The engine had been pulled and some of the parts were rusted out. Now he sat there wondering how hard it would have been to make a car look like it hadn't run in years. Probably not all that difficult with the right parts installed and others removed. He'd always had this lingering feeling that he had something to do with it, but with no evidence they had been forced to eliminate him. He still regretted that to the day. With the technology they had at the time, and no DNA left at the scene, they had nothing to go on. The case had gone cold almost as quickly as it had started.

Cordell tapped his fingers on the steering wheel for a moment, formulating his plan. He knew that Cowles wouldn't be happy to see him walk in, and sure as shit wasn't gonna be cooperative. Cordell had just sent him up to the point of the mountain; the state penitentiary as the locals referred to it, on a two year stint for possession of narcotics a few years back. He didn't exactly think Cowles had gotten over that yet. He already knew how this visit was gonna go...

So, with a heavy sigh, he reached out and pulled the door handle. "Screw it," he whispered. *Let's just do this old school...*

He stepped out of the car, adjusting his shoulder holster beneath his coat as he did. Then he closed the door and started towards the shop's entrance.

Behind him, Mike and the others were rushing down the street. They hadn't been quicker than Cordell's car, but they weren't far behind. They raced to catch up, desperate to see it through to the end, John nearly getting clipped by a car as he rushed through a red light to keep up.

Cordell stepped into the auto shop office, the bell overhead *dinging* as it opened. Don was sitting behind the desk with a magazine spread out on the counter in front of him.

He looked up, pausing as he recognized the cop's face. "Aw shit," he growled, closing the magazine. "What'd I do this time?"

Cordell looked around the shop, surprised at how neat and organized the place was. The last time he'd had to come in to question him the place was a pig sty, with boxes overflowing and piled up, dirt and grease all over the floor.

He glanced towards the lot past the door. "Actually," he said, working his gaze back to Cowles, "You remember about twenty years ago? Little girl went missing. Maggie Lorris?" He paused, waiting for a response. None came. "No? Doesn't ring any bells?" He paused again, watching as the thinnest flicker of a squint flashed past the man's eyes. It would have been all but unnoticeable to most, but Cordell caught it as clear as a flash going off on a camera. "Well. See. I've been thinking a lot about if recently. There're just some things that I can't quite work out. If I remember right, you had an alibi for that night."

No response. The man eyed him in the manner a dog would taking a treat from an abusive owner.

"Something about it's never really sat right with me," Cordell continued. "So, I figured I'd recheck with some of the people we interviewed back then. See if maybe anybody might have remembered anything they might have forgotten to mention."

Cowles' demeanor changed, a nervous flicker washing through him. Cordell watched him pull his hands back from the desk and shift uncomfortably in his seat. "Nah," Cowles continued. "I remember anything about that. Sad really, young girl like that up and run off." He paused, shaking his head. "Don't know anything now I didn't then, *officer*." He cleared his throat, shifting nervously again.

"Huh," Cordell replied, his gaze locked unflinching to Cowles'. "Well as it turns out, we got a report that came through, saying there might just be a car matching the description of the one used to abduct that young girl, parked right here in this very scrapyard. It says it might even be under a big blue tarp near the back there."

Don shifted again, stretching his neck with a small *pop*. Then he smirked, big and accented. "Nah," he grunted. "Ain't nothin' back there over ten years old. I'm sure of it. Cleared out the old inventory myself when the old man passed on and I took over."

Cordell nodded, glancing around the shop one more time. Then he locked his gaze back to Cowles. "So, I guess that means that old mustang you had parked back there when we first interviewed you is gone now?"

Cowles stared at him, the animosity flaring brightly behind his eyes. "Ain't no mustang back there."

"Well, I suppose you wouldn't mind me going ahead and having a look around then? I mean, seeing as there isn't anything back there that would be of interest."

Cowles eyed him carefully. Cordell could see the gears turning as he thought of what to say next.

"Yeah," Cowles replied smartly. "I'm afraid I'm gonna have to see a warrant for that officer. See, some of the vehicles back there are here on consignment. I don't rightly know how the owners would feel about me letting the law back there to illegally search their property. Could be bad for business for me if they found out you know. Confidentiality and all that."

Cordell nodded, deciding it was time to cut the bullshit, and tired of beating around the bush. "Yeah. The whole thing's got me thinking as well. If we'd of had the technology we do now, being able to pull hair and fiber samples and what not. We probably would have taken a closer look at that vehicle of yours." He paused. "Yeah. It's amazing what they can do now with DNA, and electron microscopes and what not."

"Yeah, I think it's time for you to leave now," Cowles growled.

"Ok, ok," Cordell said, raising his hands in the air. Then he turned, stopping two steps away before turning back. "Just one last question."

Cowles continued to stare through hate-filled eyes.

"Say I've already got that warrant in the works, and that it's being delivered as we speak. You're sure I'm not gonna find an old coat of red beneath that blue, like maybe if I scratched some of the paint off near the back bumper...?"

Cowles stared at him for a moment. He could see his mind racing. Then he did the last thing Cordell was prepared for. "Oh hell."

Cowles pushed off the desk, spinning out of his chair and charging out the back door. In a flash he was in the yard and blasting down the main aisle.

Cordell flinched, and then darted after the man.

In seconds they were racing after each other, rusted metal and faded paint blurring past.

Cowles hit the end of the aisle and bolted to the right, taking the next turn at full speed and rushing back towards the office.

Cordell struggled to keep up. The perp had home field advantage as he referred to it. He knew the lay of the land, where the obstacles were, and could run full speed without thinking about it. Cordell had to be conscientious of everything in his path. One slipped foot, one trip, could be the difference between bringing in the suspect and someone potentially making it to their car and it turning into a pursuit, which put many more lives in jeopardy. So, he picked up the speed, leaping over a crate of engine parts and a small stack of mufflers.

Ahead of him Cowles made a dash for the office door. He just needed to get through and he could slam the door and lock it from the inside. That would give him plenty of time to get in his car and get far enough that they'd have a hard time catching up. It would take the detective a good amount of time to get up and over the razor wire. Then it was into the mountains and gone. That's when he looked up and saw the kid he'd fired a few days prior standing in the doorway. "MOVE!" he shouted not slowing down.

Inside Mike saw Don rushing towards him, Detective Cordell thirty feet behind. "Jeff, bike!" he shouted, stepping aside so that the guy would rush full speed past.

Behind him Jeff moved in quickly with his bike.

Mike grabbed it, putting one hand on the handlebars and one hand on the seat. Then he waited, listening. It was about five seconds later when he inched the bike backwards and then shoved it full force towards the door.

Don was feet away, the door just three more bounds. *Screw locking it*, he thought. *Just make a break for it. Push the kid down to slow the cop.* Three seconds later he hit the doorway and ran full speed into the aluminum frame of a BMX bicycle.

Mike watched as Cowles came blasting into the office and hit the bike full force, flipping into the air, his legs wrapped around the metal frame. Both man and machine flew across the office, slamming heavily into the wall. A stack of boxes fell over, scattering old invoices and receipts across the floor in a splashed display of faded white and yellow.

Then Detective Cordell came rushing through the door, skidding to a stop and almost slipping himself. Without thinking he rushed forward, and grabbed one of Cowles' arms, twisting it and slapping a handcuff around it. Cowles bellowed, which made Cordell push down even harder on him, crushing his weight against the bike that in turn was crushing Cowles' legs. "You have the right to remain silent!" he shouted, shoving his weight down even harder. "Anything you say, can and will be used against you in the court of law." He wrenched the man's other arm out and rolled him over, twisting his legs even further. Cowles yelped again. "You have the right to an attorney, if you can't afford one, the court will." Then he locked the other cuff around his wrist.

Cordell stood up, pulling Cowles with him, and using his foot to push the bike away. He shot an angry glance to Mike. "I thought I told you kids to go home." Then he turned his attention back to Cowles. "Donald Cowles, you're under arrest for the kidnapping and murder of Maggie Lorris."

"I don't know what you're talking about!" Cowles yelled, slightly struggling against Cordell's grasp. "I didn't kill no one!"

"Save it for the judge," Cordell said, leading him through the shop and out to the parking lot while he shouted a steady stream of expletives back at Mike and the others.

Jeff walked up to Mike who stood watching the entire scene. He moved next to him and stopped, gently nudging his elbow with his own. "We did it," he said, a smile wanting to appear but staying hidden just behind his lips. "We got him."

They watched as Cordell opened the back seat of his cruiser and shoved Cowles inside, shutting the door behind him. Then he went to the front and got on the radio.

Mike stood there, contained by an unnerving still. He should have felt excitement, a surge of energy for succeeding, but he didn't. Only a dissident calm enveloped him.

"Dude," John smiled, watching as the cop finished his radio call and stepped back out of the car. "The bike man. Fucking epic..."

Detective Cordell started around the back of the car and back towards the kids. They could already hear the approaching sirens in the distance.

"What in the hell were you thinking in there?" he said, stopping just in front of them. "I told you to go home."

"Sorry," Jeff said, glancing at the man in the back of the unmarked police car. "We just wanted to see it the whole way through."

Cordell sighed. "Yeah. I guess I can understand that." He paused. "But still. One of you could have gotten hurt. What if he had a gun? Huh? Did you think about that? What went smoothly could have become a hostage situation in a second. You put yourselves in a lot of risk coming here." Then he paused, looking between them. "But thank you. I probably would have done the same thing if I was you, so..." He glanced back to the car and then back to them. "There is one thing I just can't get past, so I'm gonna ask you one more time before the other units arrive. How exactly did you come across that necklace?"

Jeff glanced at Mike, who looked at Cowles for a moment. Then he looked back to Cordell and shrugged. "Luck I guess."

Cordell scoffed, a grin growing on his face. "Well, I wish that luck had been there twenty years ago..."

Behind the detective the first of the squad cars came pulling into the lot. It was quickly followed by three more.

The group watched as Detective Cordell began instructing the responding officers on what to do.

One officer pulled a roll of yellow police tape from the trunk of his vehicle and ran it across the entrance to the parking lot. Another pulled a small briefcase from his trunk and started towards the auto shop office.

Cordell started back towards the building, pausing for a moment. "Look," he said. "You all can go ahead and take off if you want. Not much more to see, just a lot of standing around. The examiner will go over the car with a fine-toothed comb, and none of us are allowed back there while they're doing it." He paused, glancing around for a second. "If you want, go ahead and stop by the station tomorrow and I'll fill you in as to what we find." He leaned closer to Mike. "It's kind of against protocol, so if you do, try and keep it between us yeah?" He reached out, putting a hand on his shoulder.

"Detective," an officer said, sticking his head out from the shop door. "You're gonna wanna see this. I think we have a match on that vehicle."

"OK," Cordell called out, stepping back. "Have forensics comb it. I want every inch of that vehicle swabbed." He paused, glancing at Mike and then back. "Tell em to start with the trunk yeah?"

"You got it," the cop said, turning and disappearing back into the building.

Jeff, Denise and Todd glanced at each other and smiled. John watched in mild fascination as the other officers shuffled past.

Cordell turned back to the group. "You kids should be pretty darn proud of yourselves." He chuckled. "Somehow you managed to do what we couldn't ourselves in twenty years. You caught that girl's killer." He paused again, nodding as his eyes moved to the street past them. "Now go on before I take you in for interfering with an investigation." He smiled, turning back towards the shop.

"Damn," Jeff said, watching Cordell walk away. "Now what?"

Mike looked around the filling lot. "We should go tell Maggie."

The group watched as Cordell disappeared back into the shop.

Chapter 31

"Oh my God!" John yelled as the summer breeze wrapped past him. "Did you see that shit!? It was like a fuckin' movie!"

The others rode next to him, each now fully enveloped in a shared excitement.

"Mike was all, *bike*! And then Jeff was like, *yo*! And then, *BAM*! Dude hit that thing full speed. He ate shit so hard!"

"I thought he broke his legs," Todd said from just behind. "The way he was twisted up in the bike frame when he landed. I'm surprised he could walk."

"How the hell did you think to use the bike?" Jeff asked from beside him.

"I don't know," Mike replied. "I just saw him running and didn't want him to escape. I just kind of reacted."

"That was one hell of a reaction!" John burst again, a loud guffaw punctuating his words.

"I loved the look in the detective's face when he saw us standing there and realized that we had stopped the guy from getting away," Denise said with a grin. "That was priceless."

"Yeah," John laughed. "Like not only did we find the guy for you, but we helped catch him as well." He laughed again. "Just let *us* do our job he says. Ha!"

"I wonder what else they're gonna find in the car," Jeff said, watching as two more police cars passed them in the opposite direction. "Cause you know they're gonna go over every *inch* of that car with a microscope." He paused. "I wonder if they'll find evidence that he's done this before. Like what if we just caught a serial killer?"

"That dude isn't smart enough to be a serial killer," John replied. "He's just some pervy fuck who gets off on kidnapping little girls."

"What if she wasn't the first?" Denise added, turning the tone of the conversation for the briefest of moments, leaving them all to ride in silence while they each contemplated the horrific possibilities in their own thoughts.

"Well," John said after a moment. "At least we can finally get back to some kind of normal summer..." He paused. "I mean, I love you guys, but I was really starting to get tired of this whole, *Unsolved Mysteries* shit... I just wanna be hanging out around the pit, drinking Aftershock and Zima, and pretending like none of this shit ever happened."

"Seriously dude?" Jeff asked, shooting him a confused look. "We all just had an experience that people read about in books, or watch on TV, and all you wanna do is go drink *shitty* alcohol and wine coolers...? What the *hell* is wrong with you dude?"

"Yeah, are you serious?" Denise asked, jumping in quickly. "We're like, the only people in the entire world that know that ghosts are real. And you'd rather be out at the pit getting drunk?"

"Yeah," Todd added. "That's pretty lame dude."

"Jesus," John said, regret starting to seep in. "I get it. Call off the dogs all right." He paused. They were right. He had just been a part of an experience he would undoubtedly carry with him for the rest of his life. He *had* enjoyed it, loved it, every single moment of it. Well, except for the police station parts. The rest was fucking awesome! The excitement, the espionage. It was just his job to be cynical and make jokes. That's just what he did. But now he actually felt like a dick. "It was pretty rad all right," he said, carefully attempting to back-pedal out of the attack. "We spent part of our summer with a freaking ghost." He paused, coasting a few more feet. "All right. It was fuckin awesome, OK?"

"Thank you," Denise said. "God. Would it kill you to not be such a fucking buzzkill every now and then?'

"I think it would," Todd said, shaking his head.

"Whatever," John said, turning his attention back to the road. "I said it was cool all right?"

"So, what's gonna happen to Maggie now?" Jeff asked, his question aimed at Mike without looking.

"I don't know," Mike replied. "I guess she'll go to wherever it is we go when we die?"

John opened his mouth to remark and then stopped, putting his focus back to pedaling. He had just climbed out of the fire and had no desire to land back in the skillet.

"Well, wherever she goes," Denise said smiling. "I'm just glad we were able to help her." She paused. "I felt so sorry for her. Just, unbelievable that something like that could happen. Poor girl."

"Yeah," Jeff said. "People are messed up."

And with that, he put a period on the entire conversation.

The group rode in silence the rest of the way to the spot. They all looked around with a new appreciation as they rode through the cemetery that stood next to the field they hung out in. So many gravestones, so many people dead. How many of them had died like Maggie, scared and alone, murdered and forgotten? Each of them held their thoughts contained, subconsciously picking up the speed as they rode through, the stone sentries watching them pass.

A few minutes later their tires touched dirt, and they followed the path to the one place where they all felt safe.

Mike pulled up first, dropping his bike into the tall weeds, Jeff just behind him and Todd, John and Denise after.

As he walked up to the large clearing, he felt a calm sadness beginning to rise. The spot was empty. Where Maggie would have normally been standing, there was nothing. She wasn't there.

"Dude," John said softly. "Where is she?"

Denise walked up, reading the look on his face. Slowly she reached out, putting her hand on Mike's shoulder. "I'm sorry Mike."

Jeff walked up, not seeing the look that had crept onto his friend's face. "Well, I guess that's it," he shrugged. "We solved her murder. I guess she doesn't need us anymore."

"Maggie?" Mike called out.

Denise left her hand on his shoulder. "Mike, it's OK. She's in a better place now. We helped her."

"Maggie?" he repeated, this time slightly softer.

Todd stepped next to him, his gaze wandering past the spot to the rest of the empty field. "I think she's gone."

John looked at Mike who stood silent, sadness on his face. "Dude," he said, leaning his face closer. "You should be stoked. We found the guy that killed her. Be happy dude."

"I am happy," Mike replied, his tone not matching his words. "I just... I'm just a little tired from everything." He glanced around the field. "I think I'm gonna head home. I don't feel very good. I'll catch you guys later."

Mike turned and walked back to his bike, the others all silently watching him leave.

"Hey man," Jeff said, trying one last time to cheer him up. "Let's meet here tomorrow at the usual time. We should go check with Detective Cordell. Let's see what else they found, and what's gonna happen to that Cowles guy."

Mike nodded, not looking back. Then he stuck his hand in the air in a single wave before picking his bike up and turning it around. "Yeah," he said, climbing on. "I'll see you then."

Then he put his foot down and pedaled off.

The others watched him ride away.

"What's his problem?" John asked when he was out of earshot. "He should be fuckin stoked right now. I mean, wasn't the entire point of this to track down her killer and bring him to justice? Did we not just do that? What the hell?"

Denise sighed heavily. "He's upset because for just a moment, we were different. We were special." She paused, not feeling all too different. "Now we're just back to being normal, regular kids on summer vacation..."

The others watched him pull onto the road leading away, and stood quietly, all feeling the same thing as he disappeared. For the briefest moment in their lives, they could all say that no one else was having an adventure like theirs. It was an experience unique to them. And now they were back to just being a group of friends, hanging out on summer break, the next semester looming just around the bend. It wasn't just Mike that felt the loss. The rest of them, each in their own way, didn't want things to go back to normal. Because as much as they each hated to admit it, that's exactly what they were. Normal...

Overhead clouds drifted by, unaware and uncaring of the four friends standing quietly below. The summer air drifted on the wind, a warm breeze caressing the tall grass that danced around them.

Chapter 32

It was late afternoon by the time Mike pulled onto Highway Fifty-Six. There was a sour sense of regret hollowed in his stomach, residual from the manner in which he had parted from the others. After all, when all was said and done, it *was* him that had gotten his friends into everything. But he couldn't just stand there and pretend that everything was OK. Yeah, they'd had their adventure, they'd found Maggie's killer and brought him to justice. They'd finished what they had started out to do. But there was this lingering thought, a frayed strand that flickered at the edge of his thoughts, a solitary whisper that something wasn't right. So as his friends had shared congratulations and rallied in celebration, he had been left standing alone, a single splinter inside him that softly tingled, telling him that he had not yet succeeded. Something was... incomplete. So when they asked him what was wrong, as deep as he dug, as badly as he had wished to have an answer, he had only been left wondering himself. He didn't have an answer and that bothered him even more. So that was why he had left, why he had ridden away and left the others to clap each other on their backs and begin plotting out the remaining days of vacation. For him, however, there was something vacant in it all, and it dug into him like a splinter under the nail. *Maggie should have been there*, he thought as he continued on, pedaling down the blacktop in a daze. *Why wasn't she there? How could she have not wanted to be there when her killer was handcuffed and taken away?* Somehow, he knew she couldn't have moved on. The entire time he rode there was a hollow weight inside him that weighed heavily. And as he followed the white line at the edge of the road, he realized that he hadn't been riding home, he'd been riding back to where Maggie had found him. Because she had. Not the other way around. He hadn't found her; she had appeared to him. She wanted to be found, and for whatever reason he would likely never know, had chosen him. Then he lifted his eyes and the hollow void inside him dissipated on the breeze, a deep, tingling trepidation scraping across his skin as he realized that standing thirty feet ahead, somber gaze locked to him in unrelenting sadness, hands folded together in front of her slouched shoulders, was Maggie.

Mike slowed, his bike coasting forward as a heavy relief worked through him.

Then he came to a stop.

He stood there, staring deeply into her gaze, searching for the right words to say, the right question. But the longer he looked, the more he realized that the feeling enveloping him wasn't of celebration or success. It was similar to throwing a bowling ball down the freshly oiled lane and watching as it slowly curved towards the gutter, but still holding out hope that it would at least take a few pins with it... "We found him," Mike said, watching her unchanged expression. "We found the guy that kidnapped you. The police arrested him. He's gonna go to jail for a long time." He paused, searching her face for any expression at all. But only an empty sorrow returned his gaze. "What's wrong? Isn't that what you wanted? For us to find the person that did this to you? That's why you're still here right, why you can't move on?" He continued to watch as she stood there, her eyes unblinking.

Slowly he set his bike down and approached her.

"We got him. You can go now. You can go to wherever it is you're supposed to. You don't have to be here anymore."

Her eyes peered deeply into his, piercing through.

Coldness wrapped its fingers around him, squeezing tighter and tighter. He began to shiver.

"I don't understand," he whispered, the cold bringing a distant fear within tow. "I thought this is what you wanted."

It may have been the sadness in his face, or the defeat in his tone, but something pierced through the veil of separation that kept them from communicating, and with a delicate slowness, Maggie stepped towards him, reaching out with both arms and placing her hands on each side of his head.

"Wha—" he started to whisper.

A deep cold grasped ahold of Mike, the empty chill stabbing into him like a thousand frozen needles. He was blasted with visions, images racing past in explosions of light and sound, pictures fed by emotion and delivered in series of rapid glimpses. From the depths a low hum slowly grew, a high-pitched ringing hiding just behind it as it crept up, filling his hears and blocking out all other sounds. Then as quick as it began, everything went black, and a different scene blurred into focus.

Mike watched helpless, formless behind an invisible curtain as everything played out before him through a thin, translucent haze. A man sitting at a bar, a bowling alley. A little girl. *Maggie*. Then the ringing in his ears slowly faded and the blurry sight he was watching became crystal clear. Then a feeling of warmth and celebration flooded in, all the emotions and joy of a young girl celebrating an early birthday brought with it.

"Hurry up! A voice shouted from behind as the girl made her way towards the bar. She was only grabbing a soda, but she knew her friend's impatience. Her turn was coming up, so she put a little more speed behind her steps.

As she approached the bar a man in his early twenties turned his face to her, a smile growing across his lips. He picked up the beer in front of him and took another sip. "Hi there," he said in a friendly tone. Well, aren't you a pretty little thing?"

Maggie looked up at the man on the stool, smiling. "Thank you." She had never been called pretty before. Yeah, her mom and dad said it all the time, but this was the first time someone else had said it, someone she didn't know. A strange flutter moved through her.

Mike hovered just behind, watching helpless as the man continued to eye her after she had turned her attention to the man approaching behind the counter.

"What can I get for you darlin'," the man behind the counter asked, smiling as he set down the bar towel he had been drying his hands with.

"Oh," she said, still smiling. "Can I have a coke please?"

"Is Pepsi okay?" the man replied.

"That's fine, thank you."

The man turned and made his way over to the soda fountain. Maggie took that moment to look back at the younger man next to her with a smile.

"What's your name?" he asked.

"Maggie," she replied with a grin.

"Maggie huh," the man said, taking another sip from his can. "How old are you, Maggie?"

"I'll be thirteen next week," she replied proudly.

"Thirteen?" the man said, feigning surprise. "You look way older than that."

Maggie smiled, a warm blush moving to her cheeks.

The man's gaze lowered a bit.

"That sure is a pretty necklace," he said, eying the pendant on her chest. "What's a pretty little thing like you doing with something that nice?"

Again, she felt the soft tingle of blush growing. "My mom gave it to me," she replied. "It's an early birthday present." She lifted the pendant up, gazing at it herself in admiration.

"Here you go young lady," the man behind the counter said, setting the soft drink down in front of her. "I'll go ahead and put that on your friend's tab," he said, turning around to make his way back to the register.

"Well," Maggie said, turning back to the man. "It was nice meeting you."

"You too little lady," he said, watching as she turned and made her way back to her friends.

Mike felt the emptiness around him shift, a blur of movement in the void. Then as he struggled to recover, he realized that he was in the parking lot of the bowling alley, and that he was in the backseat of a parked car, watching the events continue to unfold. He watched as Maggie slowly approached, the single overhead light casting a shadow just behind her. He could feel the slight tingle of hesitation she carried with her, the faint hint of fear whispering from the shadows.

The man in the front seat leaned over, pulling the handle on the passenger door and pushing it open.

Mike watched, helpless as Maggie approached. He wanted to yell, wanted to scream at her to go back, to run, but there was no voice, no lips to form words, no throat to yell from.

"I didn't think you were gonna come," he said, smiling as she stepped closer. "I thought I was gonna sit out here all night alone."

Fear made way for curiosity.

"Do you really have a present for me?" Maggie asked, stepping closer.

The man reached over to the glove box and opened it. He stuck his hand inside, and when he pulled it back, a small, sparkling object dangled from his fingers. "Now would I lie to a pretty girl like you?" he said, shifting back to his side.

"What is it?" Maggie asked, the intrigue continuing to build.

"Well," the man replied, holding it out just in front of him. "You see. You already have one very nice necklace. But what happens when you get bored of that one? Or you lose it?" He turned his face to her, a flicker moving past his eyes. "It'd probably be best if you had another don't you think?"

Maggie looked into the car. Something deep within whispered for her to turn and leave, to run.

The man held out his hand so she could see the small flower pendant hanging on a thin silver chain.

"Wow," she said, leaning closer. "It's so pretty."

As her gaze held to the floral necklace the whisper slowly faded to silence.

"A pretty necklace for a pretty girl," he said. "Why don't you hop on in and give it a try? Let's see how it looks on you."

Maggie shifted nervously, glancing up at the bowling alley doors. "I—"

"Come on now," the man said. "Ole Don ain't gonna let nothing happen to a pretty young thing like you."

He held the necklace out just the slightest bit more, cocking one eyebrow as he did.

Maggie glanced at the bowling alley once more before smiling slightly. "OK," she said, slipping into the passenger seat.

Mike was now outside of the car, observing from above. He watched helplessly as the car rocked back and forth for a moment, the sounds of a muffled scream escaping the open passenger door. Then the car went still, the silence darting in, and a single, oil-stained hand reached out to pull the door closed.

Darkness, cold, silent, everywhere.

The moon overhead slowly filtered in, thin strands of light piercing through the canopy of trees. Mike struggled to bring everything to focus, a welling of emotion flooding all around him. Sorrow, sadness, pain. Regret. He felt an invisible shudder racking his formless body, a hollow nightmare holding him captive. He could hear the road rumbling beneath, the sound of metal creaking as the tiny confines of the trunk echoed loudly. It was dark and suffocating.

In a flash Mike was back outside, watching as blaring headlights shifted away to reveal the red mustang pulling up. He stared; his formless gaze unblinking as it came to a stop just outside of a run-down cabin. Then the engine went silent, and the lights went dark. He shifted his gaze. A cabin, dark and empty, surrounded by towering pines and a void of black beyond.

The man from the bar stepped out of the vehicle, making his way to the trunk. Mike could hear the trapped screams coming from within and the muffled sound of tiny fists pounding against metal. He watched as the man took a deep breath and readied himself as he unlatched the trunk and lifted it.

The man reached inside, avoiding a flurry of swings that flung outwards as the captive girl struggled to escape. Then he picked Maggie up and hoisted her out, slinging her over his shoulder. With one hand he closed the trunk and started inside the derelict cabin.

Somewhere between the bowling alley and the abandoned cabin in the woods, the man had stopped. He had bound her wrists behind her back and tied a canvas bag over her head. As he carried her towards the house Mike could hear her muffled screams and felt the searing burn as the thin rope cut into the flesh of her wrist. It was hard to breathe, the man's shoulder pressing into her sternum and her bound arms making it difficult to catch a breath. The cloth around her face was smothering her and as the man walked, he held her chin tucked tightly against his chest.

Mike could feel the blinding fear that gripped her and the bitter helplessness that grasped her tightly. The man carrying her exuded a vile, bitter lustfulness and as he opened the door, Mike screamed soundlessly. Then the door closed, and the cabin faded to darkness.

Seconds could have passed, or years before a small room faded in around him. Mike stood — no, floated, in the empty space. The room was no bigger than his own, but with wooden floors and walls, and was barren, save for a single dirty mattress in one corner. As everything continued to filter into focus, he saw that Maggie was there, sitting atop it, her neatly pressed dress now torn, pink skin exposed beneath, a layer of dirt and grime splotching it. Tears streaked down her face through the built-up grime, and he instantly knew that she had been there for some time. Days.

Movement pulled his gaze to the other end of the room.

Standing just inside the doorway was the man. There was no smile, no friendliness about him. All the charm and flashing charisma was gone. What stood there now was a dark, malice-filled monster full of lustful desire and contempt. Mike watched as the man tucked his shirt back into his pants, his serpentine gaze not once retreating from the small girl slouched in the corner. Then he finished tucking in his shirt, he zipped his pants up and with a sickly malevolence grinned, "Don't you go anywhere. I'll be back. I still got a lot to teach you little girl. And we gots nothin' but time..." Then he turned, stepping out of the room to close the door behind him.

Mike heard the sound of a latch being closed and the sound of a padlock being clicked into place and thumping against the door. The fear and anguish he had felt moments prior was now replaced with pain and discomfort, disgust and shame. Then he turned his gaze back to Maggie who sat curled up in the corner, her legs tucked as tightly to her chest as they could be pulled. He could see her tiny body shaking, her eyes wide and panicked, deer-like and locked to the floor in front of her. "Please," she whimpered. "Somebody help me..."

Then the car engine roared to life outside and Mike turned his empty gaze to the wall as he listened. He heard the sound of tires crunching against the dirt as it backed up, and listened as it turned around and drove off, the night air once again becoming still.

Mike looked to the door, and when his gaze returned to the corner, Maggie was fighting against her bonds. He watched as she leaned back and forth, rocking against the ropes that held her wrists behind her back. Then one hand broke free, and in a series of frantic, thoughtless movements, the other came loose and she quickly unbound her feet and rushed to the door. He felt a panicked hope rise in her, feverish and confused.

Maggie struggled against the knob, desperately trying to force it open. But it wouldn't budge. It was sealed, and nothing short of a key on the other side would change that, and as she banged against it, he could hear the sound of a lock tapping back. Then she turned and moved to the back wall, kicking at the boards. Again and again, she struck them with her bare feet.

Mike watched her struggling to escape, panic and desperation pushing her even more. Then her foot landed heavy against one of the boards near the mattress and it cracked outwards.

Maggie stopped, her gaze locking to the board. She paused, only for a breath, and then knelt down, grasping the board at the bottom and began to jerk it forward and back, the wood creaking against the nails that bound it over and over. Then with one final yank, she pulled the board free and fell back onto her haunches, the sliver of wall in her hands. Her dress fell around her shoulders, and she fumbled to work it back into place. The next instant she was yanking at the board next to it. Then she was crawling through, and a moment later, she was running headlong into the woods.

Mike tethered behind, watching as she crashed through the trees, branches reaching out and drawing thin lines of blood through the dirt as they scratched past to her skin. The forest floor beneath cut into her feet, and she had no idea of the direction she was escaping, but she didn't stop, she didn't slow, she just kept running.

Mike followed her like this, moving without steps, running without breath, just behind her for what felt like days, until the trees peeled back, and she burst out onto the shoulder of a highway.

Instantly Mike recognized the place, the dirt-lined trees, the moonlight across the pavement. It could have been anywhere in the world, but he knew instantly exactly where they were. Twenty years in the future, he stood in that exact spot, Maggie's hands on his head, helpless to move. He wondered if cars had driven past, or if he had passed out, or disappeared completely. He wondered how much time had gone by. Had thought about his friends and his family. For that brief moment his mind raced as he watched Maggie collapse to the ground. Then a distant light pulled his mind back.

Down the highway a vehicle was approaching.

Maggie turned her head, sobs beginning to creep out as she fought to stay standing. Exhaustion pounded through her and when she turned to move, the steps that followed were light and staggered.

The vehicle in the distance grew closer, its lights illuminating her small, battered frame.

Mike watched as she edged closer, her feet touching the blacktop, thin wet footprints trailing behind where the moonlight flickered crimson atop. Slowly she struggled to lift her hand in a weak attempt to flag down the oncoming vehicle.

Then Mike realized that the approaching car wasn't slowing. It was bearing down on her, and it was coming fast.

Mike tried to rush forward, his empty body not moving. He tried to scream, but only hollow silence filled the air around him. His shapeless eyes were locked to Maggie as she watched the car draw closer. Then he saw it begin to veer, edging closer to the shoulder, bearing down directly on her.

Then the sound of screeching tires filled the night, followed by the sound of crunching metal and bone, squelching flesh and a staccato scream.

Mike screamed in agonizing silence as the truck screeched to a stop, smoke from the tires mixed with dirt as it rose up and drifted over the vehicle like a low rolling cloud. Headlights illuminated the scene before, Maggie's broken body lying thirty feet away, twisted and bent, the crimson trail growing wider as it reached out to touch. He heard the sound of a door opening and the whimpered words of a man who kept repeating *no* over and over again. He watched as they moved towards Maggie, her twisted body lying on the ground, thin breaths trying to hitch under shattered ribs. He watched as the faceless man stood over her, his features hidden behind a blurry shroud. The man stood there, sobs beginning to fall forth. Then the man turned and made his way quickly back to the truck, returning moments later with a shovel in hand.

Slowly the nighttime around Mike slipped away, a darkness fading in that pushed the world below further away. Maggie lying dead in the road, the truck beneath, all faded farther and farther until nothing was left but a suffocating blackness that enveloped him.

Then, in a flash, like awakening to a freezing bucket of ice water, the world warped back around him and he was standing on the side of the road, his cheeks and neck drenched in a river of warm tears.

Maggie slowly pulled her hands away and stepped back, her gaze still locked to his.

Mike stood frozen, his entire body moving involuntarily with tiny spasms. He struggled to breathe, his breaths coming in thin, rapid hitches. His hands were still splayed outwards at his side, muscles tight and tense. Then he knew. In that instant, he *knew*. "I'm sorry," Mike whispered, his words barely audible. "I'm so sorry."

And with that he collapsed, the last of his strength falling away as gravity pulled him to the ground.

For the next few minutes he sat there, his eyes locked to the dirt in front of him, the world again distant and quiet. That was why she was still there. They had captured the person who had originally kidnapped her, the person who had held her captive and done unspeakable things to her for days. But the person who had taken her life, who had struck and killed her with their car and then carried her into the woods and buried her body like a stray animal. They were still out there. They had never been caught, never brought to justice. Maggie's murder had still yet to be given closure. Then slowly he lifted his face, moving his gaze to Maggie. "It wasn't him..." he said softly. "It wasn't him..."

Chapter 33

Jeff was in his room when the pounding began. He jumped slightly, pulling his gaze away from his computer screen, only getting up to move when his mom shouted down to him.

"I got it Mom!" he yelled back, scooting his chair out and making his way up the stairs. "This better be a freaking emergency," he mumbled under his breath as he started towards the front door, another bout of pounding beginning. "I'm freaking coming!" he shouted.

"Language!" his mom yelled from the other room.

Jeff rolled his eyes and paused for a single moment before twisting the knob and yanking the door open.

Mike stood on his doorstep, his gaze locking to Jeff's, and all the anger that had built up on his trek from the basement dissipated the moment he saw the look on his friend's face.

"What happened?" Jeff asked, slinking outside and closing the door softly behind him as he did. Though it was barely dawn, the air breathed with summer's heat.

"Donald Cowles didn't kill her," Mike said, still not blinking.

Jeff stared at him like he was crazy. "What?" he asked, stunned by his friend's remark.

"He abducted her," Mike replied. "He drove her to this... cabin, out in the woods." Mike paused, a faint moistness moving in his eyes. "He abused her, for days... But he didn't kill her."

"Dude, Mike. What are you talking about?" Jeff was now beginning to feel slightly concerned.

"She escaped. She escaped." Mike paused, the images battering silently against the back of his eyes. "She was there for days. But he left and she got loose. He didn't kill her. We got the wrong guy."

Jeff glanced back at his front door and then turned his face back to Mike. "Dude, you gotta start making a little more sense man. You're really starting to freak me out... What do you mean she escaped? What cabin? What woods?" He paused for the briefest of moments, still confused. "Mike, I need you to be a little clearer man. What do you mean we got the wrong guy? How do you know this?"

Mike glanced at the ground. He took two deep breaths, exhaling slowly, and the lifted his gaze as he began to explain. "Maggie wasn't killed by Cowles. He abducted her from the bowling alley and drove her to some abandoned cabin in the woods. He did some... *fucked up* things to her. But he didn't kill her. He left her alone one night and she managed to escape. She, tore one of the boards on the wall loose and escaped into the woods." He paused again, trying to articulate the visions. "Dude. Maggie was hit by a car," he continued. "Right there on the highway, where I found her." He drifted away for a moment, quickly catching it and pulling himself back. "Somebody hit her. And whoever it was, I think they just buried her somewhere near there." He paused again, still trying to make sense of it. He had been the entire bike ride there, but it was still a frayed mess of thought. "They had a shovel..." Tears began to fall as the flashes battered him once again. "She suffered so bad..."

Jeff reached out, gently taking him by the arm and leading him away from his front door. This definitely wasn't the type of conversation he wanted his mom *accidentally* overhearing.

When he was around the corner of his house he stopped and turned to Mike. "Dude. How can you know this?"

Mike looked at him, his brow wrinkling together as he searched for a way to explain it. "She showed me," he replied, looking back up to his friend. A tear worked its way down his cheek.

"What?" Jeff said, trying desperately to retain his patience. "What do you mean she showed you? Who? Maggie?"

Mike started nodding before he even spoke, the motion continuing as the words crossed his lips. "I was riding home. When she wasn't at the spot I wanted to see if maybe she was back where I found her. She was. I stopped and told her that we found the guy that killed her, that he was going to jail for her murder. I just wanted her to be able to, I don't know, pass on...? But... It's hard to explain. She, she touched my head and... I saw everything. The bowling alley, the car, her getting into it, the shack, the room she was being kept in, her escaping, the road. I saw, and *felt*, everything..."

Jeff stood there, stunned. The past two weeks of his life had stretched the limits of what he thought possible, but this...

"We need to tell the others," Mike said, reaching out to grasp Jeff firmly by the shoulders. "We have to go back. There's gotta be something we missed, another clue. Something."

Jeff nodded. He couldn't believe he was agreeing to it, but to be honest, he didn't know what to believe anymore. "Let me tell my mom I'm going out. Just stay here. I'll be back in five. I'm gonna call the others."

Mike nodded, his gaze moving to the grass at his feet as Jeff turned and darted as quickly as he could without being obvious something was wrong.

Mike stood there, his thoughts working back over the images he had seen, the cabin, the woods, the road. The truck. If the man had buried her then there would have to be something, some marking or indication. He had only looked on the side of the road. He hadn't gone back into the trees. There had to be something there? Why else would she have gone back there? Why else would she have shown him that? She wanted them to find *her*. That's what they were missing, it was *her*.

For the next few minutes he stood at the side of Jeff's house, working and reworking over the vivid memories. Then he heard the front door to the house close and Jeff's footsteps getting closer.

"All right," Jeff said, walking up with his bike. "I got ahold of Denise and John. She's pretty sure Todd's just not answering. She's gonna stop at his place on the way to the spot. Everybody's meeting us there in thirty." He paused. "I hope you can explain this a little better when everyone else gets there, cause right now, you sound—" He didn't want to sound mean. "It's just hard to believe."

Mike nodded, his hand coming up to wipe his nose as he sniffled. "I know. And I know I sound crazy. Imagine how I feel. I just stood there watching as she died..."

The pair stood there silently for the next moment, their eyes conveying everything they couldn't voice. Then Jeff cut the conversation short. "All right. I guess we should go tell em that this isn't over yet..."

Chapter 34

The others were already at the spot when Jeff and Mike rode up. Mike could see the look of worry on Denise's face and the irritation pouring out of John's eyes. For a single fleeting moment, he felt bad for having to tell them that they were wrong. No! They weren't wrong, they just weren't finished yet.

"This better be good," John said as they rolled to a stop. "I got invited to a college party tonight, and there's gonna be hot college chicks there, and a keg."

"John!" Denise barked, the look Mike wore as he dropped his bike and started towards them telling her this was a little more important than some lame attempt at looking cool.

John scoffed, turning his gaze to Mike. "What's going on dude? Jeff here was ranting like a lunatic on the phone, so it was kind of hard to understand whatever the hell it was he was trying to say. Something about Maggie, and we got the wrong guy." He paused. "Just tell me that we're not about to get sucked right back into this... I was *really* looking forward to enjoying this vacation..."

Mike glanced at the ground for a moment before lifting his gaze and recounting everything that had happened. He told them about his ride, the visions, the truck, everything. He told it in as much detail as he could articulate. And when he was finished, the others stood silent, each of them feeling the same thing.

"Jesus dude...," John said, turning around and walking four steps away before stopping. He stood there shaking his head as the others searched for a response.

It was Todd who finally pulled the group into the conversation they were delicately skirting. "We need to go back there," he said. "Mike's right. What if he missed something? I mean. As much of a douchebag as that auto shop guy is. If he didn't kill her, then we have to find out who did. He could go away for the rest of his life."

"Yeah," Denise spat. "And he fucking deserves it." The thought of what had happened to that poor girl soured every bud on her tongue, a tense ball growing in her gut. "Fucking animal..."

"Yeah," Todd replied. "He deserves to go to jail for what he did. But not for murder. Not if he didn't do it." He took a deep breath, exhaling steadily before continuing. "This entire time it's been about finding justice for Maggie, about finding who it was that killed her. If what Mike says is true," he glanced at Mike, "and I'm not saying it isn't. It's just really crazy..." His gaze returned to Denise who stood there stone-faced and angry. "Then we have to find out who really did. Maybe that's why she is still here."

"God damn it!" John burst from the edge.

The others whipped their faces around to see John turn and start back towards them.

John stopped between Todd and Denise. "I'm gonna hate myself for this later, but he's right."

A look of surprised amusement flashed across Jeff's face.

"That guy's a piece of shit," John continued. "And he deserves to burn. But not for something he didn't do." He turned to Mike. "If her body's buried somewhere in the woods, then we have to go find it."

He turned to Mike. "You're not making this shit up, are you?"

226

"No," Mike said, shaking his head slowly.

John growled. "I'm gonna kill you guys," he said, his eyebrows riding up his forehead as he turned and made his way towards his bike. "Do you realize what I could have been doing tonight?"

"Yeah," Jeff quickly replied, not passing up the opportunity. "Passing out drunk and pissing in some girl's bed?"

"Hey!" John snapped, whipping around with his finger pointed out. "We said we were never gonna talk about that again. And it still could have been her..."

"Sure," Jeff grinned. "Of course."

"Asshole..."

John turned and picked up his bike, not seeing the smiles exchanged behind his back. The year before he had passed out at a party, and when he woke up the next morning, he found himself lying in a rather large puddle. There was a lot of deliberation over the next few weeks who had shared the bed with him that night, John insisting that it had been occupied by a girl who left before everyone woke up, but nothing had ever been confirmed, so as it stood, John passed out and wet the bed. It was an embarrassment he would go to his grave denying.

Mike, however, only heard the exchange from the fringes. He kept trying to see the man's face that had stepped out of the truck. He could see the clothes, the dirty jeans and red checkered shirt, but it had been as if the face was behind a pane of rippled glass, a distortion just enough to keep him from seeing who it was. He wondered as he made his way to his bike if it was because Maggie hadn't seen the person's face that he couldn't. Had he only relived the experiences through her memories? Was it possible that he had only seen what she had? Though by this point he didn't know *what* was possible anymore.

He bent down and lifted his bike off the pressed weeds beneath and climbed over. The others had already begun riding towards the main road. Something clung to him, tethered by the images in his mind. There was something so familiar about the truck, about the man, like a smell that wafts past on a breeze that triggers a long-lost memory. He couldn't place it, couldn't see it, but somehow, he knew... Maggie knew who killed her. She knew...

Chapter 35

"So, what I'm still trying to figure out," Denise said, maneuvering her bike beside Mike's. "Is if Maggie could have shown you this all along, why did she wait until now? Why not show you that in the beginning?"

"I don't know," Mike replied. "I don't think it would have helped," he continued pedaling. "Nothing that she showed me would have helped us figure out anything we couldn't have on our own." He rode a short way further. "I think she was just trying to tell me that we need to keep looking, that whoever killed her is still out there."

"So, she just put her hands on your head and you saw everything?"

"Yeah. But like, glimpses. Like I said, it was like I was there, but I wasn't. Like, experiencing it but, not. I couldn't talk or move. And it was like I could *feel* what she was feeling." He paused. "I don't know how to explain it."

"What did it feel like?"

Mike searched for a way to describe it. "Fear. Pain. But not like a physical pain." He paused, the pedaling movement slowing. "I think... I felt what she felt as it was happening, but like, only a little bit. Like I was feeling her memory." He paused again. "It was horrible." He paused. "I saw her in the road. Her body... I watched her take her last breath. I watched her die..."

"Jesus Mike. I'm sorry."

Mike nodded. "I just want to find her, and I want this to be over."

Denise's gaze fell back to the road ahead. She couldn't imagine what a little girl like that must have felt, abducted, held captive by a sicko... murdered. And she couldn't imagine how it must have been for Mike to go through it either. Knowing it had happened and watching it happen were two completely different things. The thought turned her stomach and she quickly pushed it away, turning her attention to the white line on the road ahead. The burden of their adventure was becoming just that.

Chapter 36

The sun was directly overhead, at its hottest and brightest point when the five of them slowed to a stop, moving their bikes off the shoulder of the road and setting them down.

"This is it," Mike said, turning to the others. "This is where it happened." He paused, turning around, his hand extended, finger out. "That's where I found the necklace."

Overhead a small group of birds flew silently past, disappearing into the tree line.

Jeff stepped up behind Mike, his eyes moving to the woods that stood just a few yards away. "We should spread out. If we stay about five feet apart and move slowly, we have a better chance of finding something. That's how they do it when they are looking for a body."

"Dude," John said with a scoff. "You have seriously got issues..."

"What?" Jeff asked, turning his shocked gaze. "It's true..."

"Oh, trust me," John smiled. "We *all* know it's true," he added, implying the issues.

"Oh...," Jeff replied as he caught the joke. "Shut up."

"Guys!" Mike snapped; the irritation loosely concealed behind his tone pulling their attentions to him instantly. "Just... Spread out and keep your eyes open. Just, try to look for anything that doesn't belong here, or looks like it might have something to do with Maggie. OK?"

Jeff shot another smart glance at John and then nodded. "That's what I was saying..." Then he turned and started towards the tree line, his feet slowly brushing through the tall grass as he stepped.

The others turned and followed suit, each making their way apart from each other and starting in the same direction.

The next hour went by like this, each of them moving slowly through the grass and weeds, pushing debris and old growth aside. John had found a large branch and was using it as a broom, sweeping back and forth. Todd had taken his que and found his own stick that he was using to swipe at the tall weeds. The road behind them for the most part stayed relatively quiet, the occasional rumble of an engine going past lifting their eyes. A still hush had moved through the group as each of them envisioned their own version of Maggie's last moments and a sinister man garbed in black glancing over his shoulder as the tip of a shovel pierced the earth.

"This is pointless," John said after a few minutes. "We're not gonna find anything. It's been freaking twenty years..."

"Mike found the necklace," Jeff responded matter-of-factly from a few yards away.

"Yeah," John called out. "He also said the guy in his vision or whatever it was had a shovel, so anything we're supposed to be looking for is gonna be buried. Do you see how much shit is growing out here?"

"Well, what do you want us to do then, huh? Go home and come back with shovels? You wanna spend the rest of our summer out here like Zelda digging holes?"

"Link," Todd replied from the side.

"What?"

"Link dude. Zelda was the princess."

John scoffed. "Whatever." Then he turned his attention back to Jeff. "Look dude, that's not what I'm saying," John snapped back.

"Just keep looking," Jeff replied. "Freaking *Lost Woods*," he muttered under his breath as he glanced around.

"Guys!"

Everyone's faces whipped in the direction of Todd's voice.

"I found something!"

"You gotta be shitting me...," John said, dropping his makeshift broom and starting after the others.

As Mike walked up, he saw Todd standing there, his gaze locked to something at his feet. It was a small metal container, almost completely covered in growth.

"What is it?" Jeff asked as he walked up. "What did you find?"

Todd reached down, prying the object from the weeds that bound it and brushed the dirt off.

"Well, what is it?" Jeff repeated.

John brushed past him, eyeing the object. "It's a flask dumbass. Haven't you ever seen one before?

"Dude," Jeff snapped back. "I know what a flask is, dickweed, I just couldn't see what he was holding."

"Let me see that," Mike said, reaching out as he stepped closer.

Todd handed the small flask to Mike who turned it over, his gaze narrowing as he did. He turned it over in his hand and then stopped, something hidden beneath encrusted dirt catching his eye. Slowly he used his thumb to brush away the earth, revealing a set of engraved initials beneath. A.L. "Holy shit," he said, lifting his head and locking eyes with Todd.

"It looks exactly like—" Todd started when Mike cut his sentence short.

"Maggie's dad..."

John stared between them, confusion growing. "What the hell are you guys talking about?" he asked, stepping closer.

Mike glanced back at Todd before responding to the question. "When Todd and I went to go talk to Maggie's dad, he had a flask exactly like this one. *Exactly* like this one."

"Dude. It's the same exact engraving," Todd added.

"Yeah," Mike replied. "They're exactly the same." Then he paused, the man's name working across his lips delicately. "A.L. Alan Lorris."

A puzzled look moved onto John's face. "So, wait. You're basically trying to say that *Maggie's dad*, is the one who killed her then?" He paused, shaking his head. "Dude. Come on... That doesn't make *any* sense. Why would he have killed his own daughter? You said he spent weeks out here looking for her. Even if he somehow found her, why the hell would he kill her?" He shook his head. "There's no way."

"Dude," Jeff replied. "It happens a lot man. You'd be surprised."

"But you just said it yourself, her dad had his flask when you went to his house."

"It's a different one dude," Todd replied.

Mike turned, tracing the ground with his eyes. "He must have dropped it when he was burying her and then went and got another one exactly like it to replace it."

"Whoa," Denise said, stepping in. "Slow down. Maybe her dad was just out here looking for her and accidentally dropped it. We can't go assuming he was the one who killed her. He told us that he had been doing that."

"At the exact spot that she was murdered?" Jeff asked. "No. It's way too coincidental to be, coincidence."

"Really dude," John chuckled, shaking his head. "Way too coincidental to be coincidence... Do you actually hear the shit that comes out of your mouth sometimes?"

"Dude! I'm just saying, there's no way that he *accidentally* dropped this at the exact spot she was killed. There's no way. It couldn't have happened. It's statistically impossible. He *had* to have been the guy Mike saw with the shovel."

"He does drive a truck," Todd added, lifting his eyebrows to accentuate the thought. "I mean, how else would his flask have gotten out here?"

"Oh my god," Denise said, her hand coming up to cover her mouth. "Her own father killed her? But why?" Then she paused, the color fading from her cheeks in the fading light. "Oh my god," she repeated, her tone now rippling with realization. She turned to Mike, her hand lowering back down. "Do you remember when we were talking to him? He specifically said that he drove up and down old 56 for weeks after she had disappeared. There's hundreds of roads he could have picked, but he said this one specifically." She paused while Mike studied her. "Why? Why this one? He could have said that he looked up the mountain, or even said *everywhere*. But he didn't. He said, Highway Fifty-Six..."

"What if he didn't mean to kill her?" Mike said, his words lowering to a thoughtful whisper. "What if it was an accident?"

"But if it was an accident," John replied, "then why didn't he just turn himself in? I highly doubt he would have gotten arrested for killing her."

Jeff watched intently, soaking in the conversation with every word.

"Think about it," Todd said, turning to Mike. "When we went to his house, we watched him stumble out of his truck. He was drunk. What if he was drunk when he killed her? They would have pinned the whole thing on him. He would have gone to prison for drunk driving and murder. They would have stopped searching for his daughter and they never would have found the person that took her. He probably just freaked and hid her body to keep from having the whole thing pinned on him. I'd wanna know who took her if it was me too. But if they found her, they'd stop looking, and whoever it was that kidnapped her would have completely gotten away with it."

"So, he buried her out here somewhere, and then went home and pretended like nothing ever happened." He paused, shaking his head as he glanced at the flask. "This whole thing just keeps getting more and more fucked up..."

"No wonder he was all weird when we started asking questions. He was probably worried that somebody was gonna dig something up or find out."

"We have to tell Detective Cordell," Denise said.

Mike turned, startling as he did. Standing five feet behind Denise was Maggie, her sad gaze locked to him.

"God, I hate it when she does that," John said, shuddering.

Mike watched as her gaze lowered to the flask in his hand, recognition flashing past her cold eyes.

"Oh man," Jeff said, noticing the look on her face. "She knows..."

"I'm so sorry Maggie," John said, watching as her gaze never wavered from the object. "I... We think it might have been your dad who killed you."

Slowly her gaze lifted to meet his.

"We've gotta take this to the police," Mike continued. "If it was your dad, then..." He didn't want to finish the sentence. He knew what would happen if it came out to be that he had been the one to kill her and bury her body. Even though he knew in the darkest pit of his stomach that that was the truth, he still clung to the tiniest spark of hope that it wasn't."

"You're sure about this?" John asked, glancing between Mike and Maggie. "Cause if we're wrong. Oh man."

"What if we're not," Jeff replied. "Then her dad gets away with murder, and Maggie's death never gets avenged, and she could be stuck here forever."

"Dude," Todd said, his reply barely above a whisper as he looked towards Maggie.

"Yeah," Mike replied. "I know."

Denise watched Maggie's gaze lower back to the ground. She could almost feel the sad confusion coming off of her. She had to know where she was, that this was the spot that she had been killed, and that somewhere out there, somewhere amidst the clustered pines, was her forgotten corpse. "I'm so sorry," she whispered, a single tear working down her cheek. "I'm so sorry about *everything* that happened to you. No one should *ever* have to go through what you did. And if it was your dad who did this to you, then he deserves whatever is coming." She wanted to hug her, to hold and console her and it pained her that she couldn't.

Even the simplest of consolations was impossible. She just stared, watching as Maggie slowly lifted her gaze.

"We gotta go," Jeff said from behind. "We gotta get to the police station before Detective Cordell leaves for the day."

"I'm sorry Maggie," Mike said, staring deep into her eyes. Then he lowered his gaze from hers and turned to the others. "Let's ride."

The group turned and started back towards the road.

"How the hell are we supposed to explain finding *this* now," John asked as he picked up his bike and stepped over. I mean, the necklace was already a stretch, but to come back and be like, *hey, we have more evidence*... He's either gonna think we had something to do with it, or that we're just making all this up..."

He was right. Cordell had already been suspicious of how they had found the necklace and earring. Mike only hoped that if it came down to it, and they had to tell Detective Cordell the truth, that it wouldn't result in them getting locked up.

"Look," Mike replied, grabbing his bike. "We're just gonna have to deal with that when we get there. For now, we just have to get this to Detective Cordell, and hope he doesn't think we're lying. There's not really any more we *can* do."

Chapter 37

It was nearly six o'clock when the group burst into the police station, their entrance bringing the desk officer to his feet, hand wrapped around the handle of his pistol.

"Jesus *Christ*!" the officer burst, taking a deep breath and exhaling slowly as they rushed towards his desk.

"We need to see Detective Cordell!" Jeff burst through ragged breaths. "It's an emergency!"

The desk officer eyed each of the kids with unmasked irritation. They were huffing and drenched in sweat, like they had run a marathon to get there. He wanted to yell at them for startling him, and just as he was about to open his mouth, a single word from one of them diffused everything.

"Please," Mike said, the tone in his voice immediately resolving the situation and bringing the officer back to a seated position.

The man growled and then picked up the phone on his desk, again eyeing the group with a shake of his head. "Detective," he said after a moment. "The kids are back." He paused. "Yeah, same ones. This time they say it's an emergency." He paused again. "Yep. Will do." He hung up the phone and looked at Mike. "You know the routine," he hissed. "Have a seat. He'll be out in a moment."

"Thank you," Mike said, turning to walk away.

A minute later Detective Cordell emerged from the back.

"So, what brings you kids back?" he said, walking up with a smile. "Checking on the case I assume?"

"Detective," Jeff said, stepping forward quickly. "We know who killed Maggie. We have proof."

"OK, hold on," Cordell said, his smile fading instantly as he glanced quickly among the excited group, before looking to the desk officer who watched in bland amusement. Then he turned back to the kids, his voice lowering just a notch. "Why don't you come on back to my office and we can discuss this in private."

He turned, making his way back towards the hall door, nodding at the desk officer who lifted his eyebrows and rolled his eyes.

Behind him John tapped Jeff on the arm, mouthing the word *relax*.

Jeff shot his hands up in exasperation, turning to follow Cordell.

As they made their way down the hallway Mike still struggled with how he was supposed to explain the flask. It must have been the look on his face, or blank gaze, but he felt a soft touch on his shoulder and turned his head to see Denise smiling reassuringly at him. He took a deep breath, sighing heavily with a single nod. He took the remaining few steps towards the office feeling a calm sense of relief easing his anxiety.

Cordell opened the door to his office and stepped in, making his way towards his desk. "Go on and shut the door behind you," he said as he moved to take a seat.

Jeff walked in first, followed by Mike and Denise, and lastly Todd, then John. They each filtered in and maneuvered their way into the exact places they had stood prior.

Cordell stared at them from across the desk, and for the briefest of moments, the office fell deathly quiet. The overhead vents whispered with cool air as the AC filtered into the room. Outside his window they could hear the low thrum of the city street. But inside, it was pin drop quiet, each of them waiting to see who was going to break the silent parley.

Eventually it was Cordell who spoke, bringing the conversation to life. And a good thing too, because Jeff was nearly shaking with anticipation, and his outburst would have sent the conversation in an entirely different direction. "All right," Cordell said at last. "Would you like to explain to me what this is all about?"

As badly as Jeff wanted to blurt it out, he kept the desire contained, allowing Mike to explain. But it was only Denise's fingers digging into his shoulder that kept him from doing so.

"We know who killed Maggie," Mike said, his words delivered calmly. "We have proof."

Cordell looked at Mike, his expression slowly dropping. "Look," he said after a moment. "I know how badly you want to see her killer brought to justice. Trust me, so do I. Not a day's gone by in twenty years that I haven't. And I can't stop telling people about the group of kids who helped us solve this girl's disappearance." He paused, just long enough for the others to brace for the coming news. "Donald Cowles confessed," he continued. "You all should be beyond proud of yourselves. But the only problem is he says he only kidnapped and—" His words trailed off as his mind replayed the disturbing events that had been the man's confession. Then he cleared his throat and straightened a bit. "He told us that he did abduct her, but that she escaped. So as of right now, we can charge him for a multitude of things, but we have no proof of him actually taking her life."

"We know!" Jeff finally burst, no longer able to contain himself. "We know who did." He elbowed Mike. "Dude, tell him."

Cordell looked confused, and not struggling with a crossword puzzle confused, but finding out the earth is really flat confused. He slouched back in his chair, gaze moving between the two and waited. His face scrunched in on itself.

"It was her dad," Mike said, his words low and quiet.

Detective Cordell cleared his throat once more, catching himself beginning to roll his eyes, but instead opting to stretch his neck to the side to hide what he truly felt. Then he brought his gaze back to Mike. "Look," he began, his tone a little less friendly that it had been when they had entered. "It is only because, somehow, by grace of God or just, dumb luck, you managed to put a crack in a case that's been haunting this department for years, that I'm gonna hear you out. But I'm telling you, this *better* be good, because if you try and pin this on that poor girl's father after all these years, and I have to go reopen *that* wound. That's not gonna make for a good day for me, and I can guarantee you, far less for him." He paused, taking the time to eye each of them carefully. "Well, go on," he said, relaxing in his chair. "Let's hear it."

Mike reached into his pocket and pulled the flask out, setting it on the desk between them. He watched as the detective's eyes latched to it, a thin intrigue building behind them. "We went back to where I found the necklace," he began. "We found this. Well, Todd found it."

Cordell sighed quietly, reaching into his desk and procuring a latex glove. The others watched as he slipped it on and reached out to pick up the flask. "OK," he said, turning it over in his hand. "And what am I supposed to be looking for here" His words were exasperated, placating the situation.

"Right there on the front," Mike said, picking up on the detective's tone. "You see the initials?"

Cordell looked closer. Then his expression shifted. It was slight, but Mike caught it.

"Maggie's father's name is Alan. Alan Lorris. A.L..."

Now his expression shifted fully, a squint flashing past his eyes. "And you say you found this at the same spot you found the necklace?"

"Yes," Mike answered.

"We think he may have dropped it when he was disposing of her body," Jeff said, finally knifing his way into the conversation.

Cordell looked up, a thin layer of shock on his face. Then he glanced at the others briefly. "Is he *always* like this?" he asked, his gaze moving back to Jeff as concern worked across it.

"Yeah," John said from the back. "You get used to it..."

Cordell smirked at Jeff and then returned his gaze back to the flask in his hand. Then after a moment he pulled a plastic bag from his desk and placed it inside, setting it back down in front of him. "Well, we have one problem with this theory," he said, not believing he was entertaining the conversation further. "Cowles admitted to abducting her and driving her to a remote cabin off of Fifty-Six. But nowhere does that include, or for that matter, involve her father. He was at home grieving."

"That's not entirely true," Jeff said, bringing the detective's attention back to him.

"Cowles said it himself, Maggie escaped. So that means that from the time she left the cabin to now, her whereabouts were completely unaccounted for. So technically, her father could have been the one to kill her and dispose of the body. Nobody would have ever known, because no one would have been looking at him as a suspect."

Cordell shook his head with a small grin. "OK," he said, playing along. "Let's say, in theory, that her father was the one that killed her. What's the motive? What would he gain from her death?"

Jeff's gaze stayed locked to his.

"Why would her father have wanted to take her life?" he continued. "I interviewed the man myself at the time, personally. He was completely distraught. That man had just lost his daughter. Both he and his wife were deeply in grief, and neither gave any indication that they had anything to do with her disappearance. If anything, they were completely destroyed by it. So how could it be that he would go from grieving parent to his daughter's murderer just like that?"

"Maybe it was an accident," Todd said, turning the tone.

Now Cordell found himself again feeling the tiny scratch of irritation. "We have eyewitness accounts of the Lorris girl being abducted. We have the car, that you *yourself* found, *and* the man responsible. There's no way that her father fits in with this. It just doesn't work. No matter how you spin it." He paused. "It's impossible."

"Like Mike finding the necklace?" Jeff asked, the scratch digging deeper.

Cordell exhaled heavily, his lips pursing together.

"Don't you think it's a little strange that we found her father's flask in the same spot we found her necklace?" Mike said, hoping to calm the direction the conversation was quickly veering.

"No," Cordell snapped. "What I think is strange, is that you never bother to call me when you find things like this, which we still don't even know what *this* is. We have no proof this belonged to her father. I have no way of knowing if you even found this in the same place as the necklace. As a matter of fact, we still haven't checked to see if this was in fact her necklace to begin with. Cowles was apprehended before we had the chance to investigate that. And to be honest, I'm still confused as to how, *if*, this is in fact, her necklace, you happened to find the *exact* spot where it was."

"We know it's crazy," Denise said, edging in. "But you have to believe us detective. We're not making this up. I know it sounds hard to believe, but it's the truth. We found this right where the necklace was."

Cordell turned to Denise, his demeanor lightening up a bit as she continued. He wanted to tell her that no, in fact, he didn't need to believe anything. He was simply humoring them because over the years he had learned never to ignore even the most ridiculous claims, because you never know where the truth may lie. So, he held his tongue and continued to listen.

"Mike and Todd went to her father's house to ask him some questions. He had a flask exactly like that one. Exactly, same kind, same initials, everything. If you go there and look around, you'll find it. Then you'll see what we're saying." She paused, her hand moving to Mike's shoulder. "Please detective. We're just trying to help." She paused. "We can take you to exactly where we found it."

Cordell shook his head lightly. Then he lifted his hand, wiping heavily down his face. "I can't believe I'm letting you kids tell me how to do my job again..." He exhaled sharply.

"Look. I'll have this sent up to the lab. See what they come back with. In the meantime, yeah, if you wouldn't mind, I *would* actually appreciate it if you showed me where it is you keep coming up with this evidence?" He shook his head with a light scoff. "I've been on the force for twenty-five years, and I never bothered to go look where you found the evidence..." He looked between them. "You kids, and this case, has me feeling like the same rookie I was when I first took it." He scoffed again. "Unbelievable..."

Chapter 38

Mike looked past John to Jeff who was staring out the window. John wore an uncomfortable expression and when he noticed Mike looking past him, he pursed his lips and shook his head, still holding tightly to the façade of irritation. Denise rode in the front seat and Todd was in a squad car just behind. They had piled into Cordell's unmarked Crown Victoria and were being followed by two more. All this had happened after what appeared to be very awkward conversation between the detective and his commander. The kids had made that assumption when Cordell had returned, flustered and visibly agitated. "You guys had better be right about this," he had said, staring heavily at Mike. "I'm gonna end up working traffic…"

For now, all five of them sat silently, watching as the city passed by, making way for the long stretch of road that would bring them to the one place that kept beckoning Mike back. In the back seat, Mike let his gaze fall out the window, quietly wondering if Maggie would be there, her face drawn in sadness, that piercing, blank stare that stabbed into the very depths of his soul. He wondered if there was more for him to see and dreaded the thought. It would be a lifetime until he was able to shake the feelings that now festered in him, like warm grease on an empty stomach.

"You said mile marker eighteen, right?" Cordell asked from the front.

"Yes sir," Mike replied, his gaze not moving from the window.

"All right," Cordell said, glancing in the rear view at the two cars behind him. "We'll be there in a minute." He brought his eyes back to the road. "Look," he said. "When we get there, I need you kids to stay back and let us do our job, you got that?" He paused, waiting for a reply. The car stayed quiet. "I'm saying this again, because you've proven already that you're not too good with following orders. But this is important. This is an actual investigation, and you could get in a lot of trouble for interfering. I really don't want to have to arrest you after all you've done. So, when we get there, just show me where it was that you found the necklace and the flask. At that point I'm gonna need you to wait in the car. We can't afford to have one of you accidentally trample potential evidence. I know you mean well, but please remember, this is what we get paid to do, and I'd like to think we're pretty good at it." He again glanced in the rear view, scanning the turned faces in the back seat. He didn't need a reply, as long as it was said and heard.

"That's it right up there," Mike said a moment later, pointing to a spot about fifty yards ahead.

"All right," Cordell replied, slowing the vehicle to the side of the road. "Here we are." He pulled the car over and brought it to a stop, turning the engine off. "You remember what I said," he reminded them. "I'm going way out on a limb here with you, and I need you to know that this is completely against protocol. The chief's already not too happy with the level of involvement I've allowed you all to have in this case, so please try not to make it any more difficult for me. He's already breathing down my back on this one."

They all looked at him in the mirror.

"Lucky for us, *he* wants to see this case come to a close just as bad," he said, unlocking the doors and stepping out.

Mike glanced at Jeff who exhaled heavily, his cheeks puffing out to accentuate. Then they opened the doors and stepped out.

Just behind the other squad cars had pulled to a stop, the one in the rear with its overhead lights flashing. Mike watched Todd step out of the other car and make his way towards them.

"All right," Cordell said, looking around. "Lead the way."

"It was right over here," Mike said, stepping past.

Cordell followed Mike a little way to where Mike had found the necklace.

"It was right there," Mike said, pointing to a spot a few feet away. "I was riding home and saw it sticking out of the dirt. The light reflected off of it, so I stopped. Sometimes I find money and things on the road so I kind of keep an eye out now. Anyways, we had already started our project and Jeff had mentioned that she had been seen with a necklace just like it, so when we went to talk to her dad, he told us that it was. So that's when we came to you."

Cordell nodded, glancing at the spot Mike had pointed to. "And the other item?"

"That was back further," Jeff said, interjecting himself into the conversation. "Just past the tree line." He started towards the trees when the detective called out to him. "Hold up," he said. "I need you to remember what I said. Just stay back and let us do our job." Then he turned to the two officers who stood nearby. "I want you to cordon off a perimeter. Start a sweep of the area. Keep your eyes open for anything out of place, or what looks like something that could potentially be buried. Keep in mind, this would be from twenty years ago."

"You got it Detective," one of them responded, turning and moving back to a marked unit.

He turned back to the kids. "Who was the one that found the flask?"

Jeff quickly pointed at Todd as the others glanced in his direction.

"All right," Cordell said, turning his gaze on him. "Show me where you found it."

Todd glanced quickly at the others and then started towards the trees, Detective Cordell just behind.

The others watched as the pair disappeared into the trees.

Overhead the sky had begun to darken. The officers who had arrived removed a generator from the back of one of the vehicles and set up two large work lights to illuminate the area. Cordell had pulled his flashlight out and the other officers followed suit.

The kids watched as the area was slowly transformed into a crime scene, Jeff watching with a little more fascination than the others.

The next twenty minutes crept by. The group was huddled by Detective Cordell's car. Denise was sitting in the front seat with her legs hanging outside and Jeff was in the back, munching on a nature bar he had fished out of his shirt pocket.

"Let me get some of that," John said, suddenly realizing it had been hours since he had eaten.

Jeff growled, breaking off a small piece and handing it over reluctantly.

"You know," Jeff said, the words coming out between chews. "It's strange that Maggie's not here."

"I was thinking that myself," Mike replied, glancing at the trees where the officers were still making their way through.

"Maybe there's too many people around," Todd said, having returned after showing Cordell exactly where he had found the flask lying.

"Why would that matter," John replied. "It's not like anybody but us can see her anyways."

"Maybe she doesn't want to see what they find if they do."

Mike looked at Denise. "Yeah," he replied. "I don't think I want to either."

A moment later one of the officers in the trees called out to Cordell who was standing a short distance away talking with a third officer who had arrived. "Detective," he yelled out. "You're gonna wanna see this!"

Cordell pulled away from the conversation he was engaged in, glancing at the group as he started quickly towards the waiting officer.

"What do you think they found?" Todd asked, the same excitement that was building in the others now flaring in him as well.

Mike shook his head silently, none of the others offering their guesses either. They stood there, waiting on bated breath as Cordell approached the officer and looked to the ground, his face growing slack. Then they watched as he turned his gaze to them and slowly shook his head in awe.

The officer standing next to him reached up and pressed the button on his shoulder mic. Detective Cordell glanced one more time at the ground and then said something to the other officer before starting back towards the group.

"How the hell you kids know...?" he asked rhetorically as he stepped past them to the driver's side, where he reached in and picked up the hand mic. "Dispatch, this is Detective Cordell. I need you to send a forensic unit to my location. I'm at mile marker eighteen off old route Fifty-Six. Copy?"

"Roger that," the voice replied from the other end. *"I'll have units dispatched to your location right away."*

Cordell pulled the mic away, holding it for a moment as he studied the marks on his steering wheel. Then he pulled his gaze away and hung the mic back up before making his way back around the car.

He stood there for a moment, five pairs of eyes all locked to him, silently waiting to be filled in on what he had found. Then he glanced towards the trees where the officer had begun putting a secondary line of tape up. "It looks like we may have found her," he said, turning his gaze back to them.

An hour later the entire area had been cordoned off. Yellow tape ran through the trees and there was a full force of people on scene. Mike and the others watched as the entire section of woods became an illuminated bustle of activity. There were officers with dogs, people wearing what looked like hazmat suits without the helmets, a coroner's van and about a dozen other vehicles lined down the highway. Traffic officers stood a quarter mile down the road in both directions, slowing vehicles up as they passed, a procession of faces all craned over, trying to sneak a look at the unfolding events. At the center of it all were Mike, Jeff, Denise and the others. Detective Cordell stood near them, watching as the different officers scrambled about, each doing their own dedicated task. Then a woman in a white outfit with a nametag hanging from the front of it approached, pulling her goggles off as she did.

"Detective," she said, greeting him.

"Gene," he replied politely. "What are we looking at here?"

"Well," the woman said, pausing as she glanced between the group.

"It's fine," Cordell said, reading the look on her face.

"OK," the woman said, glancing once more between them before settling back on him. "The body we found appears to be female. I'd say by structure, ten, no more than thirteen years old. From decomp I'd say she's been out here at least a decade. I'll have to shoot some samples off to the lab to get a more accurate timeframe." She paused. "All in all, I'd say it's pretty safe to assume that we found your girl. Congratulations."

Cordell exhaled heavily, a weight dropping from his chest that had been affixed for the last twenty years. He ran his fingers through his hair and let his gaze lift up to the sky above the trees. "Thanks Gene," he said as he lowered it, letting it fall to where the officers were further excavating near the site. A deep sadness slowly edged its way in past the relief.

"Of course," the examiner said, turning around to walk away.

Cordell scoffed, the slightest hint of a chuckle in it as he turned to the group. Then he shook his head and tugged at the knot in the tie around his neck. "I'd say it's about time I went and paid Maggie's father another visit, don't you?"

Jeff smiled, turning to look at Mike who silently nodded.

Next to him Denise pulled her legs back inside the vehicle and closed the door.

"You might as well ride along. I'll drop you all back off at the police station after I have a quick chat with Mr. Lorris. Squeeze in tight," Cordell said to the others as he turned and made his way to the driver's side. "Double up on the seatbelts."

Chapter 39

Night had spread across the sky by the time the car pulled onto North Main, and the block that the Lorris house sat on, just near the end. They approached slowly, Detective Cordell eyeing the residence cautiously as they approached. There was a pickup truck parked in the driveway, and light shined from inside the front windows.

He edged the car into the driveway, parking just behind the truck. Then he turned the engine off and stared at the house for a moment. "I need you to let me do the talking. He's already gonna be on edge having you here. I don't want to do anything that might spook him. Remember, as of right now I'm just asking questions. He hasn't been charged with anything, and if this goes south..." He paused. "Just, hang back and let me do the talking."

"Yes sir," Mike replied.

John gave an exaggerated salute from the backseat to which he received a sharp elbow from Jeff.

"Ow!" he exclaimed as quietly as possible. "Fuck dude..."

Cordell glanced between them and then stepped out of the car. The others followed just behind.

"Not a word," the detective repeated as they approached the house. He knew that by all the rules, he should have had them wait in the car, but the fact that they had already interviewed the man once, and the fact that it was more likely to put him on edge and cause him to slip up, he allowed them to accompany him. It wasn't unusual for an officer conducting a ride-along to get a call that put his passengers firsthand into an investigation. At least that's what he thought as a response to the inquiry he knew was coming later. But the honest reason was that he knew this case would still be shelved in a back corner of a dark room if it wasn't for them, and that a little girl would still be buried in the woods, her murder never solved, and justice never served. So, he smiled slightly as he stepped towards the front door.

As they reached the porch Cordell held his hand out, signaling them to stop.

The group stayed a few feet back, watching as he reached out and rang the doorbell. It was another moment before he rang again. This time there was a reply from inside, and then the door opened, Maggie's father standing just inside.

Mike watched as her father moved his gaze past the detective and landed it on them. A flash of suspicion flickered behind it.

"Alan Lorris?" Cordell asked, pulling the man's eyes back to him.

"Who's asking?"

Cordell reached down, pulling the badge clipped to his belt free and raising it up for Alan to read. "I'm Detective Cordell." He glanced back at the others. "I believe you've already met some of the others."

The man glanced at them again, that same look flickering past.

"Do you mind if we come in for a minute?" Cordell asked, eyeing the man carefully as he slipped his badge back into place.

Mr. Lorris looked between them one last time and then stepped back, making his way inside.

Cordell glanced at the others and then followed after.

"Well," Alan began, stopping at his chair. "What's this all about?"

Cordell watched him take a seat, his eyes immediately moving to the flask on the small table next to the man. He glanced back to Mike who stayed motionless and quiet.

"I don't know the best way to say this," Cordell began, turning back to him. "So, I'm just gonna come out and say it. We found your daughter Mr. Lorris."

Alan's face dropped, his gaze drifting to the table in front of him. His breath slowed and his chest began lifting in shallow hitches. A thin layer of moisture worked its way into his eyes.

"Her body was recovered this afternoon. Your daughter was buried in the woods off highway Fifty-Six."

The man's gaze never left the table. He just swallowed hard and allowed a single tear to work its way down his cheek. The air in the room grew heavy, grief flooding in.

"However," Cordell continued. "The reason I'm here is because we recovered something from the scene that we're trying to figure out." He reached into his jacket pocket and pulled the plastic bag with the flask out. "Have you ever seen this Mr. Lorris?"

Alan's gaze stayed locked to the table.

Cordell held the bag out in front of him. "I need you to try and identify this for me Mr. Lorris," Cordell continued, insistence edging into this tone.

Slowly the man lifted his gaze, his eyes moving to the object in the detective's hand. A spark of recognition struck his eye, but his lips stayed sealed.

"Two days ago, we found the man that abducted your daughter," he said, still working the reply out. "He confessed to luring her away from the bowling alley and kidnapping her. The only problem is, he claims that she escaped while in his custody; claims she disappeared into the woods outside the cabin he had her held captive in. So, if he's not lying, then somewhere between the time in which she managed to escape, and now, she was killed by someone else." He paused. "Mr. Lorris, your daughter was found buried. Her ribcage was crushed, both legs. There was massive damage done to her body. So, whatever it was that killed your daughter, did so with massive force. And *who*ever did it, took the time to drag her out into the woods and bury her." Again, he scanned the man's face. "We found this flask about six yards away from where your daughter was buried." Again, he paused. "It has your initials on it." His gaze moved to the flask on the small table. "Exactly like the one right there. And it appears to have been there for the same length of time as your daughter's corpse." He chose the word *corpse* carefully, driving home the death of the man's daughter. "So please. I need you to tell me why it is that we found evidence that places you at the crime scene where your daughter was buried, and why it is that you never bothered to mention anything about this to me during the original investigation."

The man's breaths came shorter, staggered gasps punctuating them. Another tear fell, drug down his face by the next that followed. A thin stammer began, just sound at first, an incoherent garble that transitioned to words, and began to form sentences. "I... I didn't..."

The others stood behind Cordell, watching the man's demeanor slowly crumble.

"It was dark," he stammered, his gaze again dropping to the table. "I... I'd been drinking. My wife. She, she was destroyed. Wouldn't eat, wouldn't talk... So, I drove. I drove up and down the highways, looking for anything that looked like a red mustang, anything that might have led to our little girl. Our Maggie." He paused, a small sob racking his old frame. "I..." He winced, glancing for a moment at the flask on the table. "The cap had fallen out of my hand..." He paused again. "I'd leaned over to grab it off the floor. When I sat back up." His gaze lifted, locking to Cordell's. "She was standing right there, right in front of me." Another stream of tears fell. "I tried to stop; I swear I did. But..." Another series of sobs racked the man's body. "My little girl..."

Mike and the others stood there, listening to the man tell the story through a series of wet sobs. They all felt the pain of his loss, but Mike especially. As the man retold the story, his mind replayed the events he had been showed, his emotions and Maggie's fear pounding inside him. He lowered his gaze, noticing out of the corner of his eye that Denise was wiping tears away from her eyes.

"I didn't know what to do," he continued. "I knew they'd think I was the one that did it, that I'd killed my little girl. I didn't want them to stop looking. I wanted them to find the piece of *shit* that took her from us. I wanted him to burn for what he did. I had to. For her. You wouldn't have continued searching for him..."

Cordell listened to the confession, all of the pieces falling into place for him.

"I buried my daughter on the side of the road. My angel. I left her there, and I went home. I had to pretend to my wife that there was nothing wrong, that nothing had happened." He stopped again, sobs cutting his words. "I killed our little girl," he burst, leaning forward in his chair and sobbing heavily into his hands.

Cordell glanced to the others and nodded to the door.

Each of them turned and started out. It didn't take much convincing. The man's sobs tore into each of them as they made their way outside. By then Denise had a stream of tears falling down her cheeks and Todd was wiping the moisture from his eyes. Even John wore a look of shock as he walked out, head down, gaze blank.

Then Detective Cordell turned his attention back to Maggie's father. "Alan Lorris, I'm truly sorry for everything that you and your wife went through, but I'm placing you under arrest for the death of your daughter, Maggie Lorris…"

The others made their way outside, listening as Cordell continued reading the sobbing man his rights. They made their way a little way into the yard and stopped, all turning to look at the house, all except Mike, who stared at the clouds drifting across the dark sky overhead.

A short time later Maggie's Father was led out of the house in handcuffs by two uniformed officers. Detective Cordell followed closely after. They led him to a squad car, the few nearby neighbors all watching the show from the safety of their own porches.

Cordell approached Mike and the others and stopped. "Look. I don't assume to ever know how it was that the five of you figured this out, and to be honest, a part of me doesn't think I want to. But what I do want you to know, is that we had an entire police department, trained men and women alongside state police, all out looking for that girl." He paused, a squint flashing past his eyes. "And *somehow*, twenty years later, you kids managed to find her." He paused, shaking his head. "Again, I don't know how, and I don't expect you'll ever tell me, but I can tell *you* that when you're old enough, there's a place on the force for each of you." He narrowed his gaze on John and Jeff. "Even you two."

A grin spread across Jeff's face, from one ear to the other. Even John smiled slightly at the acknowledgement.

"Detective?"

Cordell turned to see another officer standing in the doorway of the house.

"Could I have a quick word with you?"

"Be right there," Cordell replied, turning back to the kids. "Look," he sighed. "I gotta go take care of this. But I mean it. Seriously. Thank you. You have no idea how much this has meant to me." His gaze lingered a moment longer on them. "If you want, you can hang out here and I'll drive you back to the station, or it's not too far of a walk. I've got a few more things I need to wrap up here before I'm done. Up to you. But come see me tomorrow at the station. I've got something I'd like to give you." He smiled, nodding his head before he turned and started back towards the house.

The others turned to each other, all smiling behind a look of exhausted relief.

"So does this mean I can get back to having a normal summer?" John asked, half-jokingly.

Mike nodded, glancing between the others. "Yeah," he replied. "I think it does."

"I think you're forgetting about one thing," Denise said, pulling his attention to her.

He looked at her, replying with a puzzled look.

"We still have somebody we need to go check on..."

Mike smiled as Jeff reached out, putting his hand on his shoulder.

John stepped towards him doing the same. "Yeah," he said with a smile. "It's been one hell of a summer."

"Dude," Jeff said, pulling his gaze away from the house.

Behind them two officers strung more yellow tape across the front yard of the Lorris house. Two officers were taking swabs from the front end of the truck and another two going through the interior. Somewhere in the house Detective Cordell was finally getting closure.

Chapter 40

"I want you to know that your mom and I are really proud of you."

Mike looked up at his father who had paused while tying his tie.

"Detective Cordell told us everything. How you guys found that missing girl after all these years, and how you helped bring the people responsible for it to justice; your Certificate of Merit." He paused, the smile on his face growing. "We just want you to know that we couldn't be prouder of you."

"Thanks dad," Mike replied, glancing at his mom.

"It's just so sad," she said, watching as her husband finished tying their son's tie. "After all these years, finding out that that poor girl survived such a horrible ordeal, just to be killed by her own father who was only trying to get her back."

"Well," Mike's dad replied, stepping back to admire his work. "At least her spirit can rest now."

Mike smiled. *Yeah. She can.* None of them had seen her since they had gone back to the police station three days prior. They each had assumed that she had finally moved on. It was strange though. As he stood there, his parents putting the final touches on his suit, he found himself missing her.

They had gone back the next day and been given an award by the police chief and mayor. Detective Cordell had been the one to hand it to them and they had all had their picture taken for the newspaper. But they had all just found themselves going through the motions. They appreciated it, sure. But that wasn't what it had been about. They had helped bring the people responsible for Maggie's horrific end to justice. Though they were never able to truly communicate, each of them had felt a kind of friendship with her. As strange as it was, she had become a part of their group. And now she was gone.

Mike's mom looked over her son, his hair nicely combed, the suit and tie showing off how handsome he had grown. "You look so handsome," she said, putting her arm around her husband.

"Yeah," his dad smiled. "You're gonna be just as good looking as your old man when you grow up."

"Oh, you wish," his mom joked, pulling away.

"Hey," he smiled. "I was handsome enough to lock you down."

"That's just cause there was nothing better around."

"Oh whatever," he smiled, pulling her in for a kiss. "Well," he said, pulling away. "I guess we better get going."

Mike nodded. "Yeah."

"You're sure you wanna do this, right?" his dad asked, checking one last time.

"Yeah," Mike replied. "I am."

"OK."

As they pulled into the cemetery Mike saw the small gathering; a handful of cars with a slightly larger number of people gathered a short distance back. He recognized John's dad's Porsche immediately, and the red pickup truck that Jeff's brother drove.

They pulled up and parked behind the other cars. Then Mike stepped out.

"Mike!"

He looked over to see Jeff standing there, his hand in the air waving frantically. He started forward, Jeff and Denise making their way to meet him halfway.

"Hey guys," Mike said, Jeff and Denise looking past as his parents walked up.

"Hi Mr. Tanner," Jeff said, holding out his hand.

Mike's dad reached out reluctantly and shook it. "Jeff."

"Mrs. Tanner," Jeff said, pulling his hand back.

She smiled. "Hi Jeff. Denise."

Denise smiled. "Thank you for coming."

"Of course," Mike's mom replied. "We know how important this is to you all. We wouldn't have missed it for the world."

"Dude," Jeff said excitedly. "Everyone's here. Even Detective Cordell."

Denise stepped closer, putting her hands on his shoulders. "Are you OK?"

Mike nodded. "Yeah," he replied softly. "It's just... I actually started to feel like I knew her you know?"

"Yeah," she replied. "I do."

"I think we all did," Jeff added.

Mike sighed, looking over to the gravesite where everyone was seated.

"Come on," Jeff said. "We saved you a seat."

The three of them made their way over to where John and Todd were seated. As he approached Detective Cordell stood and approached to greet him.

"Hey Mike," he said, sticking out his hand. "How you holding up?"

Mike shook his hand, glancing at the small coffin that sat atop the empty grave. "Good, I think."

Cordell smiled at his parents. "Mr. and Mrs. Tanner."

"Detective," they replied politely.

"Well," Cordell replied. "I think we were just waiting on you to get here to start. Why don't we see this finished all the way through?"

Mike nodded. "Yeah."

As he approached the seats Todd and John stood up, each taking their turns hugging him. Then they all sat down, their eyes grazing the dark brown streaks in the polished wood that sat on the polished beams before them.

The priest rose and turned to address the others.

"We are gathered here to celebrate the life of young Maggie Lorris," he began. "A girl brought into a harsh world, and pulled away before she had the chance to experience the beauty that it can offer."

Mike felt a rapid succession of taps on his arm and pulled his attention away from the priest that was still speaking. He turned to Jeff who pulled his hand back and nodded his head towards the coffin. "Look," he whispered.

Mike looked back to the casket, his gaze moving just past it.

The priest's words slowly faded away and he felt his mouth fall slightly open.

Twenty feet back, a smile lightly caressing her cheeks, stood Maggie. Her dress was no longer tattered, but clean and neatly ironed, the slightly translucent pink now bright and vibrant. Her hair fell in curls around her face and surrounding her was a warm glow that ebbed ever so slight as her gaze moved between them. Then her face turned to Mike, and for the first time he looked upon her and felt a surge of emotion that wasn't bathed in sadness and sorrow, but was soft and warm, a happiness that only tears could convey.

"Mike," John said, noticing Maggie as well.

Mike felt a smile pulling at his quivering lips, and a tear slowly worked its way from his eye, another following just behind.

Mike watched, his tears now falling freely as another figure appeared, an older woman in a dress similar to Maggie's fading in from the empty air just behind her. The woman stepped forward as her shape materialized, stopping just next to her.

Mike watched as Maggie looked up at the woman in warm recognition and smiled, the gesture softly returned as the woman reached out and put lovingly her arm around her shoulder. Then they both turned their faces to the group, their smiles growing larger.

Tears fell from Mike's eyes as he felt a flood of emotions release. Beside him the others brought their hands to their faces, each wiping away the tears that too fell. Maggie's mother had come to bring her home.

Mike and the others stared, tears now falling freely as Maggie lifted her hand in front of her and waved. Her smile grew and with a single look, shared a thanks that words would never have been able to express. Beside Mike, Denise reached out and clutched his hand, squeezing tightly. John lifted his sleeve and wiped his face, and beside him Todd sniffled quietly.

Sitting one row behind them Detective Cordell looked up, the color leaving his face as he saw young Maggie Lorris standing beside her mother, exactly how they had been twenty years prior when he had been given the investigation.

He felt his breath leave his lungs and released an audible sigh.

In front of him Jeff turned to look back, tracing the stunned look of disbelief on the detective's face to where Maggie stood. He nudged Mike and nodded, who turned to see Cordell staring, eyes wide in disbelief.

Then Detective Cordell pulled his gaze away long enough to lock eyes with Mike. In that moment he understood, and every question he had was instantly answered, and a dozen more formed in their place.

Mike smiled, the tears still on his cheeks as he turned to look back to where Maggie stood.

From across the small casket, Maggie looked up at her mother, who smiled down at her. And then the group, Detective Cordell included, watched as Maggie's mother gently took her hand and turned, leading them away. Slowly their images faded, the glow left in their wake dissipating.

Denise reached out and took Mike's hand, squeezing it again.

"And so, at this time," the priest continued, his words filtering back into their ears. "We commend this body back to the earth. Ashes to ashes, and dust to dust."

Mike rose to his feet and stepped towards the coffin where he placed a single flower Denise had brought for him on top. Beside him, one by one the others followed suit.

Overhead the midday sun shined down on the small gathering, its light giving warmth to a summer that for five young kids, would never be forgotten.

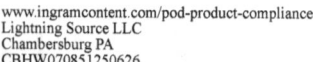